FIVE
AGAINST
ONE

FIVE
AGAINST
ONE

B. GRIGOLETTI

authorHOUSE®

AuthorHouse™
1663 Liberty Drive
Bloomington, IN 47403
www.authorhouse.com
Phone: 1-800-839-8640

Published by AuthorHouse   02/15/2012

ISBN: 978-1-4685-5409-0 (sc)
ISBN: 978-1-4685-5408-3 (hc)
ISBN: 978-1-4685-5407-6 (e)

Library of Congress Control Number: 2012903010

I would like to thank the following people who have made this book possible:

My Parents: *Many thanks for your patience and guidance throughout this process. Without the two of you this book would be just a regret in my future; unfinished, unpublished and unrealized. Your belief in my craft means more to me than you could ever know.*

My two closest friends, Eric and Joel: *As different as you both are, each of you still know the right things to say to keep me believing in myself and my craft. Brothers are traditionally born to the same mother or forged in battle or if you are lucky as I have been; found twice in the same lifetime.*

My family: *Thank you for the love and patience that has overlooked my flaws and given me the time to see this project through.*

"I may fall, crashing from the sky
only to land among those who
are happy to see me fail . . .
But I will cherish the short time
that I soared on high
and for a moment, chased my dreams . . ."
B. Grigoletti 12/2011

PROLOGUE

The dictionary defines the word Witch as . . .

Noun (Wich)—(1) A person usually female who professes or is supposed to practice magic, black magic or the black arts; a sorceress. See Warlock. (2) An ugly or mean old woman; hag

I Caitlin O'Connor define a Witch to be . . .

My new neighbor, Savannah Summers.

CHAPTER ONE

THE CAFETERIA CATASTROPHE

"I said shut your damn mouth."

I laughed, "How can anyone understand you with that fake, bullsh*t southern accent you're pretending to use? God, it's as phony as your boobs, your lips and your precious porcelain smile. No wonder your parents moved and had to sell their vast estate in Georgia. They needed the extra money to pay for the rest of surgeries you would need to complete your oh so 'natural' look." This last part I said with a wicked sneer on my face. The delivery was perfect; everyone in the cafeteria was on their feet and cheering me on. I, of course, was the home town favorite, the girl most of these kids had known all their lives and today I was going to slay the 'Mouth of the South.' I was finally, once and for all, going to make sure that the girl who had terrorized me for the last five months, was going to go down in flames.

"You are such a jealous little cow." she continued, "just look at yourself." Your clothes are all Wal-**** seconds. Everyone on the block HATES you. Oh, you think they don't? Open your eyes freak and ask yourself, who really does like you?"

She was good, but I already knew that. I knew coming in here and having it out with her was dangerous. I reminded myself though, that no great struggle has ever been won without taking some casualties. She would wound me today, but it would not change the outcome. I was going to embarrass her and end this cycle of abuse once and for all.

"That's hysterical, you calling me a freak! Look at the house your family moved into." Her face stayed cool but I could tell I had hit a nerve, "I mean the Munster's wouldn't want to live in thats piece of crap."

"My father is an architect and my mother an interior designer you ass. They are renovating it up as part of a project for . . ."

"Count Dracula?" I interjected. Many laughed, some howled and I think a girl named Agnes Moleski peed her pants by the way she scrunched her legs together and hurried out of the lunch room, plowing people over like an NFL running back heading for the end zone.

"No, for a magazine that has featured their work like, I don't know, a dozen times in the last seven years." I could tell that she was doing her best not to take a swing at me since we had both been previously warned that any additional altercations would end up in at least a suspension or worse. The principal had been quite clear on that point the last time we were in his office.

I on the other hand was on the offensive. I had to keep my momentum, had to keep focus. Today, I wanted this hag in tears and nothing was going to stop me from seeing her reduced to a babbling baboon. "Wow, they must be really good at their jobs then. Cause I see all the camera crews just lining up to film another edition of "Extreme Home Makeover." More laughter filled the large room as my heart soared.

I could sense her smoldering, I could tell she was getting close to completely losing it right here in front of all these people. This time it would be Savannah Summers turn to shriek and scream and act like a baby. This time, I would leave her with not an ounce of pride and if I was really on my game, not a shred of dignity. "Let me ask you a question, when you wake up in the morning, how long does it take for your father to run outside and turn on the air compressor so that it can build up enough pressure to fill those BALLONS sitting on your chest?" The whole assemblage of our classmates let out a unanimous howl of delight.

Now I have read a few stories regarding the ancient gladiators of Rome. It is said that these powerful, well trained killers would enter the famous Coliseum with their hands held high over their heads, their leather armor well oiled and their swords, razor sharp. They would begin waving and shouting in order to whip the crowd of spectators into an absolute frenzy, very much like I was doing now. Then, the opponent (usually a slave or peasant, far inferior to the Roman champion in both stature and martial prowess) would be released into the arena as well. They would, after a few tentative circles proceed to fight. The gladiator would toy with the challenger for a while, prolonging the tension for the paying audience. Then, when the audience was wound tighter than a spring from all the anticipation and expectation of seeing a starving outlander cut down, he would wound his opponent and knock him to the ground. Cheers would rise from the stands, "Finish him, finish him. Finish him!" The gladiator would then approach his struggling foe; raise his sword high in the air, the killing blow mere seconds away as his steel shimmered in the later afternoon, Italian sun. The audience would then take a collective, deep breath waiting for the kill . . .

"Funny you should be so fascinated with my chest Caitlin, cause Craig is too."

"What, did she just say?" thoughts began spinning wildly out of control in my head. *"Did, she just say Craig? Not my Craig, she couldn't have meant . . . my Craig."*

Suddenly, I was back in Rome again. Only this time the weak, bleeding peasant that had been lying in the dirt pulled a hidden dagger from his boot, leapt up and stabbed the gladiator right in the heart. Everyone in the

Coliseum blinked in disbelief as a hush fell over the collected masses. The spectators' hopes and dreams had been shattered. For today, unless their eyes had played a cruel trick on them, their champion had just been slain by a completely dirty trick, robbing them of their victory and their hope.

"What did you say?"

A smile began to form on her face. A perfect smile, on a nearly perfect face and I knew. I knew she was telling the truth. *"Oh my God, please tell me this is not happening to me."*

"I said," her voice slowed down but that only seemed to give it more of a bite, "that Craig liked them too. Meaning, that we made out after the basketball game two weeks ago. While you were home grounded for being a little bit*h like usual, Craig and I were under the bleachers in the gym together."

The great gladiator suddenly fell over and lay there lifeless on the blood stained earthen floor. Then, after what seemed like an eternity, the smaller, scraggily looking commoner pumped his fist into the air while emitting a loud, "Woot!" No one in the stands dared to speak. Everyone witnessing the event knew the champion, their champion, had fallen.

I had to somehow cover this one. Even though as a female I could tell she wasn't lying, I had to make it look good. I had nothing ready for this counter attack, nothing prepared for this level of cruelty. So I fell back on the oldest standby in the English language, "OH YEAH! Well, that's a lie."

"God, did it always sound so pathetic to say "Oh Yeah?" I thought.

"Really, well ask him when you get the chance sweetie. I have been over his house twice since and know what else? He loves . . . strawberry lip gloss." She ran her tongue over her lips as if to let me know that she was wearing that exact same flavor. If I had thought in advance about bringing my fathers BBQ tongs with me, I would have used them to yank her two timing lips right off her pretty little face.

I shrunk in size. I mean in fact that, someone could have picked me up and put me in an Altoids tin at that moment, and quite honestly I wish they had. It would have saved me quite a bit of humiliation as I stood there about to cry while all my classmates stood by and watched.

"Oh, Sweetie, don't cry. Just because Craig wants to be with a girl who at least is a girl already, I mean that shouldn't be a shock to you. The real shock to everyone here I think, was that he ever admitted you were his girlfriend to begin with. Let's face it; you look more like a little boy than a girl in her dating years. You don't want someone going down the street mistaking you and Craig for two boys holding hands, do you?"

I think, and I say think, because the rest of those minutes spent in the lunch room that day have become a bit of a blur. I think I heard a few people chuckle at her remarks. Mostly though, there was silence, the kind of silence that occurs when everyone gathers around a coffin to pray. The kind of silence that makes you realize when you walk in on it that if you ask "Hey, what's going on?" you would probably get rocks thrown at you.

My shoulders slouched and I felt myself draw a breath. I think it was to stop myself from throwing up, because if it was meant to stop me from crying, it didn't work.

She took three steps closer before she lowered her voice and gave me the shot that if I live to be one hundred years old, I will never forget. "I've already turned Nicole and Craig against you. All I need to do now is get your parents to dump you off like they did your other sister and my plans for you will be complete. Oh yes sugar, Craig told me all about it. Dead isn't she? Passed away? You know what you little termite, when I'm done

5

with you, you really will wish it was you who had been given up and left for dead." With that she walked past me and out of the cafeteria while everyone stood there, staring.

Tears like I had not shed in months came pouring out of my eyes. It was not a loud, look at me cry. No, this one was the kind of cry that has no sound. It's sort of like, you can't even reach down inside yourself to find the right note to wail. The humiliation was just too deep, the betrayal too complete, that there were no sounds developed to convey how much my heart had been broken.

In a mere two minutes, she had taken my victory, my boyfriend and my pride. I was left with nothing but contempt and utter hatred for this southern born harpy from hell. Before, I had thought to simply show her up, best her at her own wicked game. Now though, that would never be enough. To steal my first crush, my first love and to throw it in my face was bad enough. But to then admit you had been plotting it all along while poisoning my own sister against me, well that was more than my Irish blood could take. This was no longer about knocking her down a peg, about showing her who was really the most liked girl here in school or in our neighborhood. This was about removing her from my life. This was about making sure this would never happen again. I knew that in my heart I could not take another encounter like today.

The bell rang which thankfully reminded everyone that lunch was over and it was time to head off to their next class. Three of my friends, Melanie, Danielle and Kirsten came up finally and tried to console me by hugging me and telling me what a complete scum bag Craig was for going near her. Melanie even tried, although in hindsight pretty pathetically, to explain to me that Craig was a jock and that jocks never go for the cheerleader type, which of course Savannah was. Actually, she is the head cheerleader for the basketball squad, a fact that Kirsten kindly reminded Melanie about right after she gave her a small smack to the back of the head.

I was a mess. I was inconsolable. I began trying to talk but only gibberish came out. Nothing I said made any sense, well almost nothing. After the bell had rung again signifying that we should have already been reporting to fourth period, I screamed as the next group of kids entered the cafeteria, "I can't look at them ever again, I can't see her again, what am I going to do? I'll die if I have to see her again, I'll just die."

It was our quiet friend, the introverted friend Danielle that spoke as she stroked my hair, "No you won't. We won't let that happen. She's never going to come near you again Caitlin, I promise."

"How can you say that Danielle, how? She'll never stop now. She took Craig and Nicole . . . she is never going to stop."

Danielle never flinched she just simply said, "I won't let it happen. None of us will. Because tomorrow, we are going to make sure Ms Perfect, isn't so perfect anymore."

Three heads nodded in agreement while I just sat there, crying and ashamed.

CHAPTER TWO

WE ARE THE SOUL PATROL

*S*o, *in order to understand why things had gotten so absolutely screwed up in my life, I need to take you back. Back to our summer vacation, back to when we were all still friends and back to a time when our lives knew nothing of evil. Back to the moment just before, SHE moved into town . . .*

"Okay, so when I say your name, just raise your hand and say, here." I said in my most authoritative voice. "Nicole O'Connor?"

"Here," my younger sister replied. She was always here at these meetings and rightly so, in a way these meetings and this very organization were her brain child. Months ago, when we discovered that we had a ghost inhabiting our house, it was my eight year old sister who decided to stand watch and guard our family against any potential paranormal attacks. We set up a base camp in my room. Organized shifts so as to always have one fresh pair of eyes ready and alert and I even drafted a set of articles to help guide our decisions both on and off duty.

I made a small check on my roster sheet next to her name and smiled at what I could see of her face in the dim light inside our playground fort. Being a paranormal investigator now meant that I spent a lot of time milling about in the shadows but when hosting a meeting as important as this one I tend to like to keep the lights on, makes everyone attending a bit less jumpy.

"Craig, would you do the honors please?" I asked.

There was a hefty pause before our closest friend in the neighborhood asked, "The what?"

Craig, as you may have inferred from the name, is a boy, and not just any boy, oh no. Craig is my heartthrob, my beau, my first love, my ultimate crush and for the record he is a blonde, aquatic Adonis. He is also very sweet, believes in ghosts, specters, wraiths, the Loch Ness monster, Houdini, the thigh master and the New Jersey Devil, which in my book makes him pretty damn unique. The only real problem with Craig is that he is a bit of a thickie (like many boys) and is also the secret first crush of Nicole, making it very awkward when the three of us are in a room together.

"Would you please turn on the flashlight?"

"Was I supposed to bring one?"

I sighed because this question could only mean that he in fact had not brought one to the meeting this week which I guess makes some sense since he had failed to bring a flashlight to the last nine previous meetings as well.

"For the official record, I would like to again remind the members of the Soul Patrol that Craig Dawson is in fact, the "Keeper of the Sacred Light". A title that he himself came up with several months ago and is therefore responsible to bring some form of illumination to our weekly meetings from this day hence." I said.

He leaned in towards my sister who was sitting crossed legged beside him and I could not help but wince when I heard him ask her, "How long is a hence?"

I drew a nice long breath and continued, "Moving on," I consulted my clip board and read the next name on my list, "Dog, is Dog here?"

"I'm holding his leash Sissie. Of course, Dog is here," Nicole explained.

"I am simply taking a roll call. I know Dog is here but it is a key part of the meeting and therefore must be done properly. Okay, so that's a yes for Dog and let's see Craig we know you are present."

"Here."

"Thank you Craig. I know."

Then the cell phone which was lying open on the wooden floor of our fort began to speak. Well, the caller on the other end of the call began to speak actually, the phone's speaker just amplified it so that everyone could hear the voice of the oldest and wisest of member of The Soul Patrol, Craig's Romanian aunt, Katrina. "Quate-lin, I must agree vith my nephew on this matter, you knew Dog was dere and yet you made as if he vas not. Vhy then can't you pretend Craig is also not dere until he says, here or present or vhat ever it is he must say?"

"Yeah, I mean you asked Dog if he was here and he can't even say here," Craig added in an exacerbated voice.

I raised my voice to bring some order to the meeting, "Craig Dawson?"

"Here," he said.

"Excellent, and finally, Aunt Katrina?"

"Over here, as in not dere physically but spiritually I am of course dere with you all. You see, I am using an ancient gypsy form of planer shifting to be in two places at vonce . . ."

"OKAY! Let's get started shall we. Right. Checking my agenda I see the first order of business is to have a report on the migration of several suspicious looking fungi that are growing alongside the garden gnome in Mrs. Anderson's yard. Nicole, I believe you were keeping an eye on this bizarre phenomenon?"

"Yes Caitlin. I went to Chunky Charlie and measured his position from the front of Mrs. Anderson's house and then measured the mushrooms from that point as well. The findings were, startling."

I nodded, we had been on to these evil, vile shrooms for some time now and with any luck my sister would have the proof necessary to enact an official decree and we would go to work and destroy Satan's blossoms of death, "So, what did you uncover?"

She cleared her throat and replied, "The mushrooms have not moved at all, but the Gnome I believe is slowly making his way south."

Craig blurted out, "I knew it!"

The disembodied voice spoke from the phone as well, "as did I."

"Great, so we will write a note to Mrs. Anderson and advise her to cement her wandering statuary to the ground as we are firmly convinced it is heading south towards a winter retreat in the Carolinas. Next, Craig you were going to check on the werewolf population in the area, how did you make out with that?"

"Well Caitlin, it's been real tough as everyone can imagine. First of all, they are lone hunters, solitary creatures that prefer the untamed wilds to the small suburbian yards that we inhabit here in Braintree."

I chuckled for a moment and then said, "Nicole been helping you with this investigation Craig?"

"Just with the write up, I've taken lead on the actual field work," he replied.

"Great, continue." I said, smiling.

"Well, after a week's worth of digging around, I have narrowed it down to two suspects. I would like to say, for the record, that it is difficult to track a werewolf especially with a 9 p.m. curfew. That being said, I did my best and think madam Patrol leader you will be pleased with the results. The first suspect is a Mr. Walcott, who lives two blocks over on Pine street. He is tall, wears glasses and after snooping around his yard I uncovered this coupon for a hair removal salon in downtown Boston. My second, and I believe more likely candidate is a Yorkshire Terrier called "Poppy" who I believe when he transforms at night takes on a completely different name.

"Vhat name?" Craig's aunt asked.

"Cornelius," he stated very emphatically.

"Vell, dat makes sense. Many who suffer with lycanthropy, the wolf's curse, tend to favor names that begin with the letter C."

"Like Caitlin?" I chuckled.

"No, vith the letter C dhaling, not Q." Her voice dropped suddenly in volume before she continued, "Nicole, call me later, ve need to talk about your sisters lack of spelling skills, it could indicate a serious affliction that can only be cured by . . ."

"I do not have a spelling problem Aunt Katrina with a K."

"There is no K in aunt, Cailtin," Craig said.

Nicole busted out laughing. I knew that this meeting was not going as I had planned but in fact most of them never did. It's funny, but frustrating as this dialogue might seem, the people in this fort had helped me through one of the toughest times in my life. They had believed in me when I doubted anyone would. They supported me and in some cases guided me through the loss of my best friend Kelsey. I'm not sure I could have survived the grief of her death or the shock of her return, without the members of The Soul Patrol. We had our differences at times, all friends do. But we were also very much in tune with each other's needs and feelings.

That night as I sat there listening to their silly banter, I could not imagine a day when I would ever want to be anywhere but here, sitting with my family and friends, being myself and just enjoying the sounds of their voices. I wonder why certain voices are calming and others are not? I guess familiarity has a lot to do with it.

"Alright, it's getting late let's wrap this up. Auntie K, would you be willing to talk to us about some of the defensive techniques you learned in your Penchak Silat martial art class next time you come down for dinner?"

"Of course dhalings, of course. I vould be most happy to teach you the ancient style of Indonesian stick fighting. I vill bring some rods vith me and ve can begin vith some basic strikes to the groin."

Laughing, "That will be great thank you. Okay, now for the most important part of our meeting tonight, the weather forecast for tomorrow, Nicole how's it looking?"

"Hot and sunny."

"Excellent, then I hereby make a motion to meet everyone who can attend at the Dawson's pool tomorrow to a bit of well earned R&R, do I have a second to this motion?"

Craig immediately replied, "I, second the motion."

"Very well, the motion is carried. Let's call this one done and meet tomorrow. Good night Aunt Katrina."

"Night dhalings, I vill see you soon."

We climbed carefully down the ladder and quietly slipped out of the Addams yard which was directly to the left of our house. Craig waved and began jogging down the street towards his own yard as I put my arm around Nicole and headed inside.

"We're home," I shouted as we came through the front door.

"Okay," dad said.

"Caitlin, don't forget to walk Dog one last time for the evening before you get ready for bed."

"Mom, I brought him with us. He already went outside for the night, he'll be fine."

Ah the nightly sparring match between child and parent regarding the urination habits of the family's domesticated hound, how I enjoyed them. At least they weren't the full blown screaming matches that were pretty much common place around here a few months ago. If you are wondering what could possibly be the reason for such a change in our household, it rests with my dad. He recently moved back into the house giving up his small apartment in Boston. He has this way about him that tends to temper my mother and I. He will usually step in before mother and I have to go to our respective bedrooms to put on our guinea tees, trunks and boxing gloves.

I don't want you to think that all my mother and I do is scream at each other all day, because that's not the truth either. I mean, come on we do sleep eight hours a day. *Okay, that was just downright funny. I kill myself sometimes.*

No, the real facts are that I can be a bit, what's the right word, oh yeah precocious. That's traditional Queen's english for "a handful," my grandmother once told me. However, in my defense, she has a strong personality and likes to make sure that I, the rival to her alpha-ness, knows that she is in charge. After speaking to our therapist at length about this topic, I have come to appreciate her wisdom and tune out her criticisms. It's become a survival technique, like a turtle's shell or the poisonous spines on that deadly fish whose scientific name I can't ever seem to remember when I need to. You get my point.

"Okay, Caitlin but if Dog goes in this house, you can forget going swimming tomorrow or for the rest of this week young lady, hear me?"

"So, if Dog is sleeping and dreams of being chased by some insane rottie who weighs like a thousand pounds and corners him in some dark back yard and demands that he hand over his very last milk bone, thus causing Dog to pass water because he is so scared for his very existence, you are going to ground me?"

Nothing. Silence. I had shown her that grounding a child for not being able to predict the exact time that another animal needs to relieve itself is simply stupid and futile. I had broken the cycle of arguing and pettiness. This would be a day to remember for a long time in the O'Connor household.

Then, the single word that reinforced countless arguments between teens and their fascist parents came echoing from the kitchen, "Yes. He pee's in this house, you're toast."

Well, so much for logic. I knew better than to plea for my father's intervention on this subject, when it came to Dog and his potty habits my parents seemed like a united front.

"Fine. I'm going up to bed. Good night," I yelled back.

"Me too," Nicole added.

"Okay, well get cleaned up and I'll see you in the morning."

We finished doing our goodnights and climbed the stairs towards our rooms. Nicole and I joked a bit about Craig and Katrina and eventually said our good nights as well.

I closed over my door, got changed, grabbed my favorite doll and sat down on my bed. My eyes began to mist over a bit, as I recalled how much this small toy reminded me of my dead best friend; a fact that was not a mere coincidence either. You see, we had designed dolls to look like us on a trip to New York city a few years ago. When we got home we realized that playing with a doll that looked like we did wasn't fun so we swapped them. So, when she was killed accidently in a motor vehicle accident I was left with a replica of her sitting on my shelf.

Now if the thought of seeing your dead friend's face staring at you 24/7 is not creepy enough, at midnight this doll also talks, in Kelsey's very own voice. Yep, there's a ghost in my house and to be honest with you, I love it.

CHAPTER THREE

"THE SUMMER I MET THE SUMMERS"

"Is there some way you could possibly move your kiester any slower Nicole?" I yelled back into the house from our front landing. Our house is a nice sort of white bi-level. It has black shutters on the sides of each of the windows and while not as flashy or fine as some of the other houses on the street, it is nicely kept and has a good size front and back yard. It was one of about thirty other homes that sat nuzzled together in our neighborhood.

"Go down without me if you're so impatient," she replied. "But would it kill you to wait five stinkin' seconds while I try to find my cover up?"

Now the more mature of you out there may find the fact that I began counting out loud to be a bit childish. As a matter of fact, it was a lot childish, yet I did it all the same. "One, Two, Three . . ."

"Caitlin, be patient will you please. Nicole is just trying to find her clothes so she can walk there and back sweetie," Dad said from the kitchen.

"Dad, she is walking about four houses. Who cares if she is wearing just a bathing suit, she's eight, not eighteen with her boobs hanging out!"

"Daddy, Caitlin said . . ."

"I heard her, thank you Nicole."

"You're just in a rush to see Craigee," she said.

So, my sister thought that it was time to air out our dirty laundry in front of my father and share the fact that I have some strong feelings for our friend, *Very well Nicole, of course you know this means war.*

"Oh I'm sorry Nicole, did you say something about Craig? I mean, wasn't it you who wrote the poem, 'My heart belongs to Blondie Blue Eyes' a few days ago?' If anyone was going to be in a hurry to see him, I figured it would be you."

Suddenly, at the top of the steps, a shadow formed into substance and became my sister. She seemed calm as she stared down at me but inside I could tell she was an emotional train wreck. In an effort to prod her into action, I had awoken a dark side that until that day I was not even aware she had. It would be weeks before her vengeance would be complete and I would pay for uttering the name of the poem aloud. However, when she finally did get her revenge, it would be far more dreadful than anything I could have imagined.

Nicole gripped the hand rail and slowly, methodically, made her way down the stairs towards me. In her hands was her pink cover up, in her eyes, a look of absolute disgust. She slipped past me out the front door and waited for me to join her after I yelled to my father that we would be gone for about two hours.

So, there we were, in silence, side by side, step by step, heading towards our friend Craig's house, when I heard the deep billowing drone of a large sized truck slowly making its way down the street behind our house. Of course, this drew my attention immediately.

We headed into the backyard, went through the hedges and entered the yard of the house that bordered ours. Taking another thirty or so steps we were able to see the street and to make out the large letters on the side of truck, "G.O.D." I snickered slightly to myself, as I read what those three letters meant, 'Guaranteed Overnight Delivery'. *"Clever,"* I thought.

Oddly though, I did not foresee this as an omen of any kind. I guess the moral of this part of the story then is that even professional paranormal investigators such as myself, can miss a sign from the higher powers, even when that sign is a large brick tossed straight at your head.

"Hey boo, I think someone bought old man Frasier's house." Boo is what our family has called Nicole since she was young and an avid player of, you guessed it 'peek a-boo'.

"That makes no sense."

"Why, they have been trying to sell that old house for years now."

"That makes sense," she said starring straight ahead, "I meant what you said makes no sense. If they sold the house it's not the Frasier's anymore, that's the point of selling it." She sneered, rolling her eyes at me like I was some sort of idiot.

An aside if I may. Dear reader, have you ever in your life loved a sister or brother deeply? I know I have, which just made the sudden vision that popped into my mind of shaving her head and chasing her around the neighborhood with a Gartner snake in my hands all the more shocking.

I guess its just one of those parts of life I am not easily able to handle. I know that in the past I have been called sassy, curt, fresh and even rude. But you see, I have every given right to be that way as the older sibling. My sister in no way is entitled to the same privileges. Her role is to be sweet, nice and to allow me to vent whenever and wherever I feel like it. It may not seem fair, but hey, that's life.

I paused for a second and watched, as a very nice black SUV drove up behind the large moving truck parking itself in the driveway of what was 'once' the Frasier's house. The vehicle's engine was turned off and four people stepped outside to take a look around the neighborhood and at the adjacent houses.

Now the house that this family had decided to purchase was one of the scariest I have ever seen. I'm not kidding; I mean this thing looked just like the Tower of Terror if Disney World had decided to let the place fall apart for a while.

Picture if you will, an old and decrepit iron fence, surrounding a yard that was so overgrown with weeds and scrub grass that you could use it to play paint ball. The house itself was very large and very Victorian, which meant every peak; every angle of this one hundred year old eyesore was designed to incite fear. Whoever thought of building a house like this was obviously, criminally insane or descended from a long and illustrious line of black warlocks.

The front porch was small but very rickety with two giant wooden doors that lead for those brave enough to risk it, inside. The front of the building was covered in windows of varying size and shape. Most of them were now broken or cracked, giving the house an even more eerie supernatural appearance. The exterior walls, while originally all painted in a sort of white, had long since begun chipping and were now a sort of molted grey.

The other creepy feature to this old mansion of horrors was that sitting in the front yard was the biggest, nastiest, overgrown tree you had ever seen. This things trunk was so wide that three kids could not hold hands and wrap their arms around it. (I know this because we all tried to hug it holding hands two summers ago. We never would have even contemplated doing so if we had not been on a dare.) Now the branches of this old willow are taller than the three stories of the house that sits behind it. In the winter, when the wind is blowing hard and all its leaves have fallen to the ground, its thick old branches remind you of twisted and scarred arms. I once remember telling Kelsey that it sort of looked like a bunch of people trying frantically to claw their way out of quicksand as it swayed in the breeze under a dusky autumn sky.

We walked through our neighbor's back yards until we got closer to where the new family was standing. Now, being one heck of a charming person, I took it upon myself to wave and shout across the way towards them, "Hey, welcome to the neighborhood."

It was the father that answered me first, "Thank you, that's very kind of ya'll."

"My name is Caitlin. Caitlin O'Conner and this is my sister, Nicole," I yelled back.

This time it was the mother's turn to answer, "Well we're the Summers' and this here is Stephen and over there is Savannah." My eyes trailed along and noted the two kids she was indicating. Stephen was a good looking guy. If I had to guess I would have placed his age around seventeen. He had brown hair that was cut in a very short sort of trendy H.S. Musical style. He was almost as tall as his father, who had to be close to six feet. His clothes were very nice. He wore black jeans and a polo shirt that was a soft yellow color. Now, I don't usually go for the preppy look, but "oh la la" this guy was a hunk-ster.

Savannah stood there perfectly motionless as I checked her out. She was about my height, maybe a tad shorter. Her skin was well tanned but not overly dark. She had jet black hair and when I say black, please understand, it was black. She was wearing a deep red shirt that buttoned up the front and black jeans, which were apparently spray painted on her body. She looked to be sixteen, oh hell who am I kidding, she looked to be about twenty. Imagine my shock, when I learned in the next few

20

days that she was barely a month older than me. As my eyes locked with hers, I detected a faint sneer settle across her face. This obviously outward, hostile gesture, took me by surprise. I actually found myself blinking in disbelief.

"Stay calm Caitlin, it's just your imagination. No one in their right mind moves to a new neighborhood and picks a fight with an established resident on the very first day. You must have just misinterpreted her expression. Yes, that's it. You see, it makes perfect sense when you think it through. Where ever this girl comes from, it must be their way of greeting people." I was almost able to convince myself that the thoughts running through my brain were reasonable, until sheer perfect and beautiful logic kicked in and told my sweet, tender, I trust anyone side, that it was full of crap. *"OH yeah, it's obviously a gesture of friendship to look someone straight in the eye and mock them with a self righteous smirk. I'm sure that everyone says "Hey" the same way where she comes from, especially if she was born on MARS!!!"*

"Wow, you're very pretty."

A soft smile crossed her face. Wait a minute, did my little sister just tell this obviously stuck up girl that she was . . . . pretty. No, my sister was many things, but a traitor she was not. I must have misheard her.

Then, from across the street, Savannah spoke, "Why thank, you. Aren't you just the most precious little thing ever?"

"JUDAS." The name rang in my head like the bells of Notre Dame. You know the ones I'm talking about, right? Notre Dame is a famous church in France, where years ago this midget with a spinal condition used to jump from bell to bell ringing them whenever he got overly excited about some girl he saw dancing in the street. As for the word Judas, well if you need help with that one you have obviously lived a far more charmed life than I have.

21

I looked down at the 'creature' that was standing beside me. Never had I known my sister to be a 'glory hound' but she was eating up this attention like a starved, homeless Doberman Pincher.

Looking back up, I nearly recoiled in horror. Savannah was coming towards us. I mean she actually was walking down the street and approaching me. What on earth could have made this girl think I wanted her getting any nearer?

"OKAY, stay calm, think, think. She is coming closer, don't panic." It was all I could do to stop myself from turning and running in the exact opposite direction, waving my arms over my head like some deranged lunatic out for Sunday stroll through "Creepy Town". I believe this reaction was a result of past transgressions against my sister coming back to haunt me. My self control failed me and odd, mortifying thoughts began to coalesce in my mind. *"Did I brush my teeth after lunch or is this girl going to smell the Chimichanga I just ate on my breath? Did I put on deodorant this morning? Oh my god, I am in a bathing suit with a short cover up, please tell me I'm not sporting a wedgie that she is going to see when I turn to go to Craig's house."* I have never before in my life and I mean this with all sincerity, I have never reached out with my mind and tried to feel if my bathing suit was riding up my backside. But, at that moment, when the most prefect girl my own age I had ever seen was approaching me, I concentrated with all my mental powers on my bum. I reached out with invisible tendrils of thought and begged my derriere to give me some kind of sign that all was well, in the land of "bathing suit valley".

She stopped a mere foot from where we were standing and curled her lips into a sort of Grinchy smile. It was rather un-nerving to witness a person form a smile on their face so absolutely close to the animated green meanie of Seussian fame.

Then she allowed her eyes to look to my right as she bent at the knees, keeping her back perfectly straight (just like her teeth) and began talking to Nicole.

"And how old are you little lady?" She hummed cheerfully even though a mere second ago her eyes were lit up like torches with a certain amount of instant disdain for me.

"Well, I'm almost nine."

"Really! When?"

"In September."

"Now hold on. Are you tellin' me that you have a birthday in September of this year?" She said smiling at my sister as if she was trying to sell ice cubes to an Eskimo. I could not standby and watch this girl make fun of Nicole. Darn IT . . . . that was my job.

So I interjected, "She has a birthday in September, every year, duh." I added with a very heavy snort.

"Nicole," she pressed on as if not even hearing me "I have a cousin back in Georgia who I swear, is about to celebrated her ninth birthday this September too. Now, I have to tell you, that when I left her back there with the rest of my family I was very sad, do you know why?"

This time I remained quiet. It's useless to throw digs at someone who is capable of fending them off so easily. I decided my best strategy was to simply wait, listen and learn more about our new neighbor.

I can't remember how or exactly when it happened. I mean, I know that before she walked over here to talk to my little sister, Nicole still appeared very normal. But between that time and this moment in the conversation, somehow her eyes had tripled in size and they now resembled a Basset Hound who just found out his favorite chew toy was being recalled because it was filled with lead shavings. I mean her eyes were darn near crying and for the life of me, I'm not sure why.

"Why?" she whispered.

"Because, when I said good-bye to that cousin, to my little Peggy-Sue, I was sayin' goodbye to my best 'little' friend in the whole wide world."

I blurted out, "Peggy-Sue. Oh come on. That's a song for god's sake by some dead guy from the 50's. What a crock."

They glared at me, but I was not going to stand there and listen to this complete load of bull crap. You see, I think it's horrible when older kids treat younger ones nice merely so they can break their heart one day by calling them terrible names in front of their older, cooler friends. Nicole was not going to suffer that fate at the hands of this raven haired southerner.

Savannah reached into the front pocket of her "skinny" jeans and took out a very nice, very thin, cell phone. With nothing more then a press of her thumb, the front of this mini phone slid up and out of the way. She pressed a button three, no maybe four times and suddenly on the small window on the front of the phone came up with a photograph of a cute young girl sitting on a swing with a very sweet smile on her face.

"Nice." I thought to myself *"but it doesn't explain anything."* Then I looked a little closer, small letters began to scroll across the lower half of the screen.

Calling, Peggy-Sue . . . Calling, Peggy-Sue.

I find it odd how God's sense of humor works. I must confess that it seems a bit, off sometimes. I mean what are the chances that my new neighbor is going to be a pretentious kid from Georgia, with the name Savannah Summers who happens to run into my kid sister who coincidentally looks just like her favorite cousin she left behind on the plantation, named . . . . Peggy-Sue. *"God 3 . . . . O'Conner . . . Nada."*

"Hello, Aunt Maureen, can I please speak to Peggy-Sue? Okay, thank you. Yes ma'am we arrived just a few minutes ago. What's that? Oh the neighborhood, it's, alright I guess."

If I had to describe my facial expression at this point it would be like someone who just took a big bite out of a super ripe lemon, while sniffing blue cheese. My one eye squinted shut, while the other was as wide as my lid could pop open. I felt silly, stupid and above all else, like a real turd.

Savannah had a very self satisfied grin on her mug, probably, one that she had practiced all the way here while on her trip to Massachusetts. And if anyone had told me that it couldn't have gotten anymore of that smile called "I told you so," I would have called them a liar. But, sure enough a few moments later thanks to her pressing the button that activated the speaker, a precious little voice came dancing through the phone.

An aside for a moment if I may, even though at this point I was really angry with Savannah and our opening meeting I must take my hat off to the guys who made her phone. The reception was excellent. I could hear every word Peggy-Sue said clear as a bell tolling across the French countryside on a cold winter's morning.

"Hello?"

"Peggy-Sue, it's Savannah sweetie!"

"Savannah, I knew you would call me, I just knew it. I miss you <u>so</u> much. Is everyone all right up there?"

"Hush now, don't you go worryin' about us, we will be just fine. I'm just callin to be sure you're all right?

"Could only be better if you were back here with us, instead of in stinky old Massachusetts. Oh, I almost forgot. Momma said to tell you that we found another girl to help with my Brownie camp next week. She is the older sister of Mabel Reese, you remember Mabel don't ya? Now, I hear she can't cook, or tell stories like you can, but I know we will manage the jamboree somehow."

"God 4 . . . O'Conner . . . unconscious and probably out for the season with a concussion of the ego."

"Well darlin', listen, I got some news as well. I met my first friend up here already and her name is Nicole."

The phone just kept spilling those delightful tones from "waaay" down south even though at this point not only had I been put in "my place," but I felt like "my place" was getting smaller by the darn second.

"What she like Savvy?"

"Well, she's the same age as you are and if I didn't know any better I would swear she was made from the very same mold that God used to make yourself. I mean Peggy-Sue, you both could be cousins?"

"Wow, wait till Momma hears about this, she got a last name Savvy? Maybe we share a relation some time back?"

Nicole was spell bound. I mean it looked like she was watching Chris Angel perform the sawing a woman in half trick. Nicole has been on this earth for eight years. In that time she has made three friends. Two in preschool and one at the deli counter of our super market with an old lady that enjoys giving free samples of cheese whenever she goes shopping with my mom. She has never really needed them before. She has always had me. Isn't that the way it is for all little sisters. They don't really exist if their older sibs don't give them permission to, right? Well once we were away from this encounter with Savan-zilla, I was going to have to make sure that Nicole understood that this girl was definitely not to be trusted.

The conversation mercifully only continued about another minute or so before she disconnected the call and quietly, very self assuredly, slipped the phone back in her front right pocket.

I knew that whatever I said was going to sound silly. I had accused a perfect stranger, (please emphasize the word "perfect") of being a liar and had my bluff called. Honor, at this point, demanded I walk away but I was reluctant to leave Nicole alone with her. In truth, I was unsure what to do.

I forced a small smile and said, "Well listen we must be going. It was very nice to meet you and I'm sure we will see each other around the neighborhood over the next few weeks before school starts."

"Oh, I'm sure we will, you can bet on it," she replied before kneeling down and addressing Nicole Benedict Arnold.

"Well now Nicole, once we have some time to settle in why don't we get together and I can tell you all about my family," her eyes darted up towards me like machetes. I was almost forced to duck instinctively from their gaze, "and you can tell me all about yours."

"Sure, that would be awesome. Listen, I have a great idea! We are going swimming over at our friend's house. He lives right down the road past the yard with the gnomes out front. Why don't you come with us? He's very nice and would love to meet you, I'm sure."

I choked and blurted out, "Noooo." I tried to correct my little slip of the tongue by covering the word up. I extended no to . . . "Ohhhhhh, look at the time. We really must be running along. Come on Nicole." It seemed natural and if you ask me, I thought I masked it over pretty well. Unfortunately the scourge of the south was not buying it.

"I'll tell you what Nicole. You let me help my momma get unpacked and settled in and real soon I'll invite you over to our new home, okay?"

Savannah leaned in and gave my sister a hug. If Dorothy had witnessed the Wicked Witch of the West making out with the Tin Man I doubt she would have been in more shock than I was. Nicole was actually, I mean, had actually, made a friend. I decided to check my horoscope later, it was sure to mention that today would be the mark of the very "end of days."

They waved bye to each other as we began walking the last few hundred feet to Craig's house. Once out of ear shot I began with what I thought was a completely logical list of reasons why I felt that Nicole should in fact NOT be friends with this new girl.

"Because, I said so," okay, so it was a short list.

"What does it matter to you anyway? How many times have you told me to leave you alone or go find some traffic to play in? Now that I found a friend you think you can boss me around and tell me what to do, think again. Savannah is going to be my friend, so get used to it."

Obviously, there was no rationalizing with this child. For now, I decided to let matters lie. After a nice swim in the pool, Nicole would be more open to discuss my feelings and see the way of it.

We arrived at the driveway to Craig's house and I immediately noticed that his mother was home. It didn't matter much, except that when she was around my cannon balls off the diving board were one of those items on the "please don't do that" list. Other examples were: we don't run around the outside of the pool, we don't bring our juice boxes into the water, we don't swear or give anyone wedgies and so on and so on.

Mrs. Dawson is a nice lady, I mean she really is but she has the "mom" gene and somehow can't help but comment on every little thing that her intuition senses as a danger to the health and well being of those minors left in her charge. Let me give you another example of why swimming is so different when she is home. About two weeks ago Dad told us that we should not always go over to the Dawson's house empty handed. He said, that a good guest occasionally brings some surprise or treat with them as a way of thanking their host for letting them come over. Nicole and I got his point. We ran down to the kitchen and filled our duffle bag with cans of soda from the fridge, twinkies from the pantry and a brand new bag of Super Paco Nacho Garspachio Doritos. If you have never tried this new flavor invention from Frito Lay, just go to the snack aisle at your local grocery store and search for the bright purple and lime green bag of Doritos with the screaming face on it. These bad boys have more bite to them than a rabid wolverine who happens to be cornered, hungry and facing a veterinarian looking to neuter him.

We arrived that day and after kicking off our flip-flops and cover-ups, we called Craig over and slowly unzipped the duffle, so he could see all the snacky goodness we had brought over for the three of us to feast upon.

From the slightly open kitchen window we heard, "Craig honey, can I see you for a minute please?"

I remember our friend excused himself and headed inside only to return a moment later bearing a pitcher of unsweetened sun tea along with a pretty bowl containing a mixture of carob chips, peanuts and raisins, all nicely arranged on a serving tray that somehow matched the pattern on the pitcher and if you can believe it, the three glasses as well. Following closely behind was his mother. She had a perfectly formed smile on her face which was sort of a good thing, since the rest of her features clearly were contorted into a mask of pain.

She broke out from behind Craig and took a direct intercept path towards my duffle. "Oh, what have we here?"

"We brought some snacks Mrs. Dawson," Nicole answered.

"That is so very thoughtful of you both," she replied as Craig desperately tried not to spill the tea as he carefully placed his mothers serving tray down on the wicker patio table. I was unsure what to do. I felt like someone on that show "COPS" that my mother used to love to watch. I wanted to grab the bag and leap over the fence before the boys in blue took me for a ride downtown to talk about where I got all this stuff. I imagined her, I mean, them asking me "So, do you think it's actually okay to give this crap to kids?" I couldn't move, better yet, I was afraid to. She scooped up the small red nylon bag, unzipped it and nearly fell over.

"Why, my goodness. What an interesting choice of snacks you girls brought with you today." She reached inside and picked up an individually wrapped, delicious, yellow sponge cake treat like it was a dead mouse, pinching the outer cellophane wrapper as if it were the rodent's tail. "And, you even brought some Twinkies."

"Daddy said that we should bring something to show you how much we appreciate you inviting us over."

"Well, you tell your father that I said thank you." *Interpretation, "Please tell your dad that if he sends over anymore snacks to my house that contain trans-fat, I will be calling my lawyers and issuing a formal challenge to him via the Internet to join me on American Gladiators."*

"Let me take this stuff inside and get it right in the fridge before it spoils." She said, firmly zipping the offensive bag closed in the process.

Nicole, being the innocent that she is carried on as if nothing bad was happening, "Mrs. Dawson you don't have to put the Doritos in the fridge, they taste better at room temperature."

"Oh, well I wasn't going to open those right now sweetie."

"Why not, don't you like our snacks?"

I had enjoyed swimming at Craig's house, I really had. But at that moment, I reached for my cover up, waiting for his mother to unleash the beast on my sister and tell her exactly what she did think of our . . . snacks.

I guess her adult filter kicked in at the last second and she was able to recover from her near fit of hysteria, "Oh, sweetie it was very generous of you, it's just that Craig is allergic to, to . . . powdered cheese."

"Really?" Most times Nicole is very astute but when an adult throws a little white lie, she tends to believe it since adults in her world are nice, honest people who would never mislead you or tell a fib. "Sissy, did you hear that? Craig is allergic to powdered cheese, we could have killed him."

"Thank god we didn't open the bag up on the way over here. The orange coating on our fingers might have sent him into a state of shock." I said under my breath.

"Yeah, good thing. Craig, from now on no more Doritos, if we do bring a snack it will be Pringles," Nicole beamed.

"Sissy, are you coming or not?" Her voice snapped me back from the past and into the present. I regained my senses and headed for the fence gate that led to the back of the house and the good times that were going to be had in the pool.

I was careful not to let the swinging wooden gate slam shut behind me and making sure that it was completely latched, I headed over to the patio. It was then that I saw Craig, he was swimming from one end of the pool to the other underwater.

"Hey Caite, hey Nicole." His words were almost lyrical; his thoughts were similar to those of other great thinkers of our age. He was so busy looking cute that he did not have time to actually create long, cumbersome sentences. No, his mental computer was far too preoccupied doing advanced mathematics and spatial distance calculations. For instance, right now as he was climbing out of the water and the sun was hitting him just right. He had chosen to use the ladder on the left side of the pool, which meant that he was giving us his best profile angle for this time of day. When he began his walk towards us, he did not just grab a towel to dry his well trimmed hair. He passed it over his head four times, the exact number needed to create that shaggy, messy, dreamy hair style that guys can achieve without even using a single thirty dollar bottle of hair care product.

"Hi Craig, how's the water?" I asked, careful not to over tax him. Unfortunately, my beau went for an attempt at humor.

"Wet." His face lit up as the funny-ness of his statement played through his thoughts. Nicole on the other hand was not impressed as she walked passed us. If her eyes could have rolled any further back in her head she would have looked like a possessed girl from some campy horror flick.

I smiled, took off my cover up and threw it on the chair. From the kitchen window I heard the happy and always sweet voice of Mrs. Dawson, "Hello ladies, how are we today?"

"Good Mrs. Dawson." I like to keep things polite with Craig's mom. I have come to learn that simple, respectful sentences with grown-ups work best. They are usually not too excited to find out that you may be more clever or funny then they are and for some bizarre reason they do not get sarcasm at all. So, in an attempt not to be thought of as rude or referred to as the "mean girl" (a label which sort of stuck due to a misunderstanding at a funeral home last year when I struck Nicole across the face), I have begun a campaign of "less is more." The less adults hear from me the more they like me. Now don't take this as giving in to them, oh contraire, now I simply make sure that I only share my ideas and dark wit with my family, teachers and other adults who have had a chance to get to know me a bit better and whom I have judged to be thick skinned.

"Hello Mrs. Dawson, did you see that we have some new neighbors moving in today?" Nicole smiled and called back towards the kitchen window where his mom was still standing.

"Is this the day Nicole, where they drag me off to prison for a series of dark and violent crimes that I commit against your favorite elephant stuffie, all because you can't seem to keep your trap shut? IS IT?"

"No sweetie, I hadn't noticed. Where did they move, into the Fraiser's old house?"

"Yep, they just bought it and are moving here from Georgia."

"How nice. Craig did you hear that, we will have to go over there when your dad gets home and say hello. Maybe I'll make my famous fruit tart to bring over too . . ."

"NO!" I blurted out.

"What?" Craig eyed me funny and I could tell his mom was doing the same. I guess something inside me wanted to keep Craig away from the Georgia peach as long as possible and if he went over with his parents I would never be able to see his face on their first meeting. I wanted to be there to ensure his chin did not pop open and scrape the sidewalk, but more importantly, I wanted to be sure Savannah knows that I am his girlfriend.

"What I meant was . . . . my parents heard that they were coming to the neighborhood from a real estate agent my mom knows. She was thinking we could all sort of give them a day and then head over together, in a group, sort of like a block party get together."

33

"That sounds like a super idea. Okay, I'll call your mom later and make the arrangements and let her know not to have anyone bring a fruit tart." This she said as she slid the window shut.

*"Nice work, instead of simply avoiding this new girl, I just volunteered my family to organize the let's welcome **Satan** to our neighborhood bash."* I had fooled Craig's mother easy enough but somehow my field of effectiveness for this particular fib must have somehow missed him entirely. Craig stood there, the mid afternoon sun careful not to cause an iris around his body and give off that eerie halo that might draw attention away from his good looks. Hey, the sun was a flaming ball of cosmic gas that had been doing the same show now for some 2 billion years. I mean, 10 out of 10 for longevity, but 2.8 for originality, I would score the whole sunny day routine a low 4, been there done that. But for me and the rest of the neighborhood, this was only like Craig's seventh appearance in that swim suit, with a low cloud cover and a nice north westerly breeze gently rustling his hair. But alas, the whole effect was being thrown off by his two eyes, which were currently locked on me like laser sights.

He decided, to try the subtle approach and see if he could trick me into divulging the information. "So, what's really going on over there Caite?"

Surprisingly, Nicole did not respond for me. Instead, she had decided to let big sister worm her way threw this little gem on her own. "What do you mean?"

"Your mother is going to host a block meet and greet? Sure, and I'm Ashton Kutcher?" he quipped.

Girls, grab a pen and paper and prepare to learn what I refer to as: **Boyfriend Essential Survival Guide Rule #8**

There are three ways to handle a prying boyfriend. One is to simply pull his attention away from whatever it is that is bothering him by either a quick kiss (depending on length of time as boyfriend) or, by setting his favorite sneakers on fire. The second, is to immediately burst into tears and wail like a complete and utter flub about something he did several weeks ago that bothered you but you never brought up because you didn't want to be "that kind of girlfriend". The final way, is in my humble opinion, the most effective way of dealing with a nosy guy but requires that you use it sparingly or else risk the relationship. All you do is find the one word in his last several sentences that could be taken out of context and of course, take it that way. I will for those of you who may be a bit new to this game, demonstrate . . .

"What the hell is that supposed to mean?" I snapped.

His eyes lost a bit of their accusatory stare as he reeled from my reaction. In fact as you will see, he even stammered a bit at the ferocity of my sudden change from sweet, doting GF to "Griselda . . . the HELL CAT!" "Wh . . . what? All I mea . . . meant was that you seem to be acting weird, okay?"

"Ya, you're right. I do start acting weird when people attack my family!" For dramatic effect at this point, I placed my fists, clenched tightly against my hips and leaned in towards him. I would have done an eye twitch but when I tried to pull that off once on a teacher, they sent me to the school nurse and had them call my parents because they thought I was having a seizure.

"How did I attack your family? All I said was . . ."

"I heard you. You said that my mom would never host anything for the neighborhood. Why is that Craig? Because everyone hates us? Because we aren't fortunate enough to have a stay at home mom who makes famous fruit tarts? Is this how you've really felt all this time? That we are just a pack of carnies from a traveling circus?"

"Geez forget it okay. Fine, your mom can host the party, what do I care?" He had decided to let go of the conversation and was now simply scrambling to keep the day from becoming a complete and total loss. I had achieved my goal but at a cost. I would not be able to pull that gambit again for a few more weeks otherwise he might just decide that I was not worth the drama.

Nicole had quietly slipped into the water and was already busy climbing into the floating chaise lounge. In life there are swimmers, soakers and tanners. Nicole was without a doubt a great tanner. She could sit there for easily an hour or more (depending on the level of sun block she was wearing) and simply be content to float aimlessly around the pool. I on the other hand was a swimmer. I loved to play and swim and dive in the pool. It was one of the things that I think attracted Craig to me, that, and my obvious charm. But, to make my outburst appear more like a real quarrel and less like the emotional ravings of a certified lunatic, I simply made my way over to the side of the pool, sat down and dropped my feet into the water. Yep, I was acting like a soaker.

Craig gave me some space for about 10 minutes. Then, as he swam past I let him catch me smiling at him. He immediately spun and splashed me with a small amount of water which of course drew me into the pool and an all out splash fest ensued.

The three of us spent the rest of the day being the friends that we had become over the last nine months. Craig and I continued growing closer, even though Nicole had been promised by yours truly that I would never "go out" with him, and Nicole, well she was simply still Nicole. That in no way meant that she was a simple tag along. I know that at times I have been a bit on the cruel side when it comes to my sib but I assure you that she is a smart, clever girl. She is practical, cautious and always courteous to those who treat her with even a little bit of respect. And even though at times we have our spats, we had begun to become closer friends. I guess tragedy can do that. I guess that when people like Craig, Nicole and I share a common crisis, there is bound to be a camaraderie that develops from the struggle.

As our time at the pool ended and we were heading home, I could not help but enjoy the fact that after a shaky start, The Soul Patrol, us, had enjoyed a nearly perfect day together. As Nicole and I entered our house to get showered and ready for dinner, I decided to rethink my position on my scoring of the sun's bright, summer day show. *"Yeah, a four was being a bit of a putz. If I had to rate today, it would be a nine."*

It would be a long time before the three of us saw a nine again . . .

CHAPTER FOUR

THE BRIGHT SUN AND A HEAD IN THE CLOUDS

"Without sounding annoyed, could you please explain to me exactly how you managed to get me volunteered to organize a welcome party for the new neighbors."

"Okay," I took a deep breath and shot Nicole a glance that would have frozen Jack Frost in place where he stood, "Mrs. Dawson, you know, Craig's mom . . ." "Yes, I know who Craig's mother is Caitlin." By the tone in her voice I could tell mom had just concluded one of her more miserable days at the office. Normally on nights like this, we tidy up the living room, let her eat her dinner in peace and smile a lot, anything more than that and her nerves might just fire bolts of electricity through her brain and blow her head clear off her shoulders.

"Okay, geez you asked me to explain it. Well anyway, Craig's mom was talking about how she makes the most perfect fruit tart in the whole world, I mean even better than the Swiss, who as you know invented the fruit tart back in 1308. Well anyway, she said that she was going to make one of these special deserts and take it over to the new neighbor's house today! Now, you are always talking about how these other mom's don't know how difficult it is working and trying to be involved in the community. So I said, 'Mrs. Dawson that would make it really rough on my mom and a few of the others who work. She doesn't even know these people moved in yet. If you wouldn't mind, I can explain it to her when she gets home. I'm sure she would appreciate being included in whatever plans you and the other mom's have for welcoming this new family to our neighborhood.' She then said that I was right and she should not always try to grab the lead when it comes to things like this. So, she said tell your mom to call me and I'll let her decide what time is best for everyone to go over and say hello. That's how it happened; I was merely sticking up for you." I had been working on my smile for nearly forty-five minutes before my mom got home. I took another breath, focused and threw it.

Anxiously, I awaited the judge's ruling, would they find the smile overdone, contrite, thin and wimpy?

My mom nodded and came up to hug me. "Sweetie, that was very thoughtful of you. Thank you." *Wheaties . . . . here I come.*

I removed myself from my mother's embrace and headed downstairs to watch some T.V. I settled down onto the couch and reached for the remote control and turned on a "Teen Titan" marathon as Nicole took her usual spot on dad's recliner.

"That is not going to work; mom is going to figure out that you made the whole thing up," Nicole said.

"What?" I still find it hard to deal with my sister when she insists on speaking to me when my favorite shows are on. Bad habits such as picking your nose, slurping your drink or even scraping your teeth on a fork while eating could be forgiven. But speaking during a "Teen Titan" marathon should most definitely earn the offending person a one way ticket to perdition.

"I said your lie won't hold. It's going to fail. Mom is going to speak to Mrs. Dawson and she will mention your fib regarding the realtor friend you claimed mom has. After that, your whole story will fall apart."

"Wrong." I replied, my good humor obvious from the expression on my face.

"What do you mean wrong? You lied and you're going to get caught this time."

I muted the sound so that I didn't have to yell. "You've made one small miscalculation my dear sister. Today is Thursday." I snuggled deeper into the couch and leveled the remote at the screen to draw dramatic effect to the fact that I was sure she understood my meaning.

Nicole thought for a moment and then said, "What does Thursday have to do with anything? A fib is a fib."

"Yes, but on Thursdays the Dawson's always go out to eat and visit Craig's great Uncle Murdock at the nursing home. So you see, mom can call her but there won't be anyone home. Knowing mom's inability to NOT plan out every detail (yes a double negative, dear reader, which I thought I delivered with pure gusto and panache) she will leave a lengthy message about what works for her and settle the entire affair via the answering machine. So . . . point of fact, there will be no need to even speak face to face with Mrs. Dawson until the actual meet and greet and by then the whole street will be converging on the Summers' home leaving little time for mom to discover my little miscalculation." I stood and bowed flourishing the remote in my hand as if it were a conductor's baton.

She sat there stewing. I could see that this situation had become one of those painful life lessons for my sister. In her head she kept hearing my parents discussing over and over again the virtues of telling the truth. But here in the practical world that we live in she was seeing first-hand how a simple reworking of the facts could indeed get someone not just out of trouble but earn them a thank you and a hug. Inside, I felt this was a great turning point for my sister. If she reasoned this out properly, she will have taken her first step towards young lady hood.

"I hope you get caught." And with no elaboration, she simply got up and made her way up the stairs.

"Well so much for the first steps towards adolescence. It seems that Ms Goody Two Shoes was praying for a slip up. That bothered me. It didn't feel right to have her so upset over such a small thing like this. Over the last several months I had chased her up to her room and apologized enough. Not this time. She needed to get a grip. I remembered the great words of Theodore Roosevelt when they came to him complaining that he was working the men far too hard during the digging of the Panama Canal, "They'll get over it." *Bully Teddy, Bully!!!* Without a doubt . . . . he was a great humanitarian.

The next morning I was stirred from my slumber by the sound of my mother calling up to me from the landing. I hated being woken up this way. Truth be told, I hated being woken up any other way then by the soft, gentle streaks of daylight that tenderly made their way through my curtains to tempt my eyes into opening. I don't know about you but when sleep is working and you are fully under its spell there are few things more enjoyable.

"Caitlin you need to get up and walk Dog now. I don't have the time and your father is in the shower. Let's go!"

"MoooooM, it's Nicole's turn to walk him!" I yelled back. The spell of sleep was now fully broken as I burrowed my head under my pillow. With any luck she will believe me and begin shouting for her to take him outside.

I thought I heard footsteps and sure enough I was right. I only know this because the dog's leash landed on my exposed back with a light thud.

I was shocked, I was appalled, I was beside myself with anger. Who would **dare** throw his leash across my back like I was some common peasant? I ripped my head from its hiding place and to my chagrin, there stood Nicole. She was already dressed and by dressed I mean, with socks and sneakers.

"Get up and walk your dog . . . fibber." Her voice held no malice or venom. She simply spoke those words and stood there, almost daring me to leap out of bed, lift her up over my head like Tarzan might and hurl her from my bedroom window. Instead, I chose the more civilized option which included no immediate jail time.

"You're already dressed! Why can't you walk Dog?"

"Because, it is not my job and because I'm not a fibber," again, she spoke with a voice de-void of any emotion.

I threw off the covers moving my clenched teeth a bit closer to her face, "What does being a fibber have to do with letting Dog out to go piddles?"

"Caitlin, let's GO!" The shout echoed up through the hall.

I yelled back: "Mom, I'm getting up, one second!" Then, I set my attention back on Nicole; "Well?" I sneered.

"Fibbers never win," she replied.

My voice rose in anger, "Are you mental?"

"What did you say young lady?" *How the hell did my mother even hear that?*

"I wasn't talking to you, Mom."

"Since fate has decided not to teach you anything about fibbing and why it's wrong, I've decided to. From now on when you fib, no more favors, no more play time, no more sharing and no more covering up your lies. You want to get away with things well you're not getting away from your chores. I have to do mine and I'm NOT a fibber."

I began searching the floor for my jeans with no success. "So, this is war?"

"No, this is justice." And with that she turned and walked out of the room as I decided to head downstairs in my pajamas.

Now for those of you who do not remember what my room looks like. Let me give you a quick recap on what I like to call my "inner sanctum." The walls are a nice, very pale pink. I have two windows which sit near the head of my bed facing the front of our house. There is a good size dresser, a decent size closet and a small vanity, which for those of you who don't know is a place for a young girl to stare at herself and apply modest amounts of make up, so people don't end up staring at her for applying GENEROUS amounts of make-up. The first time I put lip stick on I did not do it at my vanity mirror and ended up looking like Angelina Jolie had just got smacked in the mouth by Mike Tyson. In fact, my mother swears that she had never seen a lovelier shade of nostril.

Now, also in my room are several shelves. And on these shelves sit all of the dolls that I have collected since I was a little kid. Yes, I realize at twelve collecting dolls may be viewed as a bit, weird. But, I assure you that it is by far the least weird thing that I do. You see that is in fact because I talk to my dolls. Well, okay let me explain that. I guess the statement "I talk to my dolls" is inaccurate. I do talk to them. But only one in fact, talks back to me. About eight months ago we discovered that my very best friend in the whole world growing up had been my fraternal twin. She had been raised next door by my mother's best friend, a woman who could not have children of her own. The two women raised us as close as sisters, which we were, even though at night we slept in separate rooms, in separate houses.

Unfortunately, Mom's best friend and Kelsey were involved in a terrible car accident. Well, the next day my sister began haunting this house. She had become stuck between this world and the next unable to find her way. Well the short version is that my sister and our friends banded together to help her across with clues she gave us by speaking through one of my dolls, her doll in fact. We had versions of us made at a large doll store in New York City years ago and exchanged them feeling that it was more fun to be with each others doll than ones that looked exactly like us. Once we had solved the mystery and helped her find some peace I expected to stop hearing from her. As you can guess, that never happened. We are still able to speak although only briefly and always between the hours of midnight and one a.m.

I headed down stairs grumbling about how absolutely unfair it is to be forced into walking a dog when everyone else in the house is already up and about. I understand that this seems like a silly and pathetic reason to be cranky but it's the only one I had and did I mention it was only 7:00 a.m. on a summer vacation day?

I slouched, throwing my shoulders as far forward as my spine would allow just to get my mother to yell about something other than my laziness and sure enough she did not disappoint.

"Caite, stop slouching." Inside, I smiled.

Dog was sitting by the back sliding door. His large brown eyes nearly tearing from the intense need to piddle. He wanted to be happy to see me but I think he knew that I was far too perturbed to greet him with a smile and hello.

I took a deep breath. "Sit still." Dog was now doing some ancient rendition of the potty dance as I tried to secure the leash to his collar.

I opened the back door and took a single step outside when BAM, the sun snapped over the top of our neighbors house and hit me full force in the face. I felt like Frankenstein being attacked by a crazed villager who was cruelly waving a torch near his head. The funny thing was I made a similar sound as I threw my free arm over my eyes trying to protect them, "Argghhhhh."

Behind me Nicole chuckled. Then I heard, not saw, her next small act of barbarism. She slid the back door closed blocking off my retreat. I was outside in my pajamas, shrieking with a weiner dog on a leash and apparently no one cared.

I staggered forward five steps. The glare was so powerful my eyes were watering like crazy as the yellow rays of light converted into red dots of pain as I clenched my eye lids together praying for a cloud or the moon to leap to my rescue and block out the cruel sun.

"Woof," Dog said.

I cocked my head to the side slightly. Why the heck was Dog speaking? He never spoke during piddles. He, like myself, believed that silence is the proper medium to be used when relieving ones self.

"Woof woof."

"For god's sake dog, JUST GO!" I jerked his lead slightly trying to remind him that the only reason we were out here in the first place was because of him.

"Do you always scream like that in the morning?"

I spun my head left and right trying to determine the exact location of the voice. My eyes attempted to crack open a bit but the fiery cosmic globe was still pounding directly in my face.

"Who, who's there?"

"Guess." *That voice, no way. This can't be happening.*

"Okay, let me think. Ummm, you're the nice new kid who just moved up the street, right?" I replied, still swiveling my skull around like an owl might, while looking for dinner, well a blind owl with scrunched eyes.

"Nice kid, now that's interesting, and here I was thinking that I was the liar who moved in up the street. You remember the liar who has a cousin back in Georgia."

No way out of this one. I was going to have to stand here and take a bit of yesterday's medicine. "Yes, I remember. What are you doing out at this time of morning and in my backyard?"

Well, I was jogging when I heard the scream. So I cut through the yard behind yours to find you here with this very cute little dog."

"Yes, he is cute. Would you like to pet him?"

"No. I don't want to mess up his coat other wise it might look like your head and that would be a real shame."

Bed head. Great, thank you pillowcase. I have to remind myself to let Dog lie on you the next time dad makes some chili fries.

Then I heard the sound of a shutter, like on a camera or worse on a very nice stream lined cell phone. *NO!!!*

"Please tell me you didn't just take a picture of me."

"Why would I do that? You look like crap. I took a picture of your dog to send to my cousin."

I drew a sigh of relief. "Thank you. I have been the victim of a bad photo scam once before. I appreciate you not making me have to convince my parents that we need to move away from the neighborhood," I said with a smile.

"Why, is that all it would take?" Savannah asked.

I stumbled to the left and felt the garish light finally leave my eyes so that I could open them and focus. Savannah was wearing a full jogging suit made by Under Armor and it looked great on her, too. It takes a brave person to slide into one of those, "please, judge my bod," running suits. But no matter how perfect her hair was, or how white her sneakers were and they were white even after running through our neighbor's yard to reach me, she had just made a real mean comment and it could not go without some form of rebuttal.

"What did you say?"

"I simply asked if taking your picture looking like you do would be all that was necessary to drive you out of this neighborhood."

"What's your freakin' problem?"

She smiled and said nothing. She just stood there and stared at me. Dog piddled and then came to sit by my feet wagging his tail at the new human standing before him. He was trying to impress, why I don't know, but it was creepy. Yesterday Nicole acted the same way like she was star struck. *"Hello Caitlin O'Connor to earth. This is not Hiedi Klum people. Hello, is this microphone on?"*

Behind me the patio door opened, "Caitlin, Dog has to . . . Oh hello. Caitlin who is this?" my mother asked.

"This is our new neighbor. This is Savannah Summers. (*Hecubus, this is my mother.*) Savannah this is my mom.

"It's a pleasure to meet you Mrs. O'Connor."

"Same here Savannah. How are things coming along in your new house, getting everything squared away over there?"

"Well, there is a lot of unpacking to do yet. But before we get started I am going to get a run in then I'll go home and make breakfast before my family gets up. They worked so heard bringin' in the furniture and all, that I wanted to do somthin' nice for them this mornin'. Especially my parents. This move has been so stressful for them and all. I mean their whole lives had been spent in Georgia. I can only imagine they must be feelin' a right bit out of place up here."

Okay. Wow, she is good.

"Well that's very sweet of you, Savannah. But I'm certain they aren't the only ones worried about the move. It must have been hard on you as well uprooting and leaving all your friends and school behind?"

Way to go Mom. Don't fall for this load of very well made bullsh*t. She is trying to impress you but let her see the cynicism that has made you one of the great hard ass parents of all time. Oh chickie poo . . . you're toast!

"Well ma'am I must admit that at first I was a bit upset when I found out we were movin. But I reminded myself that I've my whole life ahead of me. This move is only for a short time. Ya see, my parents have worked hard to become well known designers, I don't want them to miss this big chance to really do something special. They earned this chance, mine will come in time. What's the expression, good things come to those who wait."

Okay mom, HIT IT! I have to confess that my eyes lit up wider than Tiny Tim's would have if he walked in on a full pig roast and a new pony with a braided tail and hooves made of gold. I wanted to shout out, "God bless every one of us."

"Well Savannah I must say, that is a very mature and conscientious attitude towards such a major change in your life. When I see your mother later I'll be sure to let her know what a special daughter she has."

"Thank you Mrs. O'Connor you don't have to do that really."

I was going to be sick.

"Caitlin, why are you out here dressed like that?"

"Because you asked me to walk Dog."

"Well for god's sakes honey, go get dressed. Look, Savannah is already up and about. I swear you're like a lazy bones sometimes."

"Mrs. O'Conner since I can see that Caitlin doesn't like to exercise, I was wondering would you mind if I took Nicole for a run with me? It's so much more fun sharing time with someone when you're runnin' then just runnin' alone."

"You're right Savannah, Caitlin doesn't like to exercise at all. But I suppose if Nicole wants to tag along that would be okay, let me go ask her."

"Thanks Mommy!" Nicole had overheard the whole conversation and came out of the house like a bullet fired from a gun. Savannah and my mother laughed in unison at my sister's enthusiasm. I would have laughed but the large shaggy hairdo I was sporting at that moment would have made my attempt at laughter look like a badger was trying to make little baby badgers with the top of my skull. Best not to laugh at this point.

"Well I guess you got your answer Savannah. Okay Nicole. Stay by Savannah and don't go wandering off, you hear me?"

"Yep."

"Okay running partner, you ready to go?"

Nicole nodded and together they began jogging in place and then with a WHOOSH, they were gone.

I stormed into the house past my mother and unhooked the leash from Dog's collar before spinning on her with a dark, slow burning fury. "How could you let her go off jogging with that, that, thing?"

"Caitlin, what are you talking about?"

"What am I talking about mom, jeez let me think? Let's see a new kid from some place down south . . ."

"Georgia" she interjected.

"Whatever. Some new kid from Georgia moves into the neighborhood and on her second day, a mere two whole minutes after meeting her you allow her to take your youngest child off to god knows where? Do you honestly think that's good parenting?"

"Morning everyone," My dad said as he entered the room. He had just finished his shower and although he was dressed he was still drying his hair with a towel. I was grateful for his timely arrival. Like many other moments in my life where my mother and I failed to see eye to eye, dad was the voice of reason. Which in this house meant that he usually was the one who made at least some sense when it came to the bizarre and twisted problems that we've dealt with throughout the years. My father had been away for a while, while he and mom worked out whether or not they wanted to be together anymore. But about six months ago he had moved back in, it was the happiest day of my life. Why you ask? Because of conversations like this one I was having with my feminine parental unit. Conversations that always led to me being grounded, and my mother needing another trip to the mall.

"Okay, ask dad. Ask dad if it was a good idea to let Nicole go off with a complete stranger?"

"Excuse me young lady, I don't have to ask your father's permission to decide to let Nicole go out for a simple run around the block with someone. And if I were you I would . . ."

"Watch my tone?" I interjected. Alas, I discovered that day that these aggressive interjections were only usable by those who are either parents or professional wrestlers. Which I expected I might need to become by the way my mother made a move at me across the room. Thankfully, dad blocked her by moving quickly to his left and stepping in front of her path.

"Caitlin, watch it. Your mouth is going to get you into a lot of trouble, you understand?" my father said.

"Ian this is what I am talking about. She can't talk to me like that just because she had to get her lazy butt out of bed to walk Dog." My mother was absolutely furious, which seemed okay with me at that moment, since I was as well.

"Dad, she let Nicole go off with the weird kid who just moved into the Frasier's old house."

"How is she weird Caitlin?" My mom shouted back.

"What thirteen year old girl jogs at seven a.m. on summer vacation MOTHER, duh?"

"She's flipped. Ian, our daughter is a mental patient."

"Okay, come on you two, cut it out. Caitlin, upstairs and get ready for your day. We have some things to get done around here and I want to get started before it gets too hot outside. Move it young lady, let's go."

I stomped my feet and headed right over to the counter top where the cradle for our cordless phone was sitting. I snatched the phone from the charger and then with great theatrical flare I stopped and spun at the entrance to the hallway that led through the living room to the stairs at the front of the house. "Dad, I will keep the phone nearby for when Savannah calls with a ransom demand for Nicole's safe return or in twenty four hours when my sister is still not back I can call the police and give them her description."

I then left them standing there speechless and stunned. Sometimes it's good to let your parents know that you too are capable of becoming unhinged, it keeps them on their toes. Unfortunately, it also tends to lead into a lot of alone time in your room, grounded.

I laid down on my bed and looked up at the ceiling. I stared at the white, flat surface intently. Why do people do that, you think? I mean, are there any great mysteries of life that could possibly be contained within

51

the painted surface of a ceiling. For me it was a way to stop from, at least at this point, seeing red.

Running. My little sister was out there somewhere, running. The thought of it sent shivers down my spine. In all the years I've know Nicole, all nine of them, I can only remember her running once for more than a few feet and that was when I had her convinced that the Easter Bunny was not only real, but alive and well, nestled snuggly under Kelsey's shed next door. She burst through the back door like a gazelle that day, running with her list of confectionary treats and happy wishes she wanted to be certain that "Peter" would carry to the other houses in the neighborhood for her. Kelsey was not amused, nor were my parents. We found her trying to crawl under their shed screaming for the cornered bunny to "Take my list, please!" They were so angry in fact, that they made me watch a video they found on the internet of the dangers of rabies and how serious a condition it could be for someone bit by a contaminated, feral rodent.

I was sure that my parents at this point had no idea how serious this situation was becoming. Not only was Savannah Summers being nice to my kid sister, she was going to turn her into a mindless, athletic, muscle bound, zombie freak. Nicole was taking the first steps towards becoming a jock. We are not a family of jocks. My parents watch one sport all year and that's hockey. We don't like football, baseball, shuffleboard, gymnastics, cycling, cross country or soccer. Sweating quite frankly is something that other people do, not us. Swimming is only done recreationally. We do not even own a dart board for the fear of straining our arms trying to dislodge one of the small missiles from the painted cork circle. Okay, that last part may be a bit of an exaggeration but we have never owned a dart board, for whatever reason.

How was I going to handle this? What could I do to secure that my sister stays the soft, logical, lovable couch potato that we all adore?

My intense concentration was disrupted by my mother yelling up the stairs, "Caitlin when Nicole gets back you, your sister and father are going out grocery shopping. I suggest you choose a nice dessert for the Summers' and we can all take it over when I get home tonight. Caitlin did you hear me?"

"Yes." I shouted back and then rolled over screaming into the pillow, "The whole block heard you crazy lady!"

"What? Caitlin you are about to get a smack across the backside you hear me?"

"Yes."

I heard the front door shut. Mom was gone. That meant dad was home and at least at some point I could try to explain to him way Savannah was a bad influence on our "Little Boo."

I looked over at the doll that sat near my bed. Kelsey, or what was sort of left of her, was sitting there staring at me like she always did during this time of the day. I knew that I could talk to her and she could sometimes hear me but never answer. In order for that to happen, it would have to be much later at night, around midnight as a matter of fact. I knew the rules, as did she. But I still sometimes feel the need to un-bottle my thoughts and just confide in her.

"Can you believe this? Mom let Nicole run off, literally, with someone she hardly knows. Okay, you're right and I'm sorry. I know you can hear what goes on around the house. Repeating myself is only making you feel like I don't believe you're actually still here. I'm sorry okay. It's just that this new kid, well, she is very different. No, I mean it Kelsey. There is something wrong with her, she is almost too perfect to be true. I mean come on; she wants to be friends with Nicole? Alright, alright I will give her a chance but I'm telling you, sis, this is not your average new kid on the block. This girl has 'mean' written all over her and I think she is planning on focusing that meanness straight at you-know-who."

A shout came from the downstairs foyer, "Daddy, I'm home."

"In the kitchen, Nicole."

I had to figure out what I was going to do to make my little sister see that all the love, attention and positive reinforcement she could ever need was living inside this house with her. I had to get her head out of the clouds and back on me.

CHAPTER FIVE

FRUIT TARTS

I quickly straightened up my room, which meant I bent over at the waist, grabbed a hold of the bed skirt, lifted it up as far as it would go and then took my right foot and slid the large pile of dirty clothes under the bed. In a matter of a few moments I had done what that bizarre clown chick from the "Big Comfy Couch" had taught me, I had perfected and implemented, the "Ten Second Tidy." My room sparkled, well almost. I still had a glass sitting on top of my bureau that I think had Coke in it at one point. Though now it appeared to have something growing in the bottom that resembled swamp grass.

Perhaps I can show it to Ms. Georgia herself and see if she can identify it. Being from the south surely she has seen and eaten all forms of marsh critters, therefore it's safe to assume that one of them lived in an environment not unlike my Petri glass." I made myself laugh, which I tend to do a lot.

I took the glass in my hand and looked down at the brownish green and yellow fuzz that had climbed nearly two full inches up the side. I contemplated bringing it downstairs and placing it in the trash when a strange thing happened. I swear it appeared as if the fuzz moved. I mean actually changed its shape. Of course this had HUGE implications. If in fact I had somehow grown sentient fuzz in my bedroom I would become famous, a millionaire, no wait, a billionaire. I could see it now, people lining up outside my house, screaming, begging for a chance to come in and see the amazing, lucid, stinky fuzz. My imagination swam in a whirlpool of countless possibilities; a noble prize, an interview with that hot guy from those vamp movies. And there amid all the countless tens of millions of adoring fans stood one figure. High atop of a barren, desolate mountain this "thing" stared down at me. I could tell by its eyes that it mocked my success, laughed at the fact that I had created the perfect environmental conditions in my own room for "fuzz." Then, as if to punctuate just how pathetic it thought my discovery was it held up a large backlit screen that said, "Calling Peggy-Sue . . ."

I let out a blood curdling scream.

"Caite, you okay?"

"What, oh yeah dad, I'm okay."

"Well let's get a move on; we have some errands to run and some ingredients to get from the store."

"Be right down."

"What are you doing?" My sister had moved to the doorway to get a glimpse at what had caused me to scream so loudly. If I had to guess I am betting she was somewhat disappointed to see that it was in fact only a dingy glass and not some nine foot tall alien stuffing me into a burlap bag that caused me to shriek like I did.

"How was your run, did you have fun being in Savannah's shadow?"

"Hey, sissy . . ."

"What?"

"Jealousy is an ugly emotion, although, it suits **you** actually."

"What?" I was about to launch an all out vulgar assault against the little cretin but I knew now was not the time. I had picked at the scab a bit too early, metaphorically speaking. My shadow comment only raised her ire. If I was going to get Nicole to realign her universe so that once again

I was at the center of it, I was going to have to try a different tact. I was going to have to try . . . kindness.

That thought sent a shiver up my spine. This was going to be a very long day, very long indeed.

We headed downstairs after a brief pause of, "you go first." I, being the eldest finally conceded and started my descent.

We entered the kitchen and found my father staring at his laptop, a befuddled look on his face. At first glance, he seemed to be contemplating the zoological value of the manatee, which would make almost any person sit there in silence with a pained expression. We would soon discover however, that this was not the issue that was consuming his thoughts.

Nicole and I chose to be nice children and not interrupt this magical moment by standing there quietly and unmoving. Finally, he looked up and said, "how the hell am I supposed to make this thing, I don't even like fruit cake?"

"Daddy, can't we just go and buy one?" Nicole asked.

"Fruit tart, it's supposed to be a fruit tart dad, not a cake," I added.

His eyes were still drifting far away as if they were trying to recall some childhood memory, perhaps even one that he had blocked out as a form of self preservation. "Yes honey," he replied, "we will have to go out and buy one. I mean there is no way I am going to sit here and make this thing, there's just no way."

I nodded my head in approval. First of all, my dad is a decent cook but when it comes to baking, which is its own skill entirely, well let's just say if it's not a rolled Tollhouse dough, we won't be eating any cookies. He just doesn't bake and it was quite apparent that this task was well beyond his abilities. Second, it meant that instead of having to apologize for a disastrous offering to the Summers' I would instead, be able to proudly hand them a fruit tart from the local bakery which would be heavenly in appearance and taste. We, the O'Connors were going to shine tonight. We were going to show them that "Yankees" can be just as warm and welcoming as anyone from the Confederacy.

The rest of the morning was spent getting my dad's Jeep inspected and doing some other needless errands for the family. It amazes me that in a world so advanced that we still have to drive to certain places in order to conduct business. I suppose some things are just better handled in person.

Finally we arrived back home, our "to-do" list completed and with a fruit tart firmly in our possession from a wonderful German bakery downtown. We also, thanks to some amazingly gifted whining, picked up a few "black and white" cookies to enjoy.

"Daddy, now that we are done running around for the day, can Nicole and I go outside for a bit?"

"Sure sweetie, just remember mom will be home in a few hours so don't go getting too dirty, we are heading over to your new friend's house right after she gets home."

"Okay . . ." I replied aloud, although in my head I said, *She is not my friend dearest father of mine. She is a jerk, a professional a-hole, a creep, a skank and most probably a complete tramp, so please in the future refrain from referring to her as my friend.*

I turned to my sister and asked, "Hey Nicole, wanna go outside and practice some field hockey, the season is only a couple weeks away?"

She walked over towards the small side table that sat near the loveseat in our living room and reached for the cordless phone. *An odd reaction to my question,* I thought.

"Sure sissy. Let me just give Savvy a call and see if she's ready to practice."

I smiled and nodded my head, "Okay then, I'll run up and change into some shorts and my sneakers and be right dow . . . what, who are you calling?"

"Savannah."

"What the HELL for?" I asked.

"Caitlin, let's watch our language and our tone please young lady." My father's words came echoing from the kitchen, where I assume he was placing our fabulous fruity tart in the refrigerator.

Nicole placed the receiver up to her ear, "I promised Savvy that I would call her this afternoon after I got done with our errands. We were going to work on some field hockey stuff together. She was a star forward for her junior high school."

"Oh what a load of horse sh . . ."

I have never been shushed before by my little sister, but on that day, as she heard the call connect and begin to ring in that freaky house up the road where Savannah lived, she raised a single finger to her small pink lips and made the universal sign for "shut your mouth, now." Understand, she did not give me the sign for "please be quiet I'm about to engage in a very important and possibly long distance phone call where being able to hear is vital", oh no. This was shut up, plain and clear. How can you tell the infuriating difference? Simple, she took that single upraised finger and tapped it, not once, not twice, but three times against her lips as her eyes got all small and squinty.

I clenched and unclenched my hands into tight fists as I debated on how severely I should thrash her for even contemplating tapping her finger against her mouth when her call must have been answered.

"Oh hello, this is Nicole O'Conner, is Savannah home? Okay. Yes, thank you ma'am."

I was beside myself. How could this girl have so quickly moved my sister against me? Was our relationship so fragile, so precarious that any freak who paid Nicole even an ounce of attention be able to pull her away from my loving and caring embrace?

Nervous bolts of electrical current shot up and down my body, this unfortunately sent my limbs into a bizarre sort of jerky dance as I kicked, punched and threw myself in an all out assault against my family's couch. Pillows went sailing skyward, cushions attempted to maintain their shape as my fists rained blow after blow onto them. The arm of the couch saw the worst of my reaction as I sunk my teeth into it using its billowy softness to muffle most of my screams.

"Savannah, hey it's Nicole. Can you hang on a minute? My sister is having a seizure."

I went still. *She didn't just tell this chick that I was having a seizure, did she?*

"What in the hell is going on in here Caitlin?" My father was standing over me and by the look he was giving me he was not going to be very receptive to my explanation as to why I was latched firmly to the sofa by my face.

"Dad, can you get her out of here, I'm trying to have a conversation on the phone."

"Room, now!" He shouted, pointing towards the stairs.

I tried to turn it around on Nicole and say that my dad's instructions were meant for her but it sort of came out like, "Mikool, baddy smed goo twoo merr oom." Mental note, always release whatever it is you're chewing on before speaking or you'll end up sounding like a disturbed mental patient.

I was physically lifted by the back of my shirt off the sofa and placed on my feet as my father repeated his order, this time softly and only three inches from my face so that there could be no doubt, he meant it for me. "Go, to your room, now."

I nodded and headed upstairs. I left the cushions lying about the room as a silent warning to my sister about the wrath she had almost faced.

Halfway up the incline I heard, "Hey daddy, Savannah's brother found her field hockey goal and offered to put it together for us, can I go over there to practice?"

I smiled a dark and secret smile and lingered on the stairs waiting for the resounding, "no" that I knew was forthcoming from my father. I knew his belief system about walking that far alone, especially for Nicole. This perhaps was going to be worth getting grounded for in the first place.

"I don't know Nicole. With sissy grounded I wouldn't feel comfortable with you walking that far alone." I nearly burst with joy. Yet even as my heart swelled with that wonderful feeling of "hah, gotcha" my sister chimed back. "No, daddy its okay, Savannah said that she will bring the goal here so you don't have to worry about me walking there by myself, as long as it's okay we play in our yard."

Did you ever see the old vampire movies? You know the ones I mean, the old black and white classics with Bella Lagossi? Well, in those magical films, there is inevitably a scene where the count is confronted by some old geezer with a cross. Seeing the blessed crucifix, the dark and powerful vampire cowers in terror. Well, that must have been exactly how my face looked as I heard my father thank Savannah and give them all permission to come to our house and practice in the back yard. It probably didn't help that I threw my left arm across my face and fell against the wall. I always thought that move was a bit too "over the top" but in times of crisis, it is actually a natural and completely reasonable reaction to a sudden and disturbing situation.

"Okay Savvy, I'll go upstairs to change and be right out. My sister, oh no she won't be able to join us, she just got grounded for acting like a bean head and trying to eat the sofa."

Sweet mother of God, tell me she didn't just say that. Eat the sofa? Is there no limit to the number of times you are willing to stab me in the back, Brutus?

Then, as if nothing could have happened to make the matter any worse I heard from my perch on the fifth step, laughter. Yes, deep, hearty laughter. My sister was actually belly laughing at something that had been said on the other end of the phone. She whispered and then placed the phone back in its charger and ran towards the stairs.

"Excuse me," she chirped.

I moved to block her. "What was so funny?"

"Nothing, now please excuse me." It was obvious that she was repressing a sneer.

"Nicole, I am not moving until you tell me what Savannah said."

"Aren't you grounded right now? Didn't dad tell you to get to your room over two minutes ago? He is going to be really angry when he finds out you were eavesdropping on my conversation and not sitting in your room."

"If you do not tell me what she said this minute when I am not grounded, I will go downstairs log into the computer and order a ten pound tarantula from Papua New Guinea, and when it arrives I will release it in your bedroom while you are sleeping."

Fear crept across her face as she conjured a vision of this big, thick, black, hairy limbed spider scurrying across her bedroom floor. The image had nearly wormed its way entirely into her brain when her logical mind reasoned out the situation and foiled my scheme, "You don't have a credit card and the shipping alone would be over thirty dollars, especially if the package weighs more than eight pounds. Now move." And with that she muscled past me and into her room.

The times, they were a changing and it sucked.

Defeated, I walked down the hall and into my own room and closed the door behind me. As a kid I can tell you nothing sucks more than being sent to your room when you don't want to be there. And yet, I can't tell you how many times I've run to my room willingly when I didn't want to be where everyone else was. How can the same 12' x 15' space be both a prison and a sanctuary? Oh sure, I had my books and my music all in here, but out there my little sister was discovering a world in which I was expendable. This all felt so wrong.

The next two hours were hell. I snuck several times over to the guest room where my grandmother sleeps whenever she comes down to visit and watched them play through the window. That room faced the back of the house and I had a clear view of the three of them laughing, running and having a generally good time together. Yes, I said three because Savannah's older brother put on some goalie pads and tended goal for them while they worked countless give and go's and set plays that Savannah must have learned from her JV coach.

Twice I called down to my father and asked him how long I was going to have to stay in my room. His answer was so absolutely "parent" that it made my blood boil; "When you can explain to me exactly why you were trying to consume the living room furniture, you can come down." Great, that explanation could take me a week to riddle out. *This so blows.*

I thought about confiding in him about my jealousy but I was already developing a headache and didn't want to compound it by listening to a lecture about people needing their own friends and space. *Blah, blah, bleck!*

Finally, after just over the two and half hour mark the field hockey gang decided to call it quits and go their separate ways. This was of course after several pitchers of Gatorade my father brought out to them.

I lay there and stared at my ceiling, a hobby that would consume fairly large portions of my time over the next several months and waited to hear Nicole coming back upstairs. I did not have to wait too long.

"Nicole," I shouted.

The door opened slowly as she peeked inside. She was obviously tentative about coming in and rightly so. I had acted poorly and she knew that sometimes when I lose my "cookies" that it can take anywhere from twelve minutes to seven years to get over it.

"What is it?"

"Dad said I needed to tell him why I was chewing on the couch before he will un-ground me."

"Really, wow that's not good."

"Yeah, I know. How can I explain that I feel like this new girl is trying to weasel her way into my sister's heart? How can I say that I feel jealous and angry cause my sib is more interested in spending time with this new kid more than she is with me?" I let my gaze leave the flat white surface of my ceiling to connect with the vibrant blue pools that are Nicole's eyes.

"You see sissy, this is going to be really hard. Because in all the things you said it was "my" and "me". You need to understand that I need to have fun and friends as well. How many times have you chased me out of your friendships? How many times have you told me to get lost, go home or beat it? Listen sis, I'm not mad at you but Savannah really likes me. We have a lot in common, that's all. You hate playing hockey. You will never run with me or do some of the outside games that I enjoy. So, why can't you be happy that I found someone who I can do those things with?"

"You're right, I guess I expected you to be more like me, more like Kelsey was."

"Don't go there Sissy."

"What, all I said was that I wish you were more like her, you know what I mean, more into the things I like?"

"You know what? She was my sister too, Caitlin. And I never got the chance to know her. You and her were close, bestest friends while I was always the little kid tagging along. I never got to stay up late and talk with her during sleepovers. I never shared special dreams or diary secrets. I never got to go on special birthday trips with her and the Addams. I never even had the chance to say 'I love you' to her before she had to go, so don't start with this whole, you're not like Kelsey okay, cause I don't even know who Kelsey really was."

"Nicole, I didn't mean to . . ."

"She didn't even say goodbye to me. She died and she never even said goodbye. She wrote the note to you, not to me. I mean she never even hugged me before she went away. And now you want to take away the first real friend I've ever had? How selfish can you possibly be?"

"I guess I'm really selfish. I'm so sorry, Boo."

"Sorry for what, being a jerk or just being you?" She turned and closed the door. I rolled onto my side and cried for a while. It felt good to cry which in a way, bothers me. Crying should not feel good. It should not be therapeutic to cry and yet the tears acted like a pressure valve that day and kept me from going insane at least until we had officially delivered the infamous tart.

Six o'clock came rather quickly. I had slept for at least an hour in the cool comfort of my bedroom which helped to strengthen my resolve for the upcoming task. I decided that perhaps the best way to recapture my sister's attention wasn't in shaming her into it or trying to trick her. No, the only real way to get Nicole to understand that I was the better option for her best friend was to become her best option for a best friend. Which meant that tonight, I had to shine.

I climbed out of bed and rummaged through my closet for something decent to wear. It took a few minutes but in the end I settled for a nice red dress I had worn to Easter dinner earlier this year. It was a great length on me, coming down just above the knee and had a really cute off white belt that cinched the dress in the middle which Mimi had said definitely showed off my waist line.

No one knows fashion like my Mimi. She had actually been a consultant or an advisor, (I forget which) for that absolutely fabulous British sitcom that ran on the air a few years back. Mimi is very well thought of in the fashion world and her sense of style is always impeccable. When I got this dress I had even found a nice pair of matching red shoes to go with it that had a small heel to them. It was so cool when everyone at the restaurant that day said I had looked so grown up.

Yes, this was definitely what I was going to wear to meet and greet the wretch. I looked over at my alarm clock, *Damn it.* Mom would be home soon. If my idea was going to work I had to hustle, big time.

I laid the dress and the shoes out on my bed. I then ran, not walked but ran, downstairs heading for my mother's room. I had to get my hands on her make up bag for a few minutes if I was going to make the statement that I thought needed to be made that day. I went quickly down the hallway passed our living room and slammed on the brakes. I didn't want to impale myself on our kitchen table.

Now, I am not sure how the laws of physics actually applied to this particular move but somehow I made a left hand turn while sliding forward without losing an ounce of momentum. My father was preoccupied at the stove putting the finishing touches on his Mexican feast (which we do once a month) so he never saw, heard or sensed my swish through the kitchen into the back part of the house.

I leapt into the bathroom. Then, I carefully closed the door and locked it. Only then, after I was certain that he had not seen me, I reached up and flipped on the light switch casting soft white illumination across the entire room.

I felt like Indiana Jones, which is a very strange yet somewhat intoxicating feeling. There I was, now safely secured in the temple of some bizarre porcelain god ready to take the long sought after treasure from its sacred holding place. I stood up, and began a very methodic search of my mother's so called, beauty kit. Being the age I am, there are of course, rules as to which particular items I am allowed to use and the quantity of each item. I am not allowed any of the following products: eyeliner, rouge, tweezers for the eyebrows or an eyebrow comb, (please don't ask you can imagine how messed up I looked with one whole eyebrow missing), that funky, chunky thing that makes your lashes bend, lip pencils, dark colored eye shadow, lipstick, or any other products that come from Lancome or some other high end cosmetics counter.

So basically, I was stuck with, lip gloss, mascara and a touch of cover up as needed. Here is the crux of my situation, all these rules go out the window on special occasions.

Whenever we go out to a wedding, extra important dinner or fancy party I am allowed, with my mother's assistance, to apply some of the more exotic creams, potions and lotions to which I am normally exempt. This was my newest plan. To make certain that my mother and father deemed this meeting tonight as a special occasion. Once I had those words used in a sentence by them, I would be golden.

After only about a minute of scrounging, I was able to locate the eleven items I deemed crucial for my overall magnificent appearance this evening. I slid them into the front pockets of my jeans and casually made my way out of the bathroom.

"Caitlin, what are you doing down here?"

"I needed to use the bathroom and Nicole needed the other one."

My father frowned but accepted the answer as "plausible" so I continued to make my way back up the hall away from the kitchen and the wonderful smell of tacos.

"By chance, are you ready to tell me what was going on before?"

"Before, before when?" My mind was preoccupied with trying to sort out which shade of color would make my eyes pop while wearing my red dress that I honestly wasn't thinking about the tantrum from earlier in the day. "Oh, that before. Well daddy, I am having a real hard time with some girl stuff right now, ya know hormones and feeling icky, all that kind'a stuff."

"Caitlin, I would appreciate a bit more honesty. Do you really believe I am so stupid as to think that you hitting puberty would cause you to chomp down on our couch like a deranged badger? Come on Caite, what's going on that you are obviously not telling me?"

"Dad if I promised never to chew on the furniture again, could we not have this discussion?"

He studied me. He was checking to see just how important it was for me NOT to go into why I had behaved so poorly earlier. Somehow, just standing there and not over-reacting got my message across this time. My father turned around and finished rinsing out the heavy frying pan that he had used for the ground beef. I waited a full minute for the words to begin but none came.

"Thanks Daddy." I said.

He looked back over his shoulder and nodded. I was free, free from the speech, free from the arguments, free from my grounding. I had asked for a favor and he had answered it.

And yet how was I going to repay him for that moment of trust . . . by sneaking mom's make-up upstairs and using it. I knew full well that manipulating the situation like this was probably going to get my parents into a fight. My mom would ask my dad why I had been allowed to take her things; my dad would say he didn't see me do it. Mom would ask if he paid attention to us at all during the course of the day. And so on, and so on.

Yep, this would become an all out "ouch" if I snuck this crap to my room. I sighed and turned around walking back into the downstairs bathroom. I think I saw him watching me out the corner of his eye as I stepped inside and emptied the contents of my pockets back into mom's bag.

I came through the kitchen again and stopped, facing him. I placed my hands on the back of one of the chairs at the kitchen table.

"Dad"

He turned, smiled at me and replied, "Thank you Caite. Now go on upstairs and tell your sister it's time for dinner so she can set the table for us, and please walk Dog, he hasn't been out in a while."

I did as he asked and got Nicole. Then leashing up Dog, I threw on some shoes and went out the back sliding door so that he could do his famous late afternoon impersonation of Niagara Falls. He prefers to do his act against the weeping willow alongside our house, so seeing he had been such a good boy all day I decided to make him happy. I swear he thinks he's a gymnast. There has never been a Russian, Czech or Ukrainian who can hold a toe point as long as my wiener dog can. One day I am going to have to bring a score card with us, just to see his reaction.

As Dog and I made our way back inside I saw the field hockey goal lying against the back of our house. *Great.* That means that they are coming back. Dog stopped and sniffed it.

You may not know this but animals are very keen to their owner's emotional state. When you feel joy, so do they. When you are sick, they worry. When you are sad, they are concerned and when you want to lash out at something that belongs to someone else, they raise their leg and try to piddle on it. Try was the key word here, since he had exhausted himself only a few minutes ago, the water works were a 'no show.' He lowered his leg. We were both a bit disappointed but I patted him on the head, thanking him anyway.

By the time we got back inside my mother had pulled into the driveway. She and I came through doors on opposite sides of the house almost simultaneously.

"I'm home."

And now the familiar replies began to reverberate around the house, Dad's "In the kitchen," Nicole's "Hi Mom, how was your day?" and my "So am I."

"What are you cooking?" She asked, placing her computer bag down on the floor by the stairs. Nicole came over and gave her a hug and the "nightly routine" began. We made small talk while dad got the food on the table. Mom complained about work, dad went down his checklist of errands we had run and Nicole told mom all about her day playing field hockey with the new kids.

We ate dinner quickly, which was pretty standard for us. Rarely does a meal last more than twenty minutes, and that's Thanksgiving. Nicole helped me clean off the table, which normally required me verbally twisting her arm. It was obvious she was in a hurry to head over to Savannah's house to see her new friend.

We grabbed the baked goods, hooked Dog to his leash and as a family unit, exited the house and made our way down to the end of the driveway.

It was apparent that Craig, his parents and Aunt Katrina were heading toward us by the loud, bellowing shout that came wafting across the expanse of two front yards.

"Nicole, Quate-lin, ah dhalinks, how vonderful to see you both again. You are looking mahvelous Quate-lin and you Nicole, how you have grown since last I laid my eyes upon you."

"I really don't think I could have grown much since yesterday Auntie K," Nicole replied.

Of course, this revelation did not stop Craig's aunt from continuing with her train of thought, "Ack, children sprout like veeds. Vhy I remember vhen I vas a little girl my Uncle Mykano saying to me that a parent can measure their accomplishments in life by the growth of their children. Of course, he vas usually out of vork and had two boys who vere midgets but . . ."

Thankfully, Craig's mom cut in, "Hey you guys."

Ah the greeting ritual of white, suburban, New England. Everyone smiles, men shake hands, woman almost kiss each other on the cheek, children raise their right hands in a quick wave and then immediately return said hand to their back jean pocket. The adults will then meander for a few minutes catching up, while the kids rock slowly back and forth on their heels, hoping for a puma or some other large predatory cat to come out of the bushes and frighten everyone scrambling in different directions. Yep, running into your neighbors, especially when you had planned on doing it, was always pure joy.

"Hey Craig."

"Hey, Nicole. I saw you practicing Field Hockey out back this afternoon."

"You did?"

I stood there. I contemplated saying something sarcastic but after the time when Mr. and Mrs. Dawson had witnessed me slap Nicole at Kelsey's wake I thought the better of it.

"Yeah you looked like you're doing awesome. I saw a couple of those shots you made, pretty cool."

"Thanks Craig, Savannah is an awesome teacher. Have you met her yet?"

"No, not yet, although she definitely looked like she knew what she was doing."

"Did you see me this afternoon, too?" I interjected.

"Come to think of it, no Caitlin I didn't," he replied flashing his patented smile.

"Come to think of it? I guess that means you hadn't thought of it until just now. It hadn't occurred to you to find out why I wasn't outside playing field hockey in my own backyard?" This entire conversation was going on while our parents gossiped and chatted inanely above our heads.

"Ummm no. I just figured you hate field hockey so much that you decided not to play." He looked over to my sister, as if begging for her support with regards to his obviously flawed logic.

"You just figured? You just figured that I would be so selfish that I would allow my sister to play outside with complete strangers. Do you honestly believe that I am that shallow, that irresponsible, that aloof?"

"Well, that or you were grounded," he said.

Nicole burst out laughing, "She was grounded."

"Oh, okay then," he said with finality. Why is it that boys think that just because they come to a place in a conversation where it "feels right" to end it, that they can end it. Well, no way, not this time. My crush had **NOT** seen me outside, was **not** certain as to the reasons for my absence and made no attempt to call, or discover if I was okay or sick or maybe even dead. I could have fallen face first into a bucket of cement and he would have never known it. I could have been whisked off to Kentucky for an impromptu marriage to some bucked tooth Wildman and he apparently wouldn't have cared. Men are such jerks.

"Would it have killed you to call and check on me?" I shot back.

"Well, if you were grounded then you most likely couldn't have come to the phone."

Weak.

I yanked on my dad's shirt, "Dad, if Craig had called would you have allowed me to talk to him and tell him I was not dead."

"What, ummm when?" He looked very confused as he tried to unravel the conversation going on around him but to which he had not been listening.

"If Craig had called today, and asked for me, would you have let me tell him I was okay."

"No, you were grounded."

"Tah Dah." Craig threw his hands out wide as if in victory.

"Don't you tah dah me Craig Dawson, you didn't even know I WAS grounded."

"Caitlin, do you need a minute to calm down before we head over?" My mother's voice let me know that this conversation, for now was to be put on hold.

"No." I mumbled.

Mrs. Dawson then said, "Okay then, let's go over everybody, this fruit tart shouldn't be out in the heat for very long."

"Wait, you brought a fruit tart?" Mom inquired.

"Of course I did, why?"

"Because, we brought a fruit tart as well." Mom said.

"But Christine, I told Caitlin specifically that I was going to make my famous fruit tart."

Nicole beamed. Dog began to whine. My father looked like someone who just heard the verdict of a jury and was trying to come to grips with his best friend being sentenced to stand in front of a firing squad. Katrina threw her hands skyward as if to punctuate, "GOD NO, NOT TWO TARTS," and Craig, my knight in shining armor, took three steps back and shook his head from side to side, consigning me to face my fate, alone.

"I thought you told me that you asked Mrs. Dawson if we could . . ."

That night I learned that Females have several rules that are universally sacred, they are as follows:

1) Never wear the same color as the mother of the Bride on her daughter's wedding day.
2) Pearls go with anything.

3) Never duplicate a desert to a block party or meet and greet.

I, it appeared, had committed a cardinal sin and was certain that I was going to hear about it later. In the mean time, the eight of us began walking around the block so that we wouldn't cut across anyone's property on our way to the Summers' house.

Other neighbors waved as we passed. Some fell in behind us, a few were already further up the road. Since it was the middle of July the sun was still out although it was already beginning to dip low in the west. It's fading rays of light began to cast shadows as we walked, shadows that at first I watched with some fascination. I saw how my shadow and Craig's almost appeared to be holding hands. It made me feel nice to see how our long, spindly black arms swung in unison upon the ground. Then I began to remember something that my sister had told me about the grey lands and how the shadows there weren't nice but elusive and predatory.

The grey lands are the area between life and death. It is a place that few travel in for long. Most people, once their time has come, find a guide waiting to take them across this desolate landscape into the light where their family and friends await them. Some people however, like Kelsey, get lost. They are bound to wander that place until someone in the mortal world helps them discover what it is that makes them unable to move on. The grey lands are not for the feint of heart. They are cold and scary with only a few trees and shadows that moan and weep.

We rounded the corner and headed back up Wincott which was the street that ran behind ours. I began developing a terrible sense of dread, as if taking these steps would be something I would regret for the rest of my life. Each time we passed another house my legs grew heavier and my heart more sad. It made no sense at the time. I had been to other places and events in my life that I did not want to attend but this was different. This actually felt like I was walking in quick sand. One glance let me know that no one else in my party was suffering from the same ill effects. It seemed as if I was the only one noticing it.

At least half a dozen other neighbors had already entered the small wrought iron fence that surrounded the property. The panels of fence were very ornate with many designs across the top.

The house that the Summers' had moved into was to say the least, creepy. As a matter of fact, it was so creepy most kids chose not to even bother approaching it during Halloween even though there was candy on the front porch in a very welcoming bowl that always had a large sign over it saying, "Please, help yourself." Few ever did.

I do recall once though, a kid from across town who went up to the porch with some of his friends. They filled their pillowcases full of the sugary goodness and then mocked us for being so absolutely chicken-sh*t.

It's odd how none of us ever saw those kids again. Oh, our parents were nice to make up some BS story about the kid's father getting a job cross country. But I swear, I thought I saw one of their pictures on the back of a milk carton last year.

That must have been the reason I was getting so tense. I was obviously projecting my fear of ever going near the old Fraiser house on tonight's festivities. That idea calmed me down quite a bit. It made sense. Sure, I was afraid of perhaps doing or saying something silly tonight and having this Savannah bust my chops for it. But I also think that it was the house itself that made me nervous. All and all things would be fine as long as I kept my mouth shut and my eyes open.

And open is exactly what my eyes were as I crossed through the fence and entered the Summers' property. What a dump. This place made the

Munsters' place look like a Good Housekeeping Mansion. To call the building old was an understatement. It was really old. Like Victorian old, with a ton of windows and shutters all over the front of the house. It also had about eight different roof levels tilting this way and that. Let me sum up the overall effect of this visual nightmare like this: if Dr. Seuss had been an architect this would surely have been the house that the Onceler would have wanted to own. It was freakin bizarre, and if the overall character of the house needed anymore spook, years ago old man Fraiser had placed exterior lights in the ground that pointed towards different spots along the roofs corners to illuminate the thirteen gargoyle rainspouts that supposedly were placed there by the genius who paid for this blight to be constructed. The effect was that every time it rained, the grotesque little monsters would vomit gallons of water all over the yard. What a pleasant and attractive concept. I know that when I get older, I will insist on having stone demons burping rain water all over my house too.

The first of the neighbors had arrived and were being shown in by Savannah's older brother, who we shall from henceforth call, Hottie. Hottie was wearing a very nice white tee under a solid black Bahama shirt that of course, was open but still clinging to his body. Covering his lower half was a pair of jeans and a very nice pair if I may say so myself. His hair, combed and yet a bit messy was of course, exactly the way it was supposed to look. He was, a nine out of ten and that was only because he was not a musician. Only musicians get to be a perfect ten.

When we reached the door he was polite and sincere. "Good evening Mr. and Mrs. O'Connor welcome to our home, please come on in. Hey Nicole, how ya doin' kiddo?"

"Hey Stephen," she beemed and if I didn't know any better, I think she actually tried batting her eyes although it sort of made her look like she had a twitch going on.

I stood there a moment waiting to be recognized, when my father opened his big mouth.

"Stephen Summers, may I introduce the Dawsons, this is their son Craig and their very delightful Aunt Katrina."

"Pleasure, please come on in, my parents will be so pleased to make your acquaintance," he replied.

Aunt Katrina leaned in towards Senior Hottie and whispered, "I sense a great power residing in this house. It is almost as if a psychic or powervul magi dwelled vithin dese valls." Her head tilted slightly, causing her gigantic mane of salt and pepper hair to wave like dune grass.

Well the Spooky factor just went up by thirty percent . . . thanks crazy lady.

Craig's mother was quick to try to drag the conversation back from the Twilight Zone and into a more appropriate Massachusetts dialogue, "Well, I hope your mother won't mind but we doubled up on the fruit tarts, sort of a cross wired situation." Mrs. Dawson was doing a very nice C.Y.A. (For the meaning of this acronym please see the "Official Guide to Acronyms" or in this example you could try the popular book titled, "How to be a Weasel and <u>Cover Your Ass</u> during an Uncomfortable Social Situation.")

"Ma'am all I can tell you is I hope someone else made the same mistake, cause you can never have enough tarts at a get together."

Mrs. Dawson just melted at those kind words. In fact Stephen's overall calm and pleasant demeanor put everyone into a relaxed state, everyone but me.

The group began to move past the young man and filed into the cryptorium as I looped Dog's retractable leash around one of the slats in the front porch railing. He gave me the patented "what the hell" look as I walked away and reappeared in front of Stephen.

I had decided, being my marvelous self, that if I was going to repair the current relationship with Savannah I would first have to win over her brother.

Another group of adults was already closing in on the front porch so I knew I had to make this quick and impressive.

"Hello, I'm Caitlin, Caitlin O'Connor." I curtsied.

"Welcome to our home. It's a real pleasure to have ya all here tonight. My name is Stephen Summers. My parents will be real honored to make your acquaintance," he shouted over my head to the arriving guests that began to cue up behind me.

I stood there, unmoving. This was not only ridiculous but rude, and rude was something we O'Connor's can not abide.

"Stephen, down here, hello?"

"Oh hey."

Oh hey. Oh hell no. "Don't I get a formal hello?" I asked trying to be as socially mature as possible.

"I said hello before," he nodded at the people now directly behind me. I positioned my body to basically take up the entire door. No one was getting past me until I got my hello.

"Ummm, No, no you didn't." *Time to pay the check.*

"Oh gosh, I'm sorry Caitlin, how absolutely rude of me. Hello, and how are you this evening?"

Ah, success. Hottie noticed and greeted me like I was actually welcome. It's good to be the Queen.

"Caitlin, stop blocking the line, what are you doing standing there like that?" My mother said as her head came popping into the doorway.

"I was waiting for my hello."

"Stop acting strange this instant and get in here young lady. Stephen I'm so sorry if she was being a pest."

He smiled and said, "Oh don't worry ma'am, it was my fault, I failed to greet a lady entering the house."

I was exonerated. I was lifted above the heads of mere mortal men and shown to be right for once to my mother. A warm light poured over me. Angels sang the blessed Hallelujah Chorus. All was right in my world, until of course my knight in shining armor had his warhorse kick me in the head with a steel shod hoof.

"Well thank you for your patience, Stephen." Mother continued.

"No worries ma'am, I know how kids can get."

Did that over confident, smug, arrogant, well quaffed, peacock just call me a

K

I

D

Great. Freakin' great. Just what I needed tonight. Two tarts, a mother who was once again made to look like she was smarter than me, a sneering sister, lady Satan waiting for me inside a house that Norman Bates wouldn't stay the night in and a wise ass door man who thinks I am a diaper wearing, shnookie suckin, rug rat. Yep when the planets are misaligned, boy, are they misaligned.

I lowered my head and crossed the threshold. Never in my life was I prepared for what I saw next. It was without a doubt the largest foyer I had ever stood in. It seemed to go on forever. Directly in front of us, though about twenty-five feet away was a large, bi-sectioned stair case. It started on this level as one eight foot wide staircase but halfway up it split into two identical swooping staircases one bent to the right and the other bent to the left forming two distinct staircases from the top hallway. There were rooms that were situated on either side of this monstrous stair case, one I was guessing was or would be the formal living room, since there were a ton of unopened boxes strewn about the room marked, "living room."

On the other side of this massive expanse or to my right sat the dining room. Again I only knew this because of the one hundred or so boxes that sat against the various wall spaces that could be seen from this entranceway. It seemed like there were smaller hallways to the left and right of the stairs and down them I assumed were the kitchen and some other rooms that would be used for displaying the obvious gargantuan amounts of crap that the Summers' felt compelled to bring with them from their native Georgia.

I heard Stephen call to the twenty or so people who were milling about that his parents were down the hall to the right showing some other neighbors the kitchen. *Elementary, my dear Watson.*

My parents and the Dawson's began moving in that direction as suggested by the herd master. I took a moment to look up. The ceiling in this front vestibule had to be nearly thirty feet high but that was not what caught my immediate attention. *Wow.* I had never seen a chandelier like this before. To call it the 'Crystal Octopus God' would have been to insult it. It was huge, mammoth and had to require at least sixty light bulbs to fill its various receptacles. Beads and tear drops hung off of it from its twenty four golden arms sixteen on the bottom tier and eight at the top. I exhaled and let out a soft, "My God."

The reply I got to such a statement was not what I exactly expected, "I know Quate-lin. I too feel a terrible presence here. Ve are both spiritually sensitive dhalink, therefore ve must be sure to protect the others should something happen. Here take dis," and she handed me a piece of burlap tightly woven into a small length of thin rope. "It comes from the shroud and has protective powers," she added nodding her head at me.

"The shroud, are you kidding me? This came from THE Shroud, as in Turin?"

"Quate-lin, vhat are you talking about," she lowered her voice realizing that we were touching on some seriously odd conversation, "vhere vould I get a piece of that shroud. No dhalink, this came from a vheel of cheese that was blessed by a priest back in my home country."

I had to know, even though I was prepared for an answer that more than likely would only aggravate me, "Why would a priest, bless a burlap sack, that was going to be wrapped around a wheel of cheese?"

She rolled her eyes at me, "No silly girl, he blessed the cheese of course. The burlap vas just fortunate enough to be in between him and the cheese. Come, stay close."

Shrugging my shoulders, I followed Katrina down the hall in the direction that Stephen had indicated his parents were. After passing the large dining room we entered a kitchen that was almost the size of our house. It was unbelievable just how gi-normous this thing was. It had a center island that was bigger than my family's table that we ate dinner on every night. The floor appeared to be made of large porcelain tiles and the counter top was butcher block. Pots and frying pans hung from the ceiling over the top of the island on hooks dangling like the pieces of meat that they were meant to cook from some outdoor market. The cabinets were painted an off white and they seemed to cover every bit of wall surface where a window wasn't previously present.

We entered this cathedral to food preparation in the middle of a conversation that the Summers' were having with a young couple who had moved in about a year ago, the Talgert's. Mr. and Mrs. Talgert were a nice young, newlywed couple who as of yet, being only in their mid twenties, had no children and therefore no bearing on my life. They were never outside except to cut the grass or rake a few leaves in the late autumn. They kept to themselves and I believe they traveled a lot.

". . . well the idea is to install all new Viking appliances because I just love to cook."

"Stainless steel?" The Talgert's asked simultaneously.

"Definitely, as a matter of fact I found the most beautiful set of matching refrigerator, stove with two ovens, and dishwasher at the store today. I just have to make sure it's okay with the boss," Mrs. Summers smiled.

The boss? Why the heck did Mrs. Summers need my mother's freakin okay to buy kitchen appliances? That thought made me chuckle. *Ah, Caitlin you know how to make some real funnies . . .*

"Well, I never could say no to a southern beauty who can also cook," Mr. Summers replied. The cute, or should I say nauseating response, got him an, "Oh Danny . . ." from his adoring wife, followed by a kiss on the cheek.

Mrs. Summers, or Karen, as I would soon discover, saw us out the corner of her eye and interrupted their conversation, "Oh please, come on in. Hello, hello we're the Summers', this is Daniel and I'm Karen, welcome to our home."

"Hello, I'm Christine, this is my husband Ian. We're the O'Connor's."

"Oh Nicole's parents, it's a pleasure to meet you and this young lady must be Keenan?"

"No, no, it's Quate-lin." *Great, Aunt Katrina to the rescue.*

"Oh honey I'm so sorry, I just hate it when people mispronounce my name."

I couldn't help myself, "Which one, Karen or Summers?"

"Why, which ever one they fumble with Katie Jim."

"It's Caitlin, as in Kate Lynn."

"Well that's special," she grinned and I swear I couldn't tell if she was slow or just trying to provoke me.

Thankfully my mother stopped the madness and actually scored some "Oh yeah" points with me that night by beating Mrs. Dawson to the punch, "Well, we brought some desserts in stereo tonight, figured they look so good, better to have too much than not enough."

"Look Daniel, isn't that special?"

Daniel nodded, "Definitely," was all he said.

"Mrs. Summers, have you seen Savannah?" Nicole asked.

"Why I do believe she may be in the shower Nicole but I'm sure she won't be too long." Another smile, my god this family has that look down to a science.

"You have a lovely home. It is filled vith such powerful energy." Katrina said.

"Well, thank you for noticing that, we are so excited by the prospect of restoring this house. Daniel, did you hear that, this lovely lady here said she can feel the power of this house, isn't that special?" Mrs. Summers gushed.

"Definitely."

"Oh, are you planning on restoring the house entirely to its original condition?" my dad asked.

"Well, Daniel is an architect and I graduated from Alabama with a degree in interior design. I am fascinated by the grouping of objects and how they can create harmony or chaos depending on their spatial relevance. So, while the outside of the house will be completely as it was the day it was built, the inside will be modernized and a bit more, to use the layman's parlance, feng shui."

"Definitely."

My mother's eyes narrowed a bit, "Spatial relevance?"

"Oh my god, listen to me gettin' BH&G on ya all. Daniel knows once I get started I could talk about this all night, right honey?"

Surprisingly, he did not say definitely. Instead, he just nodded and thought it, really loud.

"You see, spatial relevance is when you group items together in a pleasing and useful way, so that the home owners enjoy both the form of the object and its functionality, without giving up one for the other."

"You mean like a door near the toilet, or a mattress on a box spring?" I asked.

"Well, yes and no, Betsy Kim. It's a bit more than that. It's placing a vase at the right height and angle so that it can be enjoyed both sitting and standing. It's positioning the dining room table in the space so that the meal can be eaten without any distractions to your guests enjoying the magnificent view from your bay window."

Thankfully, actually mercifully, Stephen shoved his head into the doorway and interrupted what was quickly moving towards an absolutely fascinating conversation, "Mrs. O'Connor your dog is going a bit squirrelly out here and won't let one of the guests in the house."

"Oh no, Caitlin go get Dog. Mrs. Ritter must have made chili again and it's freaking him out." Normally a command like this would be followed quickly with a "why me?" but in this instance anywhere was better than here.

"And Caitlin, don't dilly dally. Put Dog in the house and get right back here, no more than five minutes young lady."

So I nodded and excused myself. I made my way towards Stephen and down the hallway that would lead me towards the front porch and my freedom.

"Stephen, would you be so kind as to run upstairs and tell your sister that her favorite little Massachuettesian is here please?"

And so it was that for exactly eighteen steps, Stephen and I were side by side heading for the front of the house. I would have said something magical but he had ticked me off way too much with his previous comments so we parted ways, silently.

I hit the front porch as the pandemonium was reaching a crescendo, "Stop it! Stop it right now. Oh ho, there you are Caitlin O'Connor. Will you please get that vicious animal away from me before one of us is forced to defend themselves?"

"Hello Mrs. Ritter, how are you this evening?"

"How am I? I'll tell you how I am, I am about to get my dead husband William's shotgun and stop this madness once and for all, that's how I am."

I leaned over and started untying Dog's leash. He immediately began jerking and yanking trying desperately to wrestle himself loose to get a sample of her famous chili: a chili which had won so many local awards that she could have been amazingly rich already if she wasn't such a notorious curmudgeon. On no less than seven occasions large food companies from around the United States and one from Morocco have come to try and persuade Mrs. Ritter to part with her recipe. The rumor mill even claims she has been offered to keep her name on the can, but like a true **ar-tist** she has firmly denied every single offer. My parents even joke that she has left instructions to have the parchment with the list of ingredients burned upon her death.

"He can't help himself Mrs. Ritter. Your chili drives him insane. I am not sure why my dachshund loves spicy food but he does."

I was forced to pick Dog up because he was literally choking himself trying to get to the pot of savory goodness that she was carrying in her trembling, veiny hands. I moved as quickly as I could down the stairs and took a few steps back so that she could pass.

"It's not my chili he's after, it's my legs. He's a nasty, unkempt, loud, yapping little freak and everybody hates him."

Thank you God for not letting me ask her if she was looking in a mirror. You saved me a very long lecture somewhere in the future.

And so it was that I left my family, Craig and Aunt Katrina inside the creepy old house while I made my way up the street. Inside a very important conversation was going on that I unfortunately did not learn about until weeks later, for if I had in fact been allowed a glimpse of it I would have been far less upset in the next few minutes. The conversation I speak of was this: Stephen had come back into the kitchen to announce to Nicole and his parents that "Savannah was not upstairs in her room."

I walked with Dog who was finally settling down. We got to the next driveway and I cut through the yard at the side of the house following the hedgerow towards the back property line that joined with our yard. Dog of course, had to stop for a second and sniff around because it's what dogs do. But what he did next I was not prepared for. He began yanking on my arm again, just like he did over the pot of chili.

"Stop it dummy."

He barked. It was the kind of bark that makes the hairs on your neck stand straight up. It was a definite, "There is something in the bushes over there," kind of bark.

"Come on, do you honestly think I have time for this? Dog. DOG, cut it out."

Dog was sure though that he had sniffed out a rabbit or squirrel and was convinced that this was going to make me proud of him especially if he pulled my arm out of its socket while trying to lunge after it. I yanked back hard on the leash in frustration, he yelped and I instantly felt bad.

"Sorry buddy. I didn't mean to hurt you." I said as I reached down to pet him.

He sat there a moment but the harmony was shattered by his ears perking up and a low growl emitting from his throat. I knew that if I did not immediately pick him up again we were going to relive the moment we just had, him pulling me, me pulling him and both of us sorry for it. So, I gathered him up in my arms and slipped through the bushes.

I crossed our backyard and when I reached the porch let out a small curse.

I should have known that the patio door would be locked. It always was.

I sighed and made my way around to the front entrance. I then gave Dog a kiss on the top of the head to make sure that there were no hard feelings between us and softly let him down in the foyer and closed the door again. I looked up the street and thought about returning that way but I knew it was a much longer walk. So, being a creature of ease rather than energy, I chose the shorter route back through the grass and hedgerow.

The silence of that night was overwhelming. It was a cool and peaceful summer's evening. The air was warm but not overly so and there was no sign of rain or humidity. For all intent and purpose, this was the kind of night that you get only every so many years. The kind of night you never forget.

I was so taken back by the atmosphere, that I actually found myself walking at a very relaxed pace. I figured I had about three minutes to get back to the house before my mother's five minute time allotment was over, so I might as well make the most of them. By "the most of them" I mean, I wanted my mother to turn and ask my father how long I had been gone, get the answer, not like it, check her watch, exhale loudly, scowl, think of a few choice but appropriate words, excuse herself and begin her march up the hallway towards the front porch and once there, place her hands on her hips, suck in a large puff of air and prepare to scream my name, just as I walk up, smiling. Moments like that just make my life worth living.

I crossed over into the Thomas's property and grinned. It was going to be perfect to see my mother nearly nervous, with just a hint of worry on her face, as I come strolling up the walkway and through the wrought iron fence.

The grin however did not last for suddenly a hand was over my mouth as an arm snaked around my waist and pulled me backwards nearly jerking me off my feet. I wanted to scream but the hand was clamped so firmly over my mouth that only a small muffled sound emitted from my throat. I tried to kick backwards as hard as I could but fear and confusion conspired to make sure that the blow landed ineffectively against my attacker. I then began to beg through the clenched fingers that had my jaw, "let me go, please, please let me go."

But the hand jerked my head roughly backwards as a deep, sickly voice added, "Shut your damn mouth or they will never find your body, you understand?"

Tears began to flow down my face. *Oh God not this, please, anything but this.* I struggled some more trying to get my elbows to do some damage but again the hand on my face instantly made me regret my choice. It squeezed harder and jerked my head left and right straining the muscles in my neck.

The voice hissed in my ear, "Cut it out. Stop it! You're too pretty to ruin. Don't make me leave you so that they can't identify your body. You hush now and it will all be over soon."

I froze. I stopped struggling even though I knew it was the wrong thing to do. My heart was pounding so hard in my chest I thought it would certainly burst. I actually found myself praying for that to happen, I was praying for my body to fail me and let this nightmare end.

I was dragged backwards towards the hedges as my kidnapper then whispered, "Now you go ahead and scream, 'cause no one is going to hear you from way back here."

And just like that, the hands were gone. For an instant I was free. I began running as hard as I could but stumbled and fell forward onto my hands and knees. The desperation of the moment though was so intense that I cried out and started crawling like a child as fast as I could away from him and with a breath of panicked air I screamed out, "DADDY, HELP ME!"

Laughter, intense and full came from behind me. I was rolling to get to my feet and bolt towards the street when it all became clear. Even though tears slid down my cheeks like heavy raindrops on a windshield, it all made sense. *That Bitch*. There I was hysterical, beyond words and yet her laughter made me stop dead in my tracks and turn back towards the hedges where only a few seconds earlier I had feared for my soul and my body, to witness Savannah emerge, clutching her sides from the cramps she was getting from my humiliation.

"What the hell is wrong with you?"

She was too far into her own revelry to even hear my question.

"Are you so sick and deranged that you thought that was funny?"

"No, no and yes." She was able to reply between her howls and laughter. "I only wish I could have seen your face, it must have been priceless."

"You son of a bitch, you almost gave me a freakin heart attack. HOW COULD YOU THINK THAT WAS FUNNY?"

"Calm down. God have you always been such a dumb-ass, that you would fall for that trick? I mean, come on, what guy would want to attack you?"

"WHAT?"

She started to settle down and slowly made her way towards me. "Caitlin it was a joke okay, get over it. I mean you live in little suburbia where everyone knows everybody and the people all get along and have perfect little lives. Nothing would ever happen here."

"Don't try to hide the fact that you are a complete asshole with the 'I'm so bored shtick' because I am not buying it. You've been in town exactly two days. How in the hell could you possibly know what goes on here? But I will tell you this, if you think that anyone in this town would have thought this stunt you just pulled was funny then you are quite mistaken about us. We may not have your southern sense of humor but I assure you some of the other kids around here would have knocked your teeth out if you tried that shit with them," I fired back.

"They could try but I think that most people would find that to be a mistake. Don't be so quick to threaten me sweetie, I have more ways to get to you than by just hiding in some silly old hedges waiting for you to come walkin' by."

I wanted to knock the sneer right off her face and actually contemplated it when I heard my mother call out my name.

"We'll see how funny everyone thinks it is when I tell them you were out here pretending to be a rapist." My words should have stung her enough to make her back down or at least show some vestige of emotion, like concern. All it did however was widen her smile, as she placed her hands into the rear pockets of her snug fitting blue jeans.

"Well, if you think that's how you want to play it, go right ahead and we will see who they believe," she replied.

"Like they are going to believe you, you're the outsider here, the new kid on the block."

"Yep and according to your sister, you are the drama queen of Braintree. I'll just tell them that I came out of the hedges lookin' for you, placed my hand on your shoulder and you went all squirrelly."

Her face took on the look of someone who was not only good at lying but also used to being believed. This girl was a pro in every sense of the word. She had me in a tough spot. It was already well known in my house that I didn't like this chic. Therefore my parents would think that I was trying to overstate the facts so as to turn a negative light on Savannah. Add to that, the fact that Mr. and Mrs. Summers appeared about as tightly wrapped as an unraveled ball of yarn, and you can see that my chances of convincing anyone that this had in fact been a twisted and deliberate attack were quickly dissolving.

Another shout came from my mother not far away on the Summers porch, "Caitlin?"

"Oh sugah, you better hurry up. Your momma is callin' for ya. You don't want to make her think something bad happened to you, do you?"

Okay scumbag. You want a war? You got a war.

I never let my eyes drop, to do so would have been a definite show of submission. "Coming Mom," I then dropped my voice down to a volume that only my recent assailant could hear, "This isn't over."

"Oh sugah, I know that. You can count on the fact that this is far from over," and with that she pushed passed me and out onto the sidewalk.

Threats are not supposed to leave you feeling vulnerable. When you threaten someone the polite and socially acceptable behavior is to accept the threat, show concern and then not back off knowing that you have pushed the other person well past their limits. Unfortunately, that wasn't the case here. I had threatened this horrible girl from hell and instead of playing by the rules she counter threatens me and I am left more nervous than I was prior to my threat. I would have called for a rules check but Nicole was not here and probably would have sided against me at this point anyway.

"She is over here Mrs. O'Connor, I found her hiding in the bushes."

My blood went cold. *How could I have let her speak first? I was behaving like a rank amateur.*

My mother's voice went from slightly concerned to incredibly annoyed, in about a nano-second. "She was what? Oh Savannah, thank you honey for finding her. Caitlin O'Connor get your rear end inside this house, now."

I emerged onto the sidewalk and said nothing. I just started walking towards the Summers house and my irate mother.

Savannah slid carefully past my mom and whispered something for which she received another round of gratitude. As I tried to do the same Mom grabbed my arm and twisted me around to face her.

Her voice was low and full of anger as she chided me, "What were you thinking? I mean is it so hard to take your dog home when I ask that you had to make a major production out of it? I know you don't like this girl but why in the world would you want to embarrass your father and me like this in front of the whole neighborhood?"

I stood there not answering. At this moment it was the right thing to do. I had been a victim of a terrible prank and was now getting crap for it from my mother. I kept taking deep breaths while she glared at me. I had to keep reminding myself that she had no idea of the circumstances that had just occurred.

"I asked you a question young lady. Why are you destined to be a black cloud whenever we have a chance to meet new people or spend some time mingling with our neighbors?"

I held my tongue and took yet another long, deep breath.

"You are so selfish. Every time we try to spend some normal time with our friends you have to have one of your impromptu dramatic moments and spoil it for everyone."

"Friends? By friends do you mean all these people who would spend the next six months gossiping about you if they knew that you had given your child away all those years ago immediately after her birth?"

Sometimes I wonder if Aunt Katrina is really as psychic as she says is but on that night, oh baby did I believe, "Ah Quate-lin dere you are, dhank the gods. Come, dere is something I vish to show you."

I slipped under my mother's upraised arm and went inside to speak with my gypsy savior. I must admit, I did not think too highly of my chances for surviving the encounter later that night with my mother, but for now I was safe. Yet the weird thing was that as mad as I knew my mom was, as the night progressed it wasn't her I truly was afraid of. No, it was the raven haired harlot from Georgia who had orchestrated this whole evening like a white haired maestro from Vienna. If she could best me this easily, what other plots could she be brewing in her evil head. God, if I had only known. If I had only known . . .

CHAPTER SIX

A COLD SUMMER NIGHT

When we arrived home nearly an hour later, all was not well in the O'Connor household. My mother had not spoken or looked at me since our confrontation on the front porch. During that time though, I had watched several attempts by my father to discover what had made her retreat so deeply into her shell. She was so completely wounded that the conversation could not be had in public, so my father could only shrug his shoulders and carried on as if nothing had happened.

I quietly put my shoes away and headed upstairs as quickly as I could without drawing attention to my guilt with regards to her sudden and unexplained change in mood. Yet, as I entered my bedroom I began to wonder why I was feeling guilty at all. I doubt she was downstairs feeling guilty for embarrassing me. I am sure right now she was in the bedroom telling my father what a lousy kid I was. If I knew my mother, she would make him beg to hear the information and then twist it around in such a way as to turn him completely against me. *Man, she can be such a . . .* I held back. I'm not sure exactly why. But I couldn't bring myself to say the final word to that sentence. Maybe it was because I had just been humiliated and tricked into thinking I was going to be molested by my new neighbor and therefore since I knew, beyond of a shadow of a doubt, she qualified for that particular word that maybe mother was still a notch beneath her in my catalog of contempt.

I could hear Nicole making her way first into her bedroom and then the bathroom as she brushed her teeth and got herself ready for bed. She was in her nightly routine mode and therefore NOT to be disturbed. I wasn't really ready to talk to her about the events of tonight anyway. I needed to speak to someone who I could trust, someone who would listen and tell me honestly if my assault on my mother was a knee jerk reaction to the mock kidnapping or a release of pent up anger that still needed to be dealt with over the events of seven months ago.

I waited for my sister to rinse and spit, spit, gargle and spit, before grabbing my own sleepwear and heading into the bathroom to get cleaned up. I shut the door and began my own nightly grooming rituals. Fifteen minutes later I was changed, washed up and calmed down enough to announce to my reflection in the mirror, "Okay Caitlin O'Connor, you are ready for bed."

I emerged from the bathroom and walked past Nicole's room. The door was shut which was not uncommon for her. Since we discovered that ghosts were in fact real she had been closing her door. I tried to explain to her that a ghost could move through it but she wouldn't listen. There are times when I feel like the only normal person in my family, I'm sure you understand what I mean.

I walked into my room at the end of the hall and nearly jumped clear out of my skin. My mother was sitting on my bed holding Kelsey's American Girl doll. To have your heart go from zero to sixty twice in the same night from an unexpected shock is slightly more fun than having your wisdom teeth come in the very same day you get braces and a corrective appliance for your spine.

"What are you doing with that?" I blurted out.

She just sat there for a moment and said nothing. I couldn't see her face so I don't know if she was ignoring my tone or looking for the right words to say. Either way, it had nothing to do with her holding onto my doll so I stepped forward and grabbed it out of her hand.

"Doctor Forsythe told you that this doll means a lot to me and not to touch it," I added.

She glared at me as I carefully placed the doll back on its shelf facing my bed. I turned back around and crossed my arms only to witness her take several deep, deliberate breaths before addressing me, "We need to talk."

"He also said you should not just come in here, that I need personal space just like you do and that this is where I can collect my thoughts and learn to repair and rebuild trust."

"I know what he said," she replied coldly.

There was a long pause, one that hung in the air very uncomfortably, sort of like when MJ held his baby over the balcony and everyone just went dead quiet. I mean, I was like five when it happened and I can still remember thinking, "what the heck is that idiot doing?" We both waited but the tension was so heavy that I finally had to say something,

"So, what is it? Why did you come up here?"

"I wanted to tell you that I think we need to go back to seeing Dr. Forsythe on a weekly basis again. It's obvious that you are not handling this whole situation well and quite frankly, neither am I. Your rage and anger are understandable but they need to be dealt with, your suffering won't bring Kelsey back."

I couldn't help it but I found myself staring at the floor. I wanted to look her in the face but the pain was a bit more than I was ready for. I knew she was hurting, hell I could even tell how absolutely devastated she was by all that happened, but that didn't make up for the fact that she was right, inside, I was still very, very angry. I wanted to lash out at her, especially her. I know that my father had said it was a joint decision to give my sister, my fraternal twin, to my mother's childhood friend who was unable to conceive on her own, but as a female the sting and venom seemed more inclined towards my mother than my father. And even though she had been raised next door along side us, it was wrong. If they hadn't agreed to allow this friend a chance to play mommy, my sister would still be here among us, alive and not cold and dead because some trucker lost control of his rig and crushed the car she and her pseudo mother were driving in.

I thought of about fifteen different responses but all of them seemed to miss the mark. I wanted to get it all out. I wanted to remove all this guilt I was feeling and lay it at her feet. I wanted to have someone tell me that we weren't this bizarre, messed up family and that this could have happened to anybody. Let's face it though, it wouldn't, more than likely it couldn't, and most definitely, it didn't. It had happened to us, so I gave the only answer that seemed fitting, "Okay."

"Fine, I'll call him and arrange for us to come in on the next available appointment. Caitlin, we both knew this was going to be a long and rough road, I only hope that you haven't already resigned yourself to just taking the easy way out."

"What's the easy way out, mom?" I said softly, still staring at the floor.

"Hating me. Hating your father. Hating this house and everything in it, including Nicole."

"I don't hate everything in this house, and I sure don't hate Nicole." My words fell away. I realized I was about to add one more name to that list but it hung there unspoken.

She stood and headed for the door. I braced myself for the last word assault but amazingly it never came. Instead she crossed into the hallway, reached back and shut my door closed.

My chest felt so much lighter. In fact, the whole atmosphere of the room seemed to relax. Now, I understand that inanimate objects can't actually relax and that this particular perception was based entirely upon my own mental state. But whatever the explanation was, I was thankful she had left the room and all I got out of it was an increase in how many times I would be sitting in front of our family therapist.

I made my way over to my ipod docking station and was swirling my finger around the song selector wheel when I heard a very small click off to my right. There it was again. I leaned over and looking down at my front yard I saw Craig standing there about to lob another pebble at my bedroom window.

I unlocked my window and grabbed the handles hoisting it open with one clean jerking motion. Craig heard it and stopped himself mid throw.

"Hey," I said as loud as I thought it would be safe so as not to draw my family's attention.

"Hey, you okay?"

"Yeah, why do you ask?" I replied.

"Because when you got back to the Summers from taking Dog home you were really quiet and it seemed like you were not acting like yourself."

I stopped myself from shouting, "so the only time I act like myself is when I am loud?" Fortunately, I saw that his intentions were sweet and he was doing the exact thing I had yelled at him about earlier, he was checking on me. Craig was beginning to get this whole, boyfriend/girlfriend thing.

"Well, no actually, I am not okay. My mom and I had a major blow out and now I've got to go back to the "shrink" once a week again."

"Ouch, I'm sorry to hear that. I wish there was something I could do to help you." He smiled up at me.

"Well, come to think of it there is a little favor you could do for me."

He stood there in the front yard and waited to hear my proposal. The scene looked exactly like something out of a fairy tale. The princess, locked high in her tower unable to get down to her handsome prince, speaks to him and informs him of his sacred quest, a quest that if successfully completed will grant the princess her freedom. My heart took a few extra beats in my chest as I propped myself in the window and savored the moment.

"Caitlin, come on . . . if my parents find out I'm out here they are going to ground me. What do you want me to do?"

The inner wheels of my mind were spinning like a clockwork mouse. Here was Craig, my beau, outside my window, risking himself to show his affection for me. I had to make a decision, trust him now or never trust him. He was a member of the Patrol. He also had never once mentioned or told anyone of the events that transpired both in his basement and my house with regards to Kelsey's ghost.

"Caitlin, come on!" His voice raised a notch in volume and I was very thankful that if my parents were awake they were in one of three places, their bedroom, the kitchen or the basement, all of which would make it almost impossible to hear him calling out from the front yard. I inhaled and held it and then against all my girlish sensibilities I shouted down to him, "I want you to become friends with Savannah."

I can't believe I am asking this of my boyfriend.

He chuckled, "What are you kidding me? Is this some kind of joke or a test? What are you up to?"

"Listen. She is trying to get close to Nicole and turn her against me and after her little demonstration tonight, I believe she is capable of twisting my sister around and convincing her that I am a terrible person. I can't have that happen, okay? I'm more than likely going to be grounded for a few days, so get close to her whenever I'm not around but Nicole is. Listen, this is Soul Patrol business all right. I'm not kidding around here. I want to know what that bitch is up to."

I leaned my head out a bit farther and smiled at him. "Thank you Craig, this means a lot to me."

"All right Caitlin," I could hear the hesitation in his voice but I also sensed that he would do the task I had set for him, "for you, I'll do it."

Now was not the time to play coy but boys eat that stuff up so I playfully said, "For me, why would you do it for me?"

"Because we are going out that's why."

I laughed and went to pull my head back in the room when I saw Nicole leaning out of her bedroom just as I was.

HOLY SHIT! How long had she been there? How much had she heard? The answer came rather quickly when she screamed and yanked herself back into her room and slammed the window shut.

I said something offensive that I think you can all imagine would be appropriate for the situation and after saying my good byes to Craig I closed my own window and went to sit on the bed, crossed legged and heavy hearted. I clutched a pillow to my chest and thought about crying but since I could hear my little sister crying hysterically from the next room, I couldn't conjure the tears to even match the pain, betrayal and disappointment she was experiencing now. I had broken a promise to my B.S.F.F. and this time I was certain the penalty would be unavoidable and truly deserved.

The next two hours were some of the longest I can remember ever experiencing. Nicole's heartbreak could still be heard through the wall and every tear she cried cut deeper and deeper into my heart. I never meant for her to discover that Craig and I were seeing each other this way. That's not fair; in all honesty, I hoped she had never found out. I guess the real truth of it is that I was an uncaring jerk. If I was really concerned about her finding out, I would never have started seeing him in the first place.

Midnight came. My little sister was still awake or at least I believed she was by the sounds of soft music playing in her room. She had an affinity for world music, especially when she was feeling down. You know the kind, African rhythms, Irish harp and Uilleann pipes, Italian mandolins, and Chinese Pipa. For what ever reason these traditional songs from other countries seemed to speak volumes to her. I pressed my ear against our common wall and listened as the Irish ballod by some guy in Riverdance played the pipes and remembered a great hero from an ancient time.

Midnight was here and that could only mean that Kelsey soon would be as well. I looked at the doll that shared her visage sitting on the shelf and prepared myself for the discomfort that always heralded her arrival. My stomach would tighten into a knot, the small almost invisible hairs on my arm would stand straight up and the room would drop in temperature by at least fifteen degrees. All of it though was worth it. Kelsey was my best friend and even though she was gone, I was fortunate enough to still be able to share a few minutes of each day with her and tell her how much I love and miss her.

Almost on cue, I could feel the temperature dropping rapidly in my room. I threw a blanket around my shoulders and leaned against the wall facing Kelsey. In a few more minutes my windows began to ice over on the inside and crackle from the drastic and sudden change. It sounded almost like popcorn being made. Remembering that I had my music still playing, I leapt out of my comfy blanket and went to turn my ipod off. Past experiences had taught me that it was hard for us to communicate when my music is playing.

"Cate-lin?" the doll said as its head began to turn awkwardly on its thin plastic neck. It's glass eyes attempting to focus even though I knew she was unable to see me and could only sense my presence while trying to speak to me.

"Hey sis," I said through chattering teeth.

"Cate-lin, what's going on there? So much sadness today, so much hurt. I've not felt this kind of despair in the house since the night I said goodbye." The dolls head finally seemed to locate me and stopped slowly twisting from side to side.

"It's been one heck of a day, sis. I don't even know where to begin." I sighed.

"For you to be at a loss for words, it must be pretty bad. Why don't you start with the part where you woke up and we'll try to go from there?"

I chuckled for a moment, "Kelsey, I can sum it up for you. Mom's hurt but so am I and we are both to blame. The girl next door is an evil bitch who tonight played a prank on me by jumping out of the bushes pretending to be a rapist and Nicole is next door crying because she found out that Craig and I are sort of seeing each other. Oh and Dog wanted to eat Mrs. Ritter's chili and I wouldn't let him so he's a bit miffed as well."

"I thought you promised Nicole that you wouldn't see Craig?"

"I did."

Several heartbeats passed before Kelsey voice broke through the cold silence that hung in my room, "Then why are you seeing him?"

"It's not that simple okay. These things are complicated. You know, hormones and phera what-evers, it's tricky. Can I help it if he likes me? Is it my fault that the only boy who so far noticed me is the same dude my sister likes? Is that my fault?"

"No."

"See, thank you. You were always so understanding. So logic . . ."

She interrupted, "But it is your fault if you made a promise and then broke it, especially if you did it with the hope of hiding it from Nicole. Caitlin, Nicole is our little sister, you can't treat her like some person whose feelings can't get hurt. Your actions affect everyone around you. You are going to have to face the fact that when you are part of a family, everyone's triumphs, successes, and failures affect everyone else."

"You're right. But when it comes to love, shouldn't she understand that these things just sometimes happen? It's not like we planned it this way."

"Maybe I should go talk to her," the doll said.

"Not a good idea Kels. She is also steamed up because when you went away you said goodbye to me and not to her. She thinks that you haven't even recognized the fact that she was your sister as well."

"Oh my."

"Yep, right now she is feeling really miserable."

"Caite-lin, get up." her voice was rather demanding.

"What?"

"I said get up and carry me over to Nicole's room. I have an apology to make and a sister to talk to."

"Hold on. This isn't the right time Kels, and anyway you are my spirit sister, my twin not hers."

"Caite-lin O'Connor, our little sister is in there still sad and broken hearted, she needs our love and support. Get off your butt and carry me to her room and tell her I would like to apologize, NOW."

I got up off the mattress and reached up to pluck Kelsey off the shelf. Then, spinning around I went out into the hallway and stood in front of Nicole's door.

"Are you sure about this Kels?"

"Yes."

I knocked on the door and as I expected she did not answer or offer a "come in."

"Knock and tell her I want to say I am sorry," the doll instructed.

So I did. I knocked and whispered, "Nicole, Kelsey wants to talk to you and apologize. I told her what we spoke about earlier and she feels terrible about hurting your feelings. Come on Nicole, your older sister wants to say she's sorry, open the door."

To my amazement the door creaked open a tiny amount and our sister's arm extended through the gap, her hand opened ready to receive the doll.

"Just the doll," she said from behind the door.

I reached out and let her take hold of Kelsey. I thought about threatening her not to harm my doll since it was my only link to my twin but I knew Nicole would never harm anything especially something that meant so much to me, so I let the thoughts drift away, unspoken.

"Nic-ole, may I come in?"

She withdrew her hand and the doll disappeared. Then she quietly closed the door back over. I tried to hear what was being said but it was muffled and almost impossible to make out.

I sat out in the hallway leaning on the wall across from her room. I must have been there for about twenty minutes when the door creaked open and Nicole was standing there.

"Kelsey is staying with me tonight. I . . . need her right now."

"Okay boo."

"I don't want to hate you so much but you seem to be unable to be nice to me. You always hurt then apologize. It's not right, it's not fair."

"Nicole . . ."

"Don't," she interjected, "don't. I just need to calm down for now." And with that she shut the door back over.

It was the first time since learning that Kelsey had died that her doll, her focus was not in my room. It felt weird. She was my silent guardian, my ever watchful protector and my friend. I knew she was safe and that she was doing the right thing by helping Nicole out tonight. Yet something inside me made me feel like I wanted to cry. Loneliness is scary but being exiled by my sister from my sisters, felt like a hot knife in my heart. I went into my room and climbed back in bed and didn't sleep at all that night.

CHAPTER SEVEN

AUGUST

The rest of the month of July was spent avoiding Nicole's stares and my mother's wrath. Even though Kelsey had spent several consecutive nights speaking to our little sister, she was still very hurt and very angry. When we did run into each other and conversation was unavoidable, we nodded, grunted or gave a quick, "yes or no" and then went back to ignoring the other person as much as was humanly possible.

After several conversations with Craig, some face to face and some from aloft in my window due to my reoccurring role as the punished penitent, I was able to glean that Nicole had not heard my plan for Craig to infiltrate the new group of friends only that he and I were, steadies. I was incredibly thankful for that. In many ways, I was glad to not have to sneak around behind her back about it anymore but the most important thing was that she didn't know we were sneaking around behind her back about Savannah. I know, that old English guy said it best when he wrote, "Oh what a tangled web we weave, something, something to deceive." But I bet he did not have a younger sister angry at him for stealing her heart throb when he wrote it.

As for my mother and our weekly appointments with Dr. Forsythe, they went really, really great. I guess when you're closing in on thirteen you only have so many different ways to say "I'm pissed." As an adult though you find a thousand new and exciting ways to express every single emotional pit fall in your life, and they call me a drama queen. Yet, I have to ask, am I the one tearing through a full box of Kleenex in the doctor's office? Don't think so. Mom would jump back and forth from wounded parent to infuriated adult. The emotions that she was feeling must have been so overwhelming that she just couldn't put her foot on which one was the most important at any one time. One minute she is begging forgiveness for her poor choices and the next screaming that I have no right to question her. As I said before, these sessions were just, pure magic.

Then August came and with it the arrival of my grandmother, Mimi. She had been traveling in Western Europe over the last several weeks doing some work on a book idea that she has about fashion trends in different regions of the world. I'm not supposed to tell you this but the novel's working title is "Cut from the Same Cloth" and although she is only partially done writing it, I believe she has a best seller on her hands.

Mimi arrived on the third in the late afternoon on a flight into Logan airport. It was such an adventure to head into the city and pick her up. The five of us went to one of our favorite steak houses in Boston and ate a huge meal. Mimi spoke to Nicole and I about her travels and some of the great places she saw. We listened and I found myself wondering what it would be like to live that kind of life style? I imagined myself sipping champagne with some of the most interesting people in the world. Everyone dressed up and looking FABULOUS.

We paid the check and drove back to our house in my mom's minivan. I began to realize that Mimi wasn't speaking to my parents very much, especially my dad. I was about to break off and begin to wonder why when it hit me square in the chest. How would the parent, of the parents who gave away a child to a friend to raise, feel if she were never told that she in fact had three granddaughters? Wow, no wonder she had all but stopped visiting over the last few months. Her trip to Europe was probably as much work related as it was therapeutic. Don't get me wrong, Mimi had called at least once a week to speak to Nicole and I and we did receive some wonderful post cards, but this was the first real visit she had made to us in, well, yep nearly seven months.

By the time we backed into the driveway it was late, well after ten o'clock at night. So my dad carried the luggage inside while I helped Mimi with her carry-on and souvenir bags and mom guided Nicole upstairs to get washed up and get straight to bed.

I placed the bags I was carrying in the living room and made a bee-line towards Dog's leash so I could take him out for a quick piddle. He too was very excited to see Mimi and was jumping all over the place, barking and rolling around the carpet like a wiener dog on crack. She thankfully gave him a quick pet on the head and few scratches behind his left ear which let him know that he had been noticed and it was okay to go outside and do his business.

I dragged him through the back door and out into the yard. Like a ding dong I had forgotten to turn on the back porch light. I was in such a hurry to see what goodies Mimi had brought me back from Europe that I ran right passed the switch in my haste.

"Daddy, turn the light on please!" I screamed back towards the house.

The light came to life and threw illumination over a good portion of our yard thanks to the miracle of halogen bulbs. Dog was sniffing around looking for a blade of grass that had the exact scent, height and texture to be graced with his fluids when Stephen came out of the shadows from almost the exact same place in the hedgerow that Savannah had frightened me from about three weeks earlier.

"Caitlin, don't fret none it's just me Stephen."

"Great, what is this; round two of the let's make Caitlin look like a fool. I'm surprised it took you this long. What's going to be this time? Your sister is gonna jump out and throw a burlap sack over my head and say she's a middle eastern extremist or no wait, I know, you are going to tie me up to a chair that is pointing exactly north and ask your mother to lecture me on her ideas for interior decorating until I crack and tell you where I keep all my money? Well, jokes on you, a) I'm broke and b) your mother doesn't scare me, although she does make some very valid points when it comes to certain treatment choices for bay windows."

"I came to warn you, but since you seem to have all the answers I guess I'll just be headed back home."

"Warn me, about what?"

"Savannah," he said with a serious look upon his face.

"Geez Stephen, that's one heck of a revelation. You're here to tell me that your sister is out to get me. Hold on, I think I hear the Channel Five News chopper circling the house trying to get this scoop."

He turned and started to walk away mumbling something under his breath that sounded vaguely like, "it's your funeral . . ."

"Wait," I shouted, "hold on. Okay, you obviously felt the need to sneak out here and tell me something important so go ahead." I could see that in his mind the opportunity had passed, that with my defensive sarcasm I had possibly blown it.

"Stephen, I'm sorry okay. I should be thanking you for any heads up you give me regarding your sister's diabolical plans. Please, tell me what you came here to say."

He shrugged his shoulders and moved a bit closer. Then he placed his hands in his pockets and looked down at the grass which was already developing a thin layer of dew, "My sister is a witch."

Unlike what you might have expected my response to be, for the record, I did not laugh. Nor did I grin, chuckle, guffaw or call him a fool. Quite the opposite in fact, I stood there, unmoving and unblinking waiting for him to continue with the rest of his tale.

"Savannah is a Creole, true one hundred percent, witch."

"How can you be sure about this?"

"We had an old woman who was our house servant for quite a few years. She claimed to be descended from a voodoo priest. She told us all kinds of weird and creepy stories about 'the way'. How some folks were trained in white magic and some were smutty, had their souls covered in tar and ash. She said those people were black practitioners and were to be feared. Most she said of these dark souls came from playin with terrible spells and summoning hurtful curses and dangerous charms. But a rare few were born into it, naturally. They looked like you and me but their path was a dangerous one filled with cruelty and malice especially against those that they see as an equal or a threat. For weeks after that story we begged her to look at our auras and tell us that we were okay, that there was no filth upon on souls. She refused but after asking over and over again she finally agreed to do a reading. I was first and fine. I can't tell you how relieved I was to know that I was not risking a lifetime of mischief and dark deeds against my friends and family. Then it was Savannah's turn. I will never forget the look in that old woman's eyes. Caitlin it looked as if she had seen a ghost or worse. She began crossing herself, you know like Catholics do. She cried out and pointed at my little sister and told her she was 'unbeai' unclean and backed away. Can you imagine the fear I felt at hearing this woman call my sister a child of the devil? And the really upsetting thing was that all Savannah did was smile and sit there meeting the frightened woman's stares."

I was in a state of shock. This news was more horrific than even I imagined. My new next door neighbor was a voodoo priestess. Without realizing it I said under my breath, "well that explains Katrina's reaction at the house."

Stephen was a sharp one and didn't miss this little faux pau, if what he said was true I did not want him to know about Aunt Katrina my spiritual ally from Eastern Europe, "What did you say?"

I had to try and back pedal as quickly as possible, "Oh nothing, just that I was remembering something . . . So, she is evil and wants to take out her problems on me is that it?"

"She is evil and she plans on making you into one of her servants. Why on earth do you think my parents moved so far away from Georgia? Let me guess, you believe that there are no other homes made by famous architects waiting to be remodeled besides this one? No. We came this far north hoping to remove her from the things that she uses to weave her spells. Up here the ingredients are all wrong, or at least that's what my parent's thought."

"Servant, ingredients, what on earth are you talking about Stephen?"

"Savannah had enslaved about a dozen girls around the school to do her bidding. She had them giving her money from their parent's wallets, fixing her homework, collecting all sorts of bugs and plants for her use. She was so powerful at one point that she actually was able to use one of the girls to convince her boyfriend to rob a liquor store so Savannah could buy a really nice ipod."

"Not the one hundred and sixty gig?" I asked with a quivering voice.

"Yep, in black."

"Foul demoness," I hissed. That was one sexy piece of musical and video hardware. And to think that she had someone else do the time for her heinous need to have the very best in personal portable electronic entertainment was sheer villainy.

"Just know this Caitlin, she is focusing all of her hellish power on you now. I don't know why but she is convinced that you are "shiobi" a warrior of the light. I have heard her speaking to someone in her room, on the phone I think but I can't be sure, about how she is going to destroy you once and for all." He did not waver. Stephen for all I could see was telling me the truth.

I walked up closer to him so that Dog could get a good sniff. He took in twenty maybe thirty quick little snorts and then wagged his tail. Yep, I had to admit it, Stephen passed the wiener dog test; his word with me was gold.

"You've risked much to tell me all this Stephen. I want to thank you but I can't help but wonder why you would help me?" I asked softly.

"Caitlin, I don't want to move again. My family has been running from the law for so long now. I just want to settle down, finish the rest of high school and get on with my life. Savannah will have to pay for her crimes one day and if that needs to take place here in Massachusetts so that my family can finally have peace, then so be it." Wow, did his eyes always have that puppy dog look to them. I completely forgot the "kid" comment from a few weeks earlier. Here was a courageous, handsome, wet-eyed boy who obviously wanted to protect me from the machinations of his terrible mutant zombie sister. My faith in the universe and its creator found a new strength.

Thank you God; for sending me a protector in my hour of need, oh and nice touch making him a hunk.

Stephen returned home and I re-entered the house to find that the adults were getting settled in the living room. I let Dog off his leash and made my way to join them. As I sat down on the love seat next to my fraternal grandmother I noticed a distinct drop in the temperature of the room. Now at any other time this would have had me in near panic mode thinking that Kelsey was coming forward to make some earth shattering revelation. This chill however, was due to some very heavy, obviously unresolved issues that were affecting my elders. Knowing that whatever it was would wait until I was upstairs, I decided to use my presence like the old Catholic woman in India. No, I was not going to wash everyone's feet. What I meant is that I would use my time in the room as a healing presence, a force for good. Like Stephen had said outside, I was a "warrior of the light," dammit it was time I started acting like one.

"So Mimi, what's the big, over the top, ground shaking, exciting news you have to tell us?" I asked with a smile.

"Well Caitlin, I guess now is as good a time as any, although I had planned on waiting for Nicole to tell her as well."

"Nicole is already in la la land. Let her sleep. She will find out in the morning and we can all share her reaction over this news."

"Yeah mom, what's all the secrecy about?"

Poor choice of words dad. Secrecy implies that she has been hiding something from everyone sort of like you and mom did and by the look you just got, that would be a bad sort of thing to allude to right now.

"Very well. As you all know I have been over to Europe on a trip that was partially business, partially personal. I am happy to report that both went exceedingly well. My book already has a publisher interested in printing it and I was able to conclude my business in Ireland." She smiled widely, something I had not seen her do in quite some time.

"That's great news on the manuscript. What business in Ireland?"

"Well I went over there to see about purchasing some land. No, that's not entirely accurate. I went over there to purchase what was once my family's land. When my parents sold their parcel of land it was to a neighboring farmer. Since that time he has used it for sheep and some cattle. But he has no children to speak of and I went to make him an offer on the property. Unfortunately he did not want to sell only my parent's portion. He was looking to retire and sell it all. So, I am now the proud owner of 52 acres of Irish countryside and riverfront property."

Silence sat over the room for about five seconds before I screamed as if Dog had just dragged his butt over my favorite pair of skinny jeans.

"AWESOME!" I shouted.

"Congratulations mom, that's amazing news." My dad's voice conveyed the happiness he felt for her.

"Well Ian, your father and I spoke about doing this for many years and since I was already offered an advance on my book sales, I decided to fulfill one of our dreams and purchase some property overseas. Which means Caitlin, if your mother and father agree, you and Nicole will be able to spend part of your summer with me in Ireland from now on."

"Really!" I nearly jumped out of my chair and did my patented happy dance.

"Wow mom, that's a generous offer for the kids. I mean, I don't see why we can't work something out." I immediately sensed the hesitancy in his voice. I thought about getting involved in the conversation as I would have in years past, but chose to stay calm and quiet. In the back of my mind I kept repeating my new life mantra over and over again. *I am a force of positive light. I am a force of positive light.* Yes, I understand that I only discovered this fact about six minutes ago but a protector of mankind has to start believing sometime right?

"Well, what matters is that a house is going to be built and the land is already mine. I'm sure that we can all work out how best to make use of it."

"What house?" My father asked. I also began to notice that my mother had not added her two cents in up to this point in the conversation. That usually did not bode well for future decisions regarding Nicole and myself.

"I am having a brand new house built. The one we used to live in was converted into a barn about forty years ago. This new house will be four bedrooms, with all the modern conveniences of a home here in the states. I have a lot of interior decisions to make, colors, fabrics, cabinets that sort of thing. But the outside of the home is going to be stone. Oh, and wait till you see the size of the fireplace. It's going to be magnificent, almost big enough to stand up in."

I couldn't help myself. I was literally quivering in excitement. "Big enough to, let's say, burn a witch in?"

Now of course my mother chose to remind everyone that she had a voice, "Caitlin!"

"What mom, I'm merely trying to get an idea of the exact size so I can make an educated suggestion as to the best accruements for the room."

She kept her eyes locked on me, "Oh, I thought you were trying to sound like Mrs. Summers."

"Who's Mrs. Summers?" Mimi asked.

A small, almost feint voice responded from the top of the staircase, "She's my best friend's mom. They just moved into the neighborhood from Georgia."

"She's not your best friend. How the hell can she be your best friend when she's only been living in the neighborhood for like three weeks?" I yelled back.

"Caitlin!" That was what we like to call the official second warning that had just been issued.

At the banister my sister's small face appeared. "She is too my best friend. Savannah is nice to me and likes to play with me doing the things I like to do."

"You don't even know her Nicole. She is not good enough to be your best friend."

"You're not the boss of me Caitlin O'Connor."

"Stop it both of you," Dad snapped.

"Nicole honey, why aren't you in bed?"

She walked all the way down the stairs and into the living room. "I heard everyone talking and I couldn't fall asleep. So I was going to get a glass of water in the bathroom when I heard something about Ireland and vacations and then Caitlin's big mouth asking about stupid witch burnings."

My sister was no novice. She made a bee line for our grandmother's lap and crawled up onto it. Her ability to snuggle was almost legendary and she knew exactly when to employ it. *You learn well, young Jedi.*

"I'm sorry mom. My girls sometimes forget that being sisters means being courteous to one another," Dad apologized.

"She yelled at me that Savannah is not my best friend."

"I know Nicole but let it go. Both of you let it go, right now," he finished.

"So little princess, you heard about the house Mimi is having built in Ireland?"

"Yep. I think it's great I can't wait to see it."

"Well, it will be ready in a couple of months. I had a friend set up a website for us so we can watch it being built. The contractors are going to take pictures of what they are doing every few days so we can keep an eye on it from here. The only thing that Mimi needs is to start picking out the inside of the house."

"Mimi, I've got a great idea," Nicole said as she sat bolt upright in her lap. "Mrs. Summers is an interior designer and a great one at that. She is right here local. They bought Mr. Frazier's place and you should see all the stuff they are doing to the inside, it's amazing."

How does one describe the cold touch of a wraith against your skin, or the horror of a vampire as he enters your house with his fangs seeping gore and his nails as long as straight edge razors? Well, you describe it the same way you would the sound of your own sister's voice as she offers the services of an interior designer who just happens to be the mother of a Succubus born and bred in the fifth ring of hell. You tense up as if you're about to be hit by a 2x4 across the small of the back and you try not to vomit up your lunch when it happens.

In hind sight, I can't blame Nicole entirely for making this recommendation. She was after all, unaware of the run in with Savannah along the hedgerow and the latest information from Stephen confirming my suspicions that she was an agent of the apocalypse. Nicole was trying to be helpful and make someone, in this case our grandmother, happy. All good and virtuous things, truly. Yeah right.

"Well thank you, sweetie. That's a great idea. Next time you talk to your friend ask her if her mom would be interested in hiring out her services on our Irish house."

There is a famous story about a hunchback who is mistreated and falsely accused of a crime he did not commit. He is tried and whipped for his part in this trumpt up charge and all the while you can't help but think, poor, pathetic creature. Fortunately he finds refuge on holy ground and screams out the words which were so profound back then and echo true today as well, *Sanctuary, Sanctuary . . .* I felt like I needed a place to hide my wretchedness and try to figure out why when everything begins to feel like destiny is working the way it does for normal people that it turns around and sinks its teeth into my backside like a Mako shark.

"Off to bed now Nicole," Dad said.

"Okay daddy. Night everyone. Night Mimi, night mom, night sissy."

Nicole made her way for the stairs and I stood up as well. "I guess I will be getting to bed too; big day tomorrow, good night everyone." I went around and gave everyone a hug and then set my feet in motion and walked to the upper level of my house and stopped in front of my sister's door.

I thought about a lot of things before I knocked. I thought about how she was still very hurt by my lying about Craig. I thought about Kelsey and the way she had seemingly forgotten my little sister when she said her final good byes. I thought about how she had been in my shadow for all these years and how if I were her I could imagine how nice it would be to have someone older and different pay attention to her. I even thought about not knocking but after a few moments I chose not to let this opportunity pass me by.

"Yeah."

"Can I come in?" I asked through the closed door. It seemed that she and I were doing most of our talking through the closed doors these days.

"Okay."

I opened the door and stepped inside. "Can we talk for a few minutes?"

"I guess," she replied.

"Thanks," I shut the door and went over and sat down on the carpet so that I was facing her. I leaned my back against her dresser and smiled.

"I wanted to talk to you about a couple of things," I said.

"All right."

"First, I want to apologize for the way I've been behaving about your new found friend. I know it's probably been hard for you growing up in this house with me constantly trying to get all the attention and now that you are getting some from someone outside the family I guess at first I was a little jealous. But there are some things you should know about Savannah, things that are not so nice. But instead of fighting about it now, I want to finish what else I have to say and then let you talk if you need to, okay?"

"Okay."

"Second, this whole thing with Kelsey was such a big, terrible mistake. I feel like crap that you think she didn't care about you, or that you might feel like I would be happier with only her as my sister. That is SO not true. Boo, I care about you a lot, and if Kels were still alive I know that she would tell you as well how much she loves you too."

"Don't worry about Kelsey. We've spoken sissy. It's okay. I understand that being twins makes you both sort of alike and connected. I guess I was always a bit jealous as well of the time you spent with her. I am better now though. She and I have said what needed to be said and I know that she and I were, I mean are, sisters too."

"I am so glad to hear that Boo. I never meant for any of the stuff we went through with the Soul Patrol to hurt you. Without your help, Kelsey would never have been shown the way and found peace. It was your voice that kept me steady and grounded as it seemed that the whole bottom of my world was falling out from under me. It's funny, ever since you were little, you have always been like a miniature mommy, and before you freak out I mean that in a good way."

She nodded and I could tell she understood that I was referring to her protective and rational nature not that fact that she constantly reminds me to keep my elbows off the table.

"Lastly, I wanted to tell you how sorry I am about kind of liking Craig behind your back. I know I made you a promise not to go out with him. I guess we just have a lot in common. These things aren't always in your control. As you get older, you will see that being attracted to someone is a result of many things. There's looks, height, scent, style, family values and of course, hair color. Why are you grinning?"

She sat there staring down at me with this huge silly expression on her face and she said one word, just one single word, "'cause".

"Cause why?" I asked.

"Cause what in the name of heck do you have in common with Craig?" She busted out laughing.

"I am not sure what you are finding so funny?" I said, through slightly clenched teeth.

"Come on Sis. What do you and Craig have in common?"

"Okay, well there's . . ."

She fell over laughing hysterically.

"What? Craig and I are like soul mates." That statement only forced her to roll from side to side; laughing so hard tears were beginning to stream down her face.

"We both like the color red. Oh and Sponge Bob, we both like Sponge Bob."

She began kicking her legs in the air holding her stomach which was I am sure by now cramping up from laughing so hard.

"Sponge Bob? That's the best you got?" She blurted out between guffaws.

"Yeah . . . and the color red." And suddenly, without warning I started to giggle as well. "Oh swimming, we both like swimming."

She tried to speak between breathes which was very difficult because she still could not stop from gushing her amusement. "Mom, dad, I want you to meet my new boyfriend Craig. I love him soooo much and we have a lot in common. No father, you can't stop me from marrying him, don't you see, we both love Sponge Bob."

I had to put an end to this. She was making a mockery of my first true love. "Hey, that's not fair. There are many other reasons why we were drawn towards one another." I couldn't help it. I began laughing too. She was right. Craig and I had absolutely nothing in common. The real irony of the situation though was that it took my nine year old sister to point that out to me. So why am I going steady with him? I guess like many great women throughout the ages who had been entrusted with the secret of the paranormal and its existence, I was drawn towards the one male whom I could count on. Craig so far had been like that rock everyone was afraid of during the days of wooden ships. No matter how bad it has gotten, Craig has been there, never judging and never pointing a finger at me with his left hand while making the sign of the cross with his right. Maybe that's why I want to be more than just a friend. Maybe, deep down inside I think that as long as I am his girlfriend he won't betray that trust and he will keep my secrets safer than he would otherwise. I decided to take it to a vote, well in truth I decided to ask Nicole.

"Hey, do you think the only reason I am sort of seeing Craig is so that he doesn't spill his guts about the stuff that happened to us last year?"

"You mean, do I think you are trying to buy his silence?"

Well when she puts it like that, wow. Leave it to my sister to trim the fat off of this delicate subject and go right for the sweet spot. "Yes, I guess that is what I mean."

"No."

"See, I don't think that I am quite that shallow . . . what did you say?"

"I said no. I don't think that you are pretending to like Craig just so he will be quiet about Kelsey." She sat there smiling lightly. She must have noticed the look of relief that crossed my face because she added, "Because if that were true, you would have been trying to set up daddy's uncle Kyle with Aunt Katrina. If anyone was going to spill the beans it's her."

We both broke into another fit of raucous laughter. Uncle Kyle is quite an interesting fellow. He likes trains. I don't mean that he likes them like, "Oh look, a train." Oh No, no, no, no, no. I mean, 'My god girls did you see that? That was a 1994 Electrostar 357, part of the new fleet of 74 engines which has gone almost 12 months without a major reported incident and almost forty two thousand miles of service. Tell you ladies something else, that train you see there, (looks left and then right as if he is afraid someone might overhear him even though the three of us are traveling at fifty miles an hour along a state road) rumor has it that it is going to win the "Golden Spanners" award this November. Yep, that's one powerful piece of engineering.' Now there is nothing, absolutely nothing wrong with liking trains. Trains are some of the most powerful machines on land. They do amazing things and can handle hundreds of tons of weight easily. But I can't envision in my mind a date between Uncle Kyle and Aunt Katrina, not without having my spleen shoot out of the side of my body. But for your sake my friends, I shall try. It's a dark, romantic night. The car is parked at some quiet spot and two people are sitting in the front seat huddled close together, whispering soft words as they stare up at a bright, full, summer moon. The only other visible light is from the small dashboard clock which the man seems to check periodically. He casually mentions the time, consults his wrist watch, shakes it to ensure it is running and then asks his lovely date to open the glove box and remove the bundle of papers contained therein. She, being a female captivated by the ways of this noble and devilishly handsome man obliges and hands him what appears to be a railway schedule. He sits up, unfolds the map of the various lines and times for the Massachusetts area and announces, "Damn, the Gloucester fifty three is running late." A bit stunned but not daunted, she leans in close and tries to show she cares by saying, "What?" I think dear reader you see my point.

We joked around for a little bit longer and then began talking about everything under the sun, except Savannah. As far as I was concerned, that subject at the moment was taboo, like talking baseball during hockey season. I figured that with Nicole and me on the mend, I wouldn't try to press my luck and start my litany of 'five thousand reasons you should officially hate Savannah Summers, time enough for that tomorrow, perhaps.

As the hour grew late, I climbed up on the bed beside her. She was getting tired and starting to say some of those silly things that come to your mind when you're nearly three hours past bed time and in a giggly mood.

I gave her a hug and said good night. I woke up the next morning in bed beside her. I must have dozed off as well. I looked at the window and it was still pretty dark outside so I decided to go over to my room and try to sleep the hour or two I had left in the comfort of my own bed.

I carefully removed myself so as not to wake Nicole and dragging myself half asleep through my door I took five more steps and plopped myself into bed. It was by sheer luck alone that I noticed the dark red letters on the wall, which thank god, were written in crayon and not something more sinister.

It was a message from Kelsey and by the way it was written and its directness I grew concerned that she was more than a bit perturbed.

I closed my eyes but sleep did not come easy for me. I had just begun repairing one relationship when another seemed to have become derailed. And as you can see, I was now quoting train lingo from Uncle Kyle.

I rolled over and placed my back to the wall but the message had a way of making me know that it was still there and I suddenly understood how scary it must have been for Kelsey. She may have thought that she could not be heard any longer or perhaps that I had somehow left her alone and abandoned. From now on I would have to make it a point not to be absent unless she knew in advance.

I took another breath, rolled over once more and read the words, again.

"Where are you?"

With tears forming in my eyes I whispered, "I'm right here sis. I'm still right here."

CHAPTER EIGHT

SANTERIA MARIA

Over the next few days Mimi had us all over the place going from one store to another. Much of it was for school clothes which she always took us shopping for every summer, but we made the occasional stop in furniture stores and home improvement outlets. I normally, as you could have guessed, have no patience for this kind of nonsense since whenever people go into one of those home super stores they come out spending money and having work to do. This concept I will never understand. Thank you Mr. Store Clerk, here is several hundred dollars, now excuse me while I spend all of my free time putting this crap to use, blah, thank you powers that be for making me a girl.

During these day long excursions I began doing some research on the white art of Santeria. Santeria is voodoo for good guys. It kind of has its roots set deep in the mysticism of Africa with a splash of Catholicism thrown in for good measure. I was certain there was a lot to learn but thanks to the invention of the smart phone, I was able to begin surfing the net on Mimi's phone for information during the time we spent in her car. I felt that it was important for me to understand as much as I could about this South American tradition so that when Savannah finally made her move, I would be prepared.

Unfortunately, there are very few places on the internet that had reliable information on this subject and those that did varied widely depending on which region in the world the article had been written. For instance, there are many ways to defend one-self from an attack of black magic, but each one is unique: Brazilians can dance away an evil spirit, Cubans have a shot of tequila and smoke a cigar and suddenly all is right in their world, while the other islands call for some very rare herbs and components.

After about two hours of jumping from one site to another it became apparent that even though it was contrary to everything I knew to be sensible, I was going to have to get Aunt Katrina involved in this one.

I bided my time and waited for Mimi to pull up to a Raymore and Flannigan. It was then that I asked to remain in the car pretending to be involved in one of her countless app's on the phone. She laughed and exited the car with Nicole trailing behind her.

I tried to steady my nerves. I had a feeling that this was going to be one of the most difficult conversations I had ever had. Believe it or not, children can get frustrated too. Most adults don't believe it but we do have a tolerance point as well. The strange thing was that I truly did care for Craig's Aunt, she is a good woman and one of the few adults that actually believes in all this stuff but let's face it, she's nuts. Not the nuts where you're worried that she might drop down on all fours, howl and start pretending to be a border collie/werewolf. No, she is the other kind of nuts.

I dialed the number and heard it connect. One ringie, two ringies, maybe she wasn't home, three . . . "Hullo?"

"Hey, Auntie Kat it's me Caitlin."

"Ahhhhh Quate-lin. I knew you vould be calling me. My Pomeranian has been busy scratching his tush all morning."

Sweet God in heaven did the conversation have to start off this way?

"Your dog has a butt itch and that means you knew I would be calling?"

"Vhat? No dhaling, are you feverish? Vhat on earth vould my dog's bottom have to do vith a call from you?" She replied, her voice almost sounding exacerbated.

"You said you knew I would call because of your dog's rectal skin condition."

"No, I knew you vould be calling because Craig told me that the situation between you and Savannah vas getting more and more out of hand. He has kept me informed of most of your nocturnal meetings. My dog's butt is a matter that I merely mentioned; because I know you have a dog as vell and thought you vould sympathize."

I shook my head from side to side. I was instinctively trying to shake the cobwebs away so that I continued to make more sense than the older woman on the other end of the phone. "Okay. Well there has been a new development that I have not even shared with Craig and this one requires your certain type of expertise."

"Ack my little angel, vhat is it?"

I smiled. She could be sweet when she wanted to be. "Well, it seems that Savannah is a Bokur, a voodoo priest, well priestess. She has been trained in the blackest magic and I have it on good information that I am her next target."

"My poor angel, did you get it? Let me see, ah good, good."

"Did I get what?" I asked.

"Caitlin, please try to keep up, I was speaking to my dog. Now, let's talk about this voodoo problem. Before ve begin, you must be certain that she is in fact a member of this sect. If not, ve vill be wasting a lot of time and effort trying to make our preparations only to discover that it vas all for nothing."

"Well, I had her brother approach me a few nights ago and warn me that his sister was involved in voodoo, does that count?"

There was a pause in the conversation and then she continued, "Yes, that is a pretty reliable source. A confession from a loved one is usually sound enough to begin making plans. My only concern of course is if he vould lie? Is that possible?" She asked.

"I can't imagine what he would gain from lying to me about something so twisted. Better yet, why approach me with something like that? I mean wouldn't most kids have laughed and called him a dweeb? He must have sensed that I was magically attuned. He said that I was a warrior for the light, someone born good, who would carry on the struggle against the dark forces of evil."

"He said dis?"

"Yes."

I heard her chuckle softly, "Vell then, he must be on as you say, the level. Since I met you dat first time, I knew that you were a good and kind person. I told Craig that you were a child who would do great things in her time. Yes, for now we must believe the information that heaven has been kind enough to pass on to us. So, vhat is your plan?"

"Well, I was thinking that we could perhaps take a ride into the city in the next couple of days and try to look up a shop or bookstore that deals in these kind of books and begin doing some research on the subject."

"Quate-lin, you know that I am not schooled in this type of magic, but fortunately I know of a voman who has just such a shop. She lives in Salem and I'm certain she vould meet vith us and perhaps even mix up a spell or two to help keep you and your family safe."

"Great," I said, "that would be awesome. Why don't you call her and find out when she can see us and I'll work on getting permission to take a trip into the city with you."

"Quate-lin, it is not in the city, it is in Salem." She corrected.

"Yes, I know Auntie. But if I ask my parents if I could take a trip with you into Salem to go and visit a Santerian priestess to get some protective spells to stop an insidious voodoo plot, they would have me seeing Dr. Forsythe every day."

"Good point," she agreed.

"We are going to a Hungarian art exhibition at some small gallery in the city. You are interested in sharing some of the culture from the old country with me."

"I am? Oh, da, I mean yes, yes I am. Von day Quate-lin these secrets are going to catch up vith you."

It is never a good sign when a gypsy prophesizes that you are going to pay a heavy toll for your actions. In the case of a story it indicates foreshadowing and foreshadowing means in this particular instance that I was probably going to get my butt kicked for telling my parents a lie. Yet what choice did I have? If I was honest it would be taken as drama and over-reaction. If I do nothing, my sister will continue to be a pawn in this girl's twisted game and my family and I will more than likely be the recipients of some diabolical curse. Yes, I could see it now. There in my vision was my father, doubled over in pain, begging his doctor for a cure to a disease that they could not pin point. And mother, I imagined her with back hair. Thick, course, curly back hair, oh my god, how hideous? Yet I knew that these sort of calamities would befall my family if it weren't for my little white lies and spooky secrets. I would not risk having my mother the laughing stock of Braintree by being referred to as "Sasquatch". Duty was calling collect and I had to accept the charges.

We drove back home and later that night I was contacted by Aunt Katrina. It seems that this art exhibit was available for our review in two days. I asked my father since he was sitting closest and shockingly he agreed. I expected him to allow me to go, but not quite so easily. The fact that he did not roll his eyes or make a comment about Aunt Katrina made me wonder if he in fact was "up to something." I hung up the phone after telling her she could pick me up at ten on Thursday morning and sat staring at my dad.

"So, everything's all set?" he asked from behind his newspaper. We had been sitting in the living room when the call had come in, he reading the Boston Globe, me paging through a copy of Tiger Beat. Now before you go all ballistic on me let me explain. I do this from time to time to put on the air of being a normal eighth grader who actually cares about what Nick Jonas is wearing to his latest premier or if Miley kissed another underwear model. In truth, I couldn't care less but about four months ago mom had told the therapist that I didn't do normal things like 'read girlie magazines or try to squeeze myself into skinny jeans'. So what was the first thing I did, ran out and got a girlie mag and a pair of jeans so tight that if I had a tattoo on my butt on you could read it through the denim. I'll never forget the night my mom seemed almost to breathe a sigh of relief when I screamed that Selena Gomez wore the same cherry flavored lip gloss that I loved. I tribally danced around the kitchen table, called a girlfriend and even spent some time writing about it in my dairy just in case she was sneaking peeks at my entries. Deception, when utilized, must be complete or else why bother?

"Yes. Craig's Aunt will be picking me up at ten a.m. the day after tomorrow."

"Great. Did she happen to tell you how much it will cost to get in? I don't want to have Craig's aunt paying for you."

"No, she didn't mention if there was any cost to get in." *Why did my dad have to be so clever as to play these little chess games with me and more to the point how did he always know when to play them?*

He folded his paper and reached for the phone. "No worries, I'll just call her back. The number will be in the caller history on the phone and I'll get all the particulars."

"Ah, she said she was going to jump in the shower. So you won't be able to get in touch with her right now." I stayed cool. To panic here and set off his parental senses any more and we might be forced to scrub the mission and then I would end up spending the rest of my teenage years braiding my mother's back hair. (Please see earlier voodoo reference.)

"Really. Okay, well I'll call Craig's mom then and ask her how much she's sending with Craig."

Stay Calm. Now I was seeing the root of his skepticism. He had not heard me mention that Craig <u>and I</u> were going with Katrina, so of course he was wondering why she would take me, a non family member if Craig was not going as well. *It was then that I realized where I get my clever from. I get it from you dad but it is time for the student to outfox the master. Eat this OBI-WAN!*

"Oh dad, please don't do that. This whole thing is a surprise for Craig. Aunt Katrina did not tell him where we are going or that I was invited. You know Craig, if he thought it was something educational he would only complain all the way there. I will call Mrs. Dawson in the morning and ask her how much money I should bring."

My dad folded the paper over and laid it down in his lap. He seemed to be sizing me up but then nodded and agreed. "Okay Caitlin. But don't forget to ask tomorrow. I don't want us imposing on their aunt. Was she planning on taking you both for lunch as well?"

"Yes. We are going into the city to get some pizza or something like that, nothing too extravagant."

"Alright then, I'll give you some money and you can buy the Dawson's some lunch."

"Thanks dad."

Crisis averted. I was going to have to be a bit more on guard around my dad. It seemed that he was beginning to develop a bit of blood hound in him, which made me a wee bit nervous. It was bad enough having mom doubt most of the things I say let alone now having dad do the same thing.

After several impromptu meetings between the members of The Soul Patrol minus of course Nicole, it was agreed that the best course of action at this point was to stick to the story I had concocted and head into Salem with Craig's aunt. For the record, Kelsey was a bit against the lying to our parent's part and Craig declared that the whole venture was insane and that he wanted NO part in it at all. So, let's tally the votes, those against two, those for one, but since that one was me, tough nuggies to the two of them and I made my preparations for a road trip.

Thursday came very quickly and at ten a.m. just as we had arranged, Aunt Katrina pulled up and honked the horn. When I came outside to greet her, with my father not far behind me, I stopped dead in my tracks and was forced to take in a sight that was more suited to the "Twilight Zone" than a small suburban driveway in Braintree. There sat quite possibly the ugliest car ever designed, unless of course you were an aquatic creature who appreciated spending their time in a bowl.

My father sucked a breath through clenched teeth, the way you would if someone you knew just got a bad burn or fell down the stairs while singing a "Barney" song. I was afraid to approach any closer. In all honesty, I was transfixed the way a vampire is when you show them the crucifix. If I had any sense I would have shielded my eyes and ran inside the house.

Aunt Katrina stepped out of the car and waved, "Hullo Dhalings. Quate-lin are you ready for our big day at the Hungarian Art Show?"

I nodded, words at this point were still far too elusive. Fortunately my father was able to keep up the appearances by greeting her. "Hello Katrina, wow is that a 1976 AMC Pacer?"

"Yes Ian it is, in the original lime green. It's a bit worse for the wear after thirty five years of ownership and of course the 223,000 miles but she is still a thing of beauty is she not?"

For the first time in my life I felt as if my father ditched me. As my eyes begrudgingly scanned the rest of this Detroit abomination I heard him say, "Well, you two have a great time. When do you think you'll be getting back Katrina?"

How can you call yourself my father and allow me to get inside that thing. Have you not noticed that the patches of rust seem to cover more of the surface than the remaining paint. And the windows, I mean look at all that glass; one good pot hole and they might just explode showering us in tiny razor sharp shards of doom.

"Oh, I can't see us being later than five or six o'clock. I have my cell phone turned on of course, oh yes here I vote down the number for you." She walked up and handed my father a small piece of paper with her number scrawled on it. She then smiled, wrapped her left arm around my shoulder and half herded, half led me to the idling car.

"What's that noise?" I asked.

"Vhich noise?" she said as she wrestled the door open so I could get in.

"The noise that sounds like someone is trying to stick a bowie knife into the side of a warthog?"

"Ah that. That my dhaling is eighty-three horses of pure American ingenuity."

I climbed into the car and noticed that it was at least fifteen degrees hotter inside this menagerie than it was standing on my front porch. Katrina warned me to keep my arms safely inside the car and with what I could only assume was a foul and ancient curse in her native tongue, she took a four step running start and launched herself at the car door in an attempt to close it. Seeing a fifty year old, five foot Hungarian woman lunge at a car door in this way, was to say the least, terrifying. The impact was like two sumo wrestlers fighting for a position of strength. She dug her feet into my yard and heaved. With reluctance and a grinding sound of metal on metal the door slowly began to move and finally close with a terrific bang.

"Bad hinge," I heard her yell to my father as she rubbed her shoulder trying to jump start the blood flow to the area and possibly avoid a bruise.

She made her way around the back of the car and then opened the driver's door and got in. She was sweating. Her dress was crumbled and hanging slightly off her left shoulder. I remember thinking that I hoped she had not dislocated it as the car lurched to life and backed down our driveway.

"Don't forget we have to go and pick up Craig," I yelled.

"I know dhaling, I just have to get the car to cooperate."

I waved goodbye to my father for what I feared may be the last time as a blue cloud of smoke burped out of the back of the car. My guide shifted the vehicle into drive and mashed the accelerator down to the floor. Craig only lived three houses down from us, or the equivalent of maybe a football field yet in Aunt Katrina's Pacer it felt like it might have been quicker to go inside, hook up Dog, walk him up to chubby Jim the gnome, let him do his business and walk the rest of the way to Craig's house.

As we turned into Craig's driveway Katrina screamed, "Don't open that door again dhaling I'm not sure I can handle another attempt to shut it just yet. I vill let Craig get into the back seat behind me."

She left me alone inside this mobile terrarium for about five minutes, collected Craig and stuffed him into the back seat.

"Hey, Caitlin."

"Hey you. How's things?" I replied.

"Here we go, hang on everyone." Katrina said as she pleaded with the car to be kind enough to actually move its self forward.

"I wanted to talk to you both about this before you went to Salem. I think you are making a big mistake, Caitlin."

"How are we making a mistake?"

"Okay look, this is not some kind of joke. This voodoo stuff is like weird, I mean like weirder than the séance and all that crap that my aunt believes in, no offense Auntie Kat."

She smiled, "None taken dhaling."

"Craig if we don't take some precautions this girl is going to continue to run all over us. You can see that she has already got a firm grasp on Nicole, what's next?"

"Did you ever think that maybe she actually just likes your sister. They hang together real nice Caitlin. I mean her family seems pretty cool and stuff. You know her brother is like being scouted for some major colleges and may get a full scholarship for swimming at an Ivy League school."

"Craig get your head out of the pool, okay. This is a creature of darkness we are dealing with not some simple kid looking to beat me up on the playground after school. If I, no let me correct that, if WE don't get some serious, what's the word Auntie Kat?"

"Juju." She offered.

"Right, Juju. If we don't get some serious juju on our side then this girl will have me wandering around the neighborhood at night searching for money and who knows what else, like some sort of real cute zombie slave. Now, if my boyfriend thinks that that is not a good enough reason to head into Salem then I have to wonder how much he cares about being my boyfriend."

"Damn, why is it that every time I disagree with you, you throw that boyfriend stuff in my face. Can't I just have a different opinion?"

I turned around, smiled sweetly and gave him a kiss on the cheek, "No."

Aunt Katrina had driven up to the corner and made a right. She then went two streets over from our house and applied the brakes bringing the aerodynamic muscle car to a halt.

Auntie Kat, you know her parents would be very upset if they knew the truth."

"I know Craig, so please don't allow yourself to be seen on the vay back. Listen to me dhaling. This girl has power, vhat dat means I am not sure but power she does have. I know not vhat vill come of dis road trip but if it makes Quate-lin feel safer den it is vorth it, no?"

He waited a moment before answering. "Yes."

She got out pulled the seat forward so he could walk home. Craig exited the car and just as he was about to make his way back home he leaned in and said, "Be careful, okay?"

"I will, I doubt this car can even do the speed limit. Don't worry we'll be all right."

"I am not worried about the stupid car. Just be careful," and with that left without turning around to say goodbye. I may not be very old but I've been around long enough to know that if you say your good-byes without turning around to catch a last minute glimpse of the person who is departing, it usually means that you will never see that person again. When I voiced my concerns, no correction again, when I shouted my concerns to Katrina she replied with a very confused and yet insightful adage from the old country, "It pays to take a breath, before you cut off the chicken's head."

Sound advice.

We spent the rest of our forty minute road trip in silence. I tried to speak once and ask her a question about the necessity of her saying a prayer every time before the car shifted into third gear but by the expression on her face, I thought better of it. I never knew exactly how much mental concentration it took to keep a car from exploding. Every noise, hiss, spit and sputter becomes another crisis stalking the driver like some great jungle cat. Show fear, lose focus, miscalculate and you could end up like that guy Roy in Las Vegas, as a life size cat chewie.

Salem is a quaint and very picturesque town. It has dark brown homes, a central town square, a nice college and of course a museum dedicated to the brutal torture and mass hysteria that occurred in the 1692 when several young girls declared that they had been touched by a she devil. In today's age of science it's easy to dismiss these claims as mere pranks played by young girls whose lives were very demanding. Work, prayers, studies, work and then an evening of listening to their elders talk about the bible made life in Salem a bit on the tedious side. The shame of it all is that people got hurt.

There is an under lying message here about how one should not over play the drama and believe me, its impact has not been lost on this writer.

The other thing that Salem has is a number of book stores, book stores of all types, shapes and sizes. In the long cold winter months, the good people of Salem love to read. And why not, reading is a great way to spend the time sitting beside a nice warm fire or snuggling up in your bed trying to steal a few more pages before you fall asleep.

One book store though was more important than all the rest. It was the shop owned by a woman named Maria and she was, according to Aunt Katrina the local expert on all things Voodoo.

We drove through the center of town and took a series of lefts and rights before we finally found a parking lot in which we could park this "Chariot of the Gods."

Obeying a request from my chauffer, I lifted my bottom over the gear stick and plopped down in the driver seat so I could get out of the car on her side and avoid another match between the gypsy and the car door.

"Vell, vhat do you think?" Katrina asked as she looked around taking in the old architecture and small cobble stone streets.

"I think you need a new car."

"Quate-lin, if I buy a new car vhat vould I do vith this one?" She shook her head as if I was not making any sense.

"You're right, what was I thinking. So, where is this place?"

Katrina answered me as she began walking, "about three blocks back dat vay. Ve passed it already as we came up that small hill."

I hurried to catch up. "Why didn't you park along the street then, there have been spots all along the way?"

"Because dhaling," she spun and nearly decapitated me with her black, seventy five pound purse, "we would have spent the day filling out insurance forms if I parked dere."

Before I could ask the obvious, 'what are you talking about' question she answered it for me, "no emergency brake."

So down the hill we went. The walk was nice I have to admit. Katrina was softly singing a folk song that if I understood the words she was uttering, had something to do with a gigantic pig and a traveling horse salesman.

We crossed in front of another small alleyway that cut the street into blocks and at the corner she stopped in front of a smallish black door that had no glass in it at all. The small shop window sat to the left of this ominous portal. *Oh, I like that . . . ominous portal.* Painted in yellows and reds was a large hand, palm up, with all kinds of symbols and foreign words all over the picture. Above the hand was the word "Santeria" and below the wrist which was the lowest portion of the hand that the artist had decided to depict was the name "Maria".

"Ah, here we are, good. Come let's go inside we are already a few minutes late."

I let her reach for the door handle and press down on the thumb latch. With a small hiss, like the sound of air escaping from a Tupperware burpie lid, the door to the shop opened and a tiny bell rang.

At once, my sense of smell was overwhelmed. Scents, strong and strange attacked my nose. Spices and herbs, incense and sandalwood, musk and murky oils, all this and more made a savage mad dash to be the premier odor that I was to choose as the fragrance of the day.

The room itself was a simple square with every inch of wall space covered by some sort of old wooden shelves. Books of various size and age; lined much of their surface. All around the room strange jars, vials, and plants peaked out as if to remind the shop keeper that they still existed. It quickly became obvious, at least to me that this place was meant more for a teacher than a student of the Caribbean magical arts.

Katrina closed the door behind her after she allowed me to pass by. I stood fairly still not wanting to venture too far into this alien place without my guide in tow. It was strange. When I told Craig about my idea to come here three days ago it seemed like a stroke of pure genius. Now that I was here however, the creepies were beginning to run amok.

"Can I helps you?" I heard from the back of the room. I allowed my eyes another second or two to adjust to the lack of natural light inside the store before I began searching for the source of the question.

"Maria dhaling, is dat you?" Katrina asked as she carefully made her way past me towards the counter that sat in the same direction as the disembodied voice.

"Aye, I be known as Maria. Who dere claims to speak to me as only a friend would?"

A woman of medium height stepped out of what I could only assume was the storage room and appeared behind the counter. She was dark skinned and wore what would be considered as very formal attire for the part of the world she came from. The main piece of fashion was a serape dyed bright orange that hung on her body from the shoulders. She wore a blue turban on top of her head that was intricately woven or tied. I could tell her demeanor was cautious but pleasant from the way she entered the room. All and all, she was exactly the sort of person you would expect to meet in a voodoo shop in the middle of Salem.

"Vell dhaling, dat friend vould be me Katrina, we spoke on da phone just the other day?"

"Oh yes, da pale child who has a feer dat someone is trying to werk her, wit out her wanting to be werked," Maria replied.

"Da. She is here vith me and ve came to see if dere vas any ting you could do to advise her on vhat steps to take to keep her people safe?"

"Ah come closer child. Let me see your eyes and know da truth of it," Maria beckoned me to move towards her with one curling finger.

"Okay, first I have a name, it's Caitlin. Second, the truth of what?"

"Of who ya tink ya are."

As I watched her I was introduced to a very new and quite different experience. I became upset with myself for not heeding Craig's warning. Never before had I felt such a powerful feeling of, '*Oh crap.*'

I settled my nerves and walked a few paces forward. On the walls surrounding the counter there were several small light fixtures that only held those light bulbs that look like small crystal flames. I guess her idea was to get me under the light and size me up. If I was going to get what I needed I knew that I would have to impress this woman, she was not going to be a pushover.

I decided to show no fear even though my insides were doing what could only be called the equivalent of a Tony Hawk 720°. I stopped just in front of the plain wooden counter and extended my hand in greeting. Bad idea.

"What are ya doin' child, tryin' to play me? Not once in yer life before have ya shared dat hand without it first bein' offered by anudder. Don't start actin like someone else, dat da quickest way to losin yer soul. Take heed on dat."

Katrina stood there quietly nodding to herself. I remember wondering if she was as bugged out as I was at that moment. She looked calm and in a way I guess that made sense. She was not the one getting scrutinized by a Bocur.

Maria spent a few tense seconds looking me over. Her expressions went from indifference, to studious, to impressed and then finally concerned.

All in all just about the normal reaction when people meet me for the first time . . . yeah right.

"She strong dis one," she said to Katrina.

"Da, I said the same thing to my nephew vhen I met her but alas she can not cook."

The priestess just nodded.

I thought, *Where in the hell did it say that a modern female mage or whatever the heck I was, had to know how to whip up a soufflé? People, we are fighting the Duchess of Darkness here, not trying to cater a room at the Hilton.*

"She can do more den she knows as well. In fact, she tink dis is all some game but it ain't." she continued to address Craig's aunt over the top of my head.

"I don't think this is a game. Savannah Summers needs to be stopped . . ."

"Hush child. I ain't yappin about some silly girl who is pesterin ya. I is talkin about you, yerself. Dis whole ting dat you are in with your friend and your sisters. Dat is my first concern."

Did she say sisters, as in plural? I shot a dirty look at Aunt Katrina. We had agreed not to let this woman in on too much of my past for fear of diluting her appraisal of my situation.

"Don't be lookin at her," Maria said, drawing my attention back to her and away from what I assumed was a loud mouth gypsy. "What you tink, it hard to see that a piece of ya heart is missin? Silly child, dat is da point. It ain't missin, she here with ya, always. Da girl who ya tink left ya behind, she ain't ever left ya, she just a little harder to see. But ya got da skills and da powah to make her dere, all da time. Real as you and me," Maria smiled at me as if she could tell that I needed one at that moment.

"Listen, that's lovely, but instead of talking about the situation that I currently have under control, might we discuss the one which is out of my control and trying to turn me into a mindless servant of evil," I declared.

The woman in the turban turned and addressed Katrina again as if I was not even in the room, "Does she always have such a hard time liss-en-en?" Craig's aunt nodded silently as the woman continued to babble, "dere ain't no teachin a child who can't hear, so why bodder?" She walked out from behind the counter and began looking through various oddities, some she straightened, some she spoke to, others she just grinned and chuckled.

I stood there not knowing exactly what happened. I came here for a defense against a possible magical assault and instead I received cryptic instructions on how to handle Kelsey, which was not a problem at the moment.

After several minutes of standing there being ignored I said to Auntie Kat, "Please tell her why we are here. Can you make this woman understand the real reason for all the lies we told and miles we drove just to get here?"

"Quate-lin dhaling, she already knows."

I was beginning to lose my cool. "No, no Auntie. She doesn't know why I am here, because if she had been listening she would have heard you say earlier . . ."

"Dat dere be a girl who threatenen yer family and ya worried cause ya clueless on how to stop her." Maria interjected.

"Exactly," I said.

"So we prove I lissen to you. Now, repeat to me what me already told ya and we see how well ya lissen to me."

"YOU HAVEN'T SAID ANYTHING I NEED TO KNOW YET!"

She smiled and began to laugh, "See, you ain't liss-en-en. Months ago you went through a terrible shock, ya found out dat da world around ya ain't so simple, ain't so safe. It scare ya and good ting too. Now ya here cause yer scared again. Well, dere ain't nothin' I can do to stop da frights. What I can do is help ya believe."

"I already believe, that's why I am here," I replied, finally feeling like we were getting somewhere.

"No! I ain't talking about believen in magic and spirits, ya got dat part already. I be talkin' about believen in yerself. Dis girl, she in yer head. She already took from ya yer power. Ya gots to get yer power back. Udder wise she nevah gonna let ya go."

Katrina nodded and suddenly it all began to make sense. They were right. From the moment I saw Savannah six weeks ago stepping out of her nice four door SUV, with her perfect hair, perfect face and perfect family, she had me a nervous wreck. Savannah sensed my inner feelings of inferiority and played on them. I allowed her to get to me. I was the one who felt less; less pretty, less girlie, less rich, less cool. And now that she had made friends with Nicole it only added to my feelings of "less." With Kelsey gone and Nicole avoiding me because of poor choices on my part, I feared being, sister-less. God, what a fool I've been. I spoke out loud without even meaning to do so, "No one can make you feel inferior without your consent."

"Exactly child. Dat was one smart woman dat Eleanor Roosevelt."

"Yeah, I remember that from history class like two years ago. Wow, that is true. As much as Savannah is a jerk, she is just doing what jerks do. I need to control how I handle it and come to grips with her being friends with my little sister."

"See Maria, Quate-lin can listen, it just sometimes you have to let her verk dese tings out for herself," Katrina smiled and moved in to place her arm around my shoulders and give me a soft hug.

"Okay, so now that I have this new sense of confidence are you saying that I don't need to protect myself?"

"No," Maria flatly answered.

"All right then, I mean the whole confidence thing is great don't get me wrong but . . ."

Maria came towards me and lowered her face so that our eyes were at the exact same level, "Without da belief in yerself and da powah of who ya be, dere would be no magic I could teach ya dat would have werked. To be strong is da first line of defense but against a true Bocur, it not enough. Come, let me show ya something dat ya can do dat is simple and make it hard fer her to get to ya."

Maria spent the next hour showing me things that she said would help protect both myself and my family from Savannah's magical influence. Her charisma, her persuasive power and her ability to make me uncomfortable I now understood I would have to deal with on my own.

In the end, I blew three months of my allowance or almost sixty dollars on a small wooden cross with four tiny, black wooden beads set on a leather string which I was instructed to wear as a necklace. She said it had been carved from the bark of a tree whose roots went deep into the ground a church stood on. I also got a book on defense spells that could be used with minimum components. (For those of you who are not magically inclined, components are the things that fuel a spell, you know the old monks wood, hemlock, eye of newt, tongue of bat that stuff.) I also got a packet of incense and an incense tray mostly because I liked the smell but also because she claimed it was good for channeling spirits. *Yeah, okay whatever, like I want more spirits in my life than I've got already.*

We prepared to leave and Maria gave Katrina and me kerchiefs that were made from fabric spun by young girls from her home country of Haiti, who had not yet been married or proposed to. She said "innocence passes away easily but it also passes easily on from a pure heart to another soul in need."

We thanked her for the lovely gifts and all her guidance. Then without any further delay we said our goodbyes to Santeria Maria and took our leave of her amazing bookstore.

CHAPTER NINE

FOG

With only two weeks left before school things had begun to settle down a bit. Some of it was my new found confidence and the rest in truth was because I was spending every free second I could avoiding Savannah. No, I was not hiding in my basement or running down the street whenever I heard her voice. I was just avoiding the things that were becoming part of the Summers/O'Connor routine. Allow me to elaborate for a moment. Every morning at promptly seven thirty my little sister opens the front door and joins her "friend" for their morning jog. Then it's back to the house to hydrate and grab field hockey gear, shin pads, sticks, bag and balls, cleats you get the idea. Then it's over to Mrs. Summers' house so she can do the morning drive to the high school where Nicole and Savannah are involved in a field hockey camp. Then they are there until about one o'clock, my dad (doing the afternoon pick-up) collects them and they spilt for lunch and some down time. At six thirty every night, my sister (and much to my shame my mother), head over to the Summers' house and join them in the back yard. There Mr. Summers has set up on their newly renovated covered back porch, candles and mats for everyone. Then he leads the gathered throng in an end of the day spiritual yoga and tai chi class. Oh yes, it was getting real hard to avoid the routine.

Fortunately for me, my father was still a self proclaimed hermit during the summer months. For dad, there was only two states of being in the middle of these hot months, air conditioned or slowly dying. So, we keep him constantly cooled to avoid any melting. When I was younger, it had been so ingrained in my head about his hatred of the heat that I actually feared he would turn into a puddle of ooze like the wicked witch in "The Wizard of Oz" if he stepped outside during the daylight hours of July or August.

Every night as the "Geeks and the Guru" (an immature nickname that my dad and I had adopted for this collection of flexible spiritual voyagers) gathered, we would sit down in front of the television with a bag of jiffy pop or a bowl of ice cream and watch our favorite game show re-runs. Please don't judge us. Match Game 78 can be quite addictive and Richard Dawson (no connection to Craig) was such a rascal.

Yet as these last few days began to dwindle away I was forced to bear witness to a very upsetting and almost earth shattering event. My mother and sib had just come home from another session of mediation and found dad and I sitting on the upstairs couch playing a game of Scrabble.

"Hey there they are," dad said smiling, "how was your class? Feel better."

"Ian you have to try this. It is so relaxing," my mom answered.

"Yeah daddy, it makes you feel so much better after a long day."

"Ummm, you guys enjoy yourselves. Caitlin and I are expanding our minds with a game of tile toss Scrabble. (For those of you unfamiliar with tile toss scrabble the rules are very simple, the winner gets to snap the board and send all the pieces flying. The loser gets teased while they spend the next ten minutes finding all the tiles.)

The front door opened and Mimi came in. She was carrying yet another collection of swatches which I could only imagine meant another meeting with Mrs. Summers about fabrics for the new house.

"Hello everyone. How was yoga?" she asked as she placed her samples on the chair and smiled. Over the last few weeks the tension in the air had become a bit better and at times things actually felt normal.

"We are trying to get dad to come with us and try it out," Nicole said.

"I think that's a great idea, you should do it Ian," Mimi added.

"It's okay but thanks, I'm good here," he shook his head almost laughing.

Then my mother spoke up and I am not exactly sure what she meant but it made me wince inside like when someone says something that's either weird or makes you cringe, "I don't know Ian, I am getting pretty flexible. Shame you can't see me doing downward facing dog."

"Yeah daddy, mommy is doing it really good Mr. Summers said so," Nicole said.

"Did he?" I saw my dad look at my mom and the wheels in his head were beginning to move and I suspected his resolve was being tested. Mimi broke the trance he was in by saying, "Well, I think I will join you both tomorrow. It's been a few years since I've done any Tai Chi but it will be great to get back into it."

"See daddy, even Mimi is going to try."

"I don't know," he weakly protested.

"Well, I guess I will just have to let Daniel help me with the more advanced poses. I can't move on without a spotter. I'm sure he won't mind," mom teased.

Ick. My mom just tried to play the jealousy card on my dad. She was actually taunting him to join them or else. Of all the low, under handed, despicable, conniving . . . Damn, it was sheer brilliance.

"Well, maybe I could come over just to help you out," he had been bested. It was tragic to watch this grown man whom I admired so much get played by a woman using the jealousy card. It broke my heart but not nearly as bad as the next little tidbit I accidentally stumbled upon.

"Oh good and don't worry there are plenty of other guys there," she added.

"Yeah Stephen the preppy can join you as well dad," I chuckled.

Mother cast me a quick dismissive little glance and then added, "Yes, he is there but so is Craig, and the Dawson's are thinking of coming as well."

"CRAIG? WHAT THE HELL IS HE DOING THERE?" I blurted out.

Everyone turned to face me. I stood and tried to compose "cute face # 11" but it didn't seem to have the desired effect.

"Yoga. What else would he be doing there?"

I'm sure you can imagine my complete and utter shock at this little piece of news. I can't believe Craig had not told me that he was taking yoga instructions from Savannah's father. This was simply unbelievable. No, it was beyond unbelievable it was downright treasonous. My beau was spending his evenings trying to find the path to enlightenment while sitting next to Miss 'Boobs' in what I could only imagine was a skin tight body stocking.

I became lost in a fog, not that wimpy fog that hangs lazily over a Massachusetts lake on a cool autumn morning. No, this was the type of uber-fog they get in England. The fog that has mass and you can actually taste it when you breathe. All around me the world was coming undone, all around me I was losing ground. If I had to draw a parallel to another situation that mimicked my own it would be the plight of the American Indians. Every time they turned around the settlers took a little bit more, pushed them a bit farther back. Every treaty was a lie and every day saw another slaughter or atrocity.

I excused myself and headed up to my bedroom. I shut the door and sat down on the bed. This was not a simple 'poor me' moment. This was the moment when everything I had experienced since Kelsey's death came flooding back. I was lost in an ocean of sadness and self doubt. The rage, the pain and the guilt tossed me all around and slammed me back to the shore over and over again. I was a complete mess.

Nine months ago my best friend died, taken from me by a terrible accident and ever since then I am the one alone. No, this was not melodrama, please dear reader hear me out. In the time since I uncovered the fact that she was my sister everyone has moved on but me. Everyone has begun to heal, begun repairing the wounds and all I have done is to delay the inevitable. Mom and dad are back together, the tragedy and their poor choices have somehow strengthened their bond. Nicole has found a new best friend. She has dealt with it somehow and has grasped the dark and terrible truth of it; that life goes on. Mimi has bought a new house and is fulfilling a lifelong promise. Who knows if she would have done that with out the pain of Kelsey's death to motivate her into action? When Kelsey was alive it was always about the two of us. The web of relationships in my life was a simple one. A single, unbreakable (or so we thought) strand of silk between us and then there was everyone else. She was my confidant, my conscience, my security blanket and without ever knowing it until it was too late, my twin. I had lost a twin. The hollow part of me was so full of nothingness that sometimes it felt hard to breathe. I sit here night after night waiting to speak to my sister and that is the highlight of my day. How can I move on when all I do is look forward to my time speaking to the dead, for the fact remains; that is what she is.

In truth, I have not fully faced her demise because she is still here, still in my life, still with me in the darkest parts of the night, even if it's only for an hour. Then at that moment, in the stillness of my bedroom it hit me. *What if Kelsey didn't need me anymore? What if, when I saw her in my dream months ago playing with other children from my family's past, what if that had been her way of saying to me that she was trying to move on from me? What if I was keeping her from fully crossing over? Maybe it wasn't me keeping Kelsey company, maybe she was babysitting me? Maybe she was afraid to leave me alone, not the other way around?*

I laid my head down on the pillow and pulled my comforter up over my body. I was cold, it was the end of August and I was cold. I shivered under the blanket and closed my eyes for a moment trying to draw the courage I needed to see if when I reopened them if I would notice my own breath hanging in the air. It didn't. The cold I was feeling this time then was not a warning that Kelsey was on her way. This cold was just the chill of loneliness.

I heard a soft knock on my door before it opened partially. My mother was standing there. "You okay?"

"No," was about all I could muster.

"Want to talk about it?" She asked.

"About what, which part? The part that I can't seem to let Kelsey go, the part that everyone loves the Summers' and no one recognizes that Savannah is a manipulative little bitch or the part that my boyfriend is hanging around her and seems to be avoiding me?"

She came in and sat down on the edge of my bed. "Well, that's an awful lot of things for someone your age to be dealing with at once. I guess let's handle the one you are the most upset by first."

I sat up and leaned against my head board. "I know we've gone over this a dozen times but I can't seem to just let it go. You have dad, Nicole has Savannah which makes my stomach turn, Mimi has the house and all I have is stomach cramps. When does it get easier? When does it not hurt so much?"

"I don't know. I still find myself crying in the middle of the day. Your father has written pages and pages about his grief and how that choice has done so much damage to you and Nicole. Mimi went on a holiday and cried her eyes out and Nicole has taken to sports as a way of sweating out the pain. Maybe you need to find something that will help you heal," she offered.

"You mean forget," I shot back.

"Caitlin you will never forget her, I promise you that. She will be in your mind on the day you graduate college. She will be with you on the day you get married and I bet if you have a girl you might even find down the road that you want to name her Kelsey or some variation of it. She will always be with you and she will always be with your dad and me. Yes, some days she will be there a bit less than others. But do you know when I see her the most?"

"When?" I asked softly.

"Every time I look at you, honey. Every time I look in your eyes and see the sadness or the pain, I see Kelsey. Every time I hear your voice, hers follows in my mind. I so wish I could take the pain away but I can't. Understand me, I love you so very much but there are days that all I see is the empty space at your side and know that she should be there. Maybe that's why I am the way I am with you. It's not that I am always so angry or upset with what you do or say. Maybe I just can't stop seeing Kelsey. I have to though because I want to be close to you, you're my daughter and I love you."

We didn't move right away it sort of slowly happened. She leaned forward and I met her halfway and then we hugged tightly.

"And this thing with Craig," she whispered as she gently rocked me back and forth, "boys are boys. I bet if you asked Craig he probably isn't even thinking about how it would make you feel if he was taking yoga with Savannah. He was probably invited, and went just because it was new and athletic. Talk to him about it, but remember he is a person as well and if he likes it and is not there because of Savannah, then he is not doing anything wrong, honey."

I nodded. She was right on this one. As much as I might want to blame him for being unconcerned for my feelings, I guess I wasn't thinking very clearly about his either. *God, relationships are tough. It's not just about yourself you have to think about other people as well, that stinks.*

"Mom," this next question was going to be hard to ask but I feel like I need to know the answer to it. Is Mimi ever going to forgive you and dad for what happened? I mean I know it's probably none of my business but I feel kind of responsible for everyone finding out."

"I am not sure she will ever understand why we did what we did. And I doubt she will ever feel comfortable around us like she used to when you and your sisters were first born. But I think she has forgiven us for being wrong. I think that she understands that people can screw up even with the best intentions. So I guess to answer your question, yeah I think she has or will forgive your dad and I."

That was a relief. Even though the doctor had told me it was not my fault for everyone finding out, I still felt a bit of guilt about it.

"In the morning I think I'll go down and talk to Craig. Oh, and Mom, if I wanted to invite some girls for a sleep over, would that be okay before school starts?"

She looked at me with an expression of dismay, "you want to have some friends over?"

"I need to start making some new friends, I need to start meeting new people and learning how to get along with girls my own age, ya know?"

"Sure honey, ummm, you tell me when and dad and I will help you make the arrangements. This is a big step for you, I'm very proud."

I'll give you the list of names in the morning if that's okay. Then we can use the school's friend finder to contact them."

She hugged me again and said good night. I guess she knew that I would not be coming downstairs again that evening, and she was right. I needed the time to shower and think about all the feelings and emotions I had gone through. I needed to make sure Kelsey was okay with all this. For all my talk about not knowing who needed whom more, I still felt like I should ask her opinion and see if she had any words of wisdom for me about how things were unfolding for my family, and for myself.

I heard everyone say their good nights and head off to bed. Mimi and Nicole checked on me and both told me that loved me and to sleep tight. I dozed in and out until it was time to speak with Kels. We chatted for a few minutes and then I spoke to her about the idea of a sleep over and if it would be okay. She was happy for me. She said that she had people there, family there that were helping her understand and cope with the change and that I deserved at least the same treatment here. She told me not to be upset about having fun and to try to enjoy each day as a special day. We talked right up until one in the morning.

I finally fell asleep about an hour later. I dreamt of being in a large field in the middle of Ireland on a slightly overcast day. At first, I thought I was alone but then I saw Mimi and my family coming towards me. They smiled and gathered around me, each trying to say words that for some reason I could not hear. I could feel the love they had for me and it was cozy and safe being next to them. After a time, a few more people were walking up to join us including my grandfather, Kelsey and several great uncles and aunts. Mimi wept to see grandpa again. Mom and dad picked Kelsey up in their arms and held her close. After another couple of minutes more people joined us, and more after that, people were surrounding me and my family as far as the eye could see. It was amazing how many of them there were, how many faces I didn't recognize but more amazing were how many faces shared many of the same features over and over again. All of them were trying to speak, trying to tell me so much but it was no use, I could hear nothing but the light sounds of the wind. A fog came in and it began obscuring them. It covered those far off in the back first, but in time it had worked its way up through the ranks concealing more and more of my ancestors with each passing moment. I grabbed grandpa's hand and held it tight. I didn't want to lose him again, in this dream I was so desperate not to let go. I tried to tell him that I loved him, tried to tell Kelsey and the others how much we missed them but the fog kept coming until only Mimi and my family remained.

Mimi was silently crying. I wasn't crying even though I thought maybe I should, but then I looked down. Sticking out of the fog was grandpa's arm and I was still holding his hand. He was still there. Even though he was obscured by this thick vapor, he was still there. They all were still there. Maybe that's the secret we need to remember in life, that those who love us are always there even when we can't see them; even when they are far away, or we think they are gone.

CHAPTER TEN

THE SLEEPOVER

With only eight days left before Labor Day and nine days left of summer it was time to clean my room and head to the grocery store with dad to purchase what I anticipated to be the largest haul of snack food ever. I had plans for the following goodies to be presented for my guests: Doritos, Cheetos, Ruffles, Slim Jims, Tostitos, Funyons, Cool Ranch dip, French Onion dip, Kettle Chips, Cape Cod crab boil flavored chips, Fritos, pixie sticks, Fresca, Sprite, Coke and Code Red Mountain Dew which was only because my mother put the kibosh to Red Bull power shots. I also wanted, for the more health conscience girl who may be attending, trail mix and a small jar of macadamia nuts. Now, all of these were of course just starters, the main course was to be a smorgasbord of fine foods prepared lovingly and with great care from the local Dominos Pizza. In my room I planned on my guests dining on buffalo chicken kickers, cheesie bread and pizza piled high with one exotic topping after another. Then around eleven o'clock we would head downstairs and create ice cream sundaes from a host of various flavors and fudgie toppings. This was going to be simply heaven.

Of course you can imagine that reality set in. My parents explained to me that having four people over for a sleep over did not give me the right to turn them into hospital patients who most likely would need their stomachs pumped. They were then kind enough to advise me on the legal ramifications of such an event and their liability exposure. *Wow, are adults naturally this hung up?*

So my shopping list was reduced to popcorn, Doritos, brownies which I discovered would have to be baked, ice tea, and lemonade. As for the pizza, well it was going to be from our local pizza shop and they would all be plain in an effort not to upset any one child who may not get the topping of her choice.

I could go on about my reaction to this disastrous editing of my list. I could write pages and pages of dialogue about the screaming match that ensued between myself and my mother, when I was forced to use words like, tyranny, fascism and communist block. In hindsight, I am very surprised that I did not lose the privilege of having the sleep over when I told her that Joseph Stalin had been more lenient with his kid's parties than she was being with mine. I guess she didn't want the hassle of having to call all the parents and explain why the O'Connor's were once again, having to change their plans due to a family crisis.

My room though, was another matter. My mother took a half a day off of work that Thursday to stay home and supervise the cleaning process. In current event discussions in school I have heard about large oil tankers that vomit millions of gallons of oil onto the shore endangering the local wildlife and ecosystem. We talked about the precautions that the clean up people are forced to take in order to stay safe while helping repair and rebuild the environment. Welcome to Caitlin's room . . .

"Mike, I am in the chopper now and by the looks of things, it's bad in there. The curtains are off the window so I've got a pretty good view of the destruction. The mattress has been pulled away from the wall and the sheets and pillow cases removed. Wait, wait what's this, it looks like a woman in a hazmat suit is sorting through the mountain of clothes that were under the bed

*frame. Yes, she is stuffing the clothes into one of four distinct hampers meant,
I am sure, for whites, delicates, colors and jeans. We are going to try and get a
better angle now and . . . Mike, can you still hear me?"*

"Yes we can Carl, what are you seeing out there?"

*"It appears the closet door was opened earlier. Oh the humanity. To think
that one child in this small suburban town could hide so many empty bags of
snacks and cans of beverages in one small nook is startling. I think, yes there
she is, it's the child responsible for this eco-sabotage, Caitlin O'Connor. I can
see her now, she's throwing her body across the front of her dresser in an effort
to stop the worker from digging any deeper into her privacy. But Mike, let's face
it, when you have allowed your room to deteriorate into this sort of trash heap,
something has to be done. I can only say that this reporter has seen enough of
this room to last him a lifetime. Mike, back to you."*

It was six hours or three hundred and sixty minutes or twenty one
thousand, six hundred seconds of hell. Our work efforts were described by
my father as, "A dark and disturbing opera of tears, tragedy and triumphs
of the human spirit and its ability to endure. Much, much better than
Cats."

I spent the night before the shindig trying to derail Nicole's plans of
inviting someone over for a bit as well. My parents, much to my surprise,
were steadfast and kept explaining to her that this particular party was
only about me. She could do something fun and have some friends over
for her birthday which was only a few weeks away.

I also met one last time with Kelsey. I wanted to be certain that she
was okay with all of this. She was and we agreed that she should spend the
night in Nicole's room so as not to freak out the other girls.

So Friday came. I was a ball of nerves. I had never had so many girls
over for a slumber party at once. *This was going to be a night for the history*

books. That thought was the harbinger of all the evil that was ready to manifest itself on my life.

At five o'clock my guests began to arrive. The first to enter our home was Kirsten. Kirsten and I had known each other since kindergarten. We were school friends. We saw each other during the year and then hugged and made plans to see each other again back at school. She lived about two miles from my house which makes it too far to walk and with the heavy traffic roads between our developments too dangerous to ride my bike.

"Hey girl," I said, opening the door to find her mother standing behind her carrying her sleeping bag and a sack full of other items that surprisingly did not include their kitchen sink.

"Hi Caitlin, thanks for inviting me," she replied.

"No sweat you were the first one on my list so it's cool you're the first to arrive. Come on in." I stepped back and allowed my two guests to enter. My dad came up the hallway and said, "Hello, Kirsten and this must be your mom, Rebecca right? Hi, I'm Ian O'Connor nice to meet you."

"Hello, Rebecca Giovanni."

I shut the door and offered to take Kirsten's sleeping bag from her mother but I guess she never heard me because she began speaking to my father like we were not even there.

"Here are Kirsten's things. This is her sleeping bag and these are some of her essentials."

My father took possession of the two bundles and smiled, "Okay, well thank you for dropping her off are there any special instructions or food allergies that we should know about?"

Her Mothers eye's narrowed to small slits about as wide as a paper cut, "Is your wife not home?"

"No, Christina doesn't get in till about five thirty but tonight on her way home she is picking up the pizzas so she might be a little later."

"So who will monitor the children?"

"Ummm, the same person that monitors my children every day, me. I am a writer for the Globe so I tend to do a lot of my work from home," He said politely.

"Oh yes, the article about the interesting places to eat and shop around Boston."

"That's right," he beamed.

"We hate the city. Its only saving grace is that my husband's company is located there and the salary they pay him is substantial enough to afford us a modest life style in the suburbs. What time did you say your wife would be home?" She was looking around the house as if she were expecting a monster to step out from behind one of the pieces of living room furniture and scream, 'Ha, you found me.'

My dad sighed which meant that he was already counting backwards from ten to one in his head, "She should be in around six, I would think."

"Alright, well I suppose Kirsten can stay for that hour without the instructions that I gave your wife. "Kirsten," she was now addressing her daughter, "do not eat or drink anything until Mrs. O'Connor comes in do you understand?"

"Yes mother," she replied, lowering her eyes as she spoke.

"Can she have a glass of water if she gets thirsty?" My dad inquired half joking half concerned.

Mrs. Giovanni stood there for a moment thinking, "very well, water is okay. BUT NO ICE. Ice can disrupt digestion and force Kirsten to have a stomach flutter."

"Okay, got it no ice."

Mrs. Giovanni then bent her knees slightly and leaned down to give Kirsten a kiss on the forehead. "If you need me just call, if it's an emergency . . ."

Kirsten interrupted, "I know, I know hit the life line button on my medallion."

A wide smile danced across her mother's face as she said her goodbyes and headed out the door.

"So Kirsten, it's very nice to meet you. Your mother seems very lovely."

"Thank you Mr. O'Connor, she is a bit over protective at times but after a couple calls to her therapist she should calm down and then she will be okay for the rest of the night."

My dad blinked a few times to clear the odd thoughts from his head and suggested we go downstairs to the rec room and hang out until the other girls arrived. Kirsten and I nodded as my dad lugged the duffle and sleeping bag up the stairs and into my room.

As we passed through the kitchen I jokingly offered Kirsten a glass of water which she laughingly refused.

The door to the basement was closed. Which was no surprise since Nicole was probably down there relaxing after her morning run and camp session with Savannah. I opened the door to find Dog standing at the top of the steps waiting to be introduced to my new friend.

"There's my boy," I said in that weird voice people use when talking to their pets. "Kirsten this is Dog, Dog this is Kirsten."

Dog sprang up the step and leapt to his hind legs as Kirsten pet the top of his head. She seemed truly happy to make his acquaintance which was a good thing because as everyone in this house knows Dog is a vengeful pee'er, it is always best to stay on his good side. As I watched them though, a thought entered my mind, "You're not allergic are you Kirsten?"

"No, my mother called my allergist three times to verify that I wasn't before she called your mother back and said I could come over. It seems that Dachshund fur is absolutely, completely, not like mold spores."

We both laughed and were about to head downstairs when the door bell rang again.

"I GOT IT," I yelled as I turned and prepared to bolt towards the front door. With Dog now loose, it became a foot race to see which creature god had given better tools to handle this type of challenge. Thanks to a nice laminate floor in our kitchen that looked like wood but acted like a sheet of wet ice, Dog was unable to get his claws dug in with any kind of effectiveness which allowed me an opening burst of speed. My over-confidence though was to be my undoing. As I leaned to my right to navigate the sharp turn into the hall that lead to the front of the house, I clipped my shoulder on the arched doorway. I lost more than half of my momentum and instinctively reached up with my left hand to rub and comfort my bruise. That allowed Dog to snake his way between my legs and scurry past me for a clear and decisive victory.

My dad was also making his way back downstairs and scooped up Dog in his arms before opening the door.

"Hi-iiiiiii. I'm Margaret Cassidy and this is my daughter Danielle."

"Hi," Danielle said.

"Hello, right this way ladies." My dad held the door open and bid them enter all while balancing a wiener dog under his arm.

"This is Melanie," she said patting the other child coming into the house tenderly on the head, "I brought her over as well since she and

Danielle are such good friends her mom and I try to split the car pooling duties. What an adorable dog!"

"Oh thank you.," my dad replied as the three girls and I gathered around and began making our plans for the nights festivities.

'What's his name?" She inquired.

"Dog," my dad said flatly.

"Nice. Simple and direct. Works for me," she laughed.

"Can I offer you something to drink?"

"Nope, gotta run. Don't want to cramp their style. Girls these days need a bit of room or they get all squirrely. So, I'll just be on my way as long as you're all right here alone with four of them."

"No, I'll be fine. My little one is downstairs so she can help me if a fire breaks out." Both parents laughed before my dad asked, "Any special needs or instructions?"

"Yep just one, don't lose them or else the whole neighborhood will have to go out searching the woods and who wants that. Okay, girls behave, no hostages and I'll see you tomorrow morning at eleven. Byeeeee," and with that, Mrs. Cassidy was gone.

It was weird. When I think about how different my new friend's parents are I can see more now than at any time before or since that each family has its own quirks and oddities. No child is safe from their parents, whether it be their hang ups or their hiccups.

Either way, the girls and I went upstairs to my room with Dog in tow while we waited for my mother to arrive with the pizzas. The conversation was well, silly, which is a good thing. We talked about boys and movies and books that we read over the summer. We also spoke about who we thought would come back from the break hot and who was not.

The pizza finally arrived. We ate downstairs in the kitchen and I must say we did a fine job of not embarrassing ourselves too much. Kirsten ate her slices with a knife and fork because her mother had called to remind her of the choking hazards of processed mozzarella cheese. Danielle and I, I soon discovered, love to add parmesan cheese to our slices until the smell was so pungent that other people at the table begged us to stop shaking the infamous green can.

The girls were nice to Nicole which meant a lot to me. Even though we were having our differences at the moment, I would never want my friends to disrespect Nicole. Actually, Nicole and Danielle already knew each other from field hockey. So they kind of sat near each other and spoke about camp and some of the fun things they had shared over the last three weeks.

Mimi arrived as we were nearly finished with the pizzas.

"Hello everyone," she said as I introduced her to my gathered assembly of friends. In her hands, Mimi held two plastic shopping bags filled with various pints of ice cream from Stone Cold Creamery. "Now ladies, as long as you promise to share with my littlest princess over there, then this ice cream is all yours to enjoy later on this evening."

Heads nodded in agreement but no words were spoken. A hushed silence had descended over the room. It was not a silence brought on by fear or shame. It was a silence of respect, of awe and majesty. It was the same kind of silence that you see exhibited at the Tomb of the Unknown Soldier in Washington D.C. Somehow you just felt the reverence; my grandmother toting seventeen different pints of ice cream had that effect on myself and my new circle of friends.

"Mom you had to spend a fortune on those, you really shouldn't have. The girls would have been fine with the vanilla, chocolate and strawberry that we bought from the grocery store," my dad said.

I love my father. He is a good person and he is my mentor. Many times through the years he has guided me and shown me right from wrong. He has helped me to grow and mature and often I find myself agreeing with his thoughts and wisdom. However, this was not one of those times. In fact, on this subject he was completely off his rocker.

"Dad, come on. This is Stone Cold Creamery. This is ice cream that has been blended together, by hand, upon a frozen piece of slate just like the ancient Franciscan monks used to do it. In our freezer, is a mechanically processed gallon of blah. Great machines vomit the semi frozen mixture into a cardboard sheath where it is carelessly packed and shipped to a grocer with little concern for its well being. This, this was made today, by a skilled craftsman who has spent countless hours honing his craft during his apprenticeship. Do you realize that the angles of the spatulas alone can change the ice creams flavor from subtle to sublime? Do you?"

"Okay then ladies, welcome to the 'O'Connor Theater'. Performing tonight in her classic role of the ice cream fairy will be the lovely and talented Ms. Caitlin O'Connor."

Everyone laughed, including me. The girls and I cleared a spot on the table and placed all of the pints out for display so that we could in turn talk and debate about the magnificence of one flavor over another. My parents, Nicole and Mimi began cleaning up the pizza boxes and then Mimi and Nicole headed up stairs, while my parents went down the hall to change into more comfortable clothes for their yoga session. I guess the girls saw the look on my face and of course needed to know what was going on.

"Well, last month a new kid moved into the spooky old Frasier house."

"By herself?" Melanie asked.

"No, not by herself, with her family." I replied.

"Oh, all right, that's okay then. I could understand if you were mad if she was living there alone." I watched Melanie as she tried to go on to explain why it would have been not only morally wrong but illegal to allow a minor to live on her own especially in so large a house. She is shorter than me which is a real issue since I am by no means the tallest girl in my class. She has chestnut brown hair and sad sort of solemn eyes; kind of weird when you think about it because most of the time Melanie is pretty funny in that goofy sort of way. As a matter of fact, Melanie is the opposite of her best friend Danielle who looks like the kind of girl who is bubbly and cheerful but on the inside is far more private and withdrawn. Danielle is the tallest of the girls at my sleep over, at the age of thirteen she is already almost five foot six. I mean she is T A L L. She plays basketball, field hockey and softball and is great at every single one of them. Danielle is always nodding and smiling even though she very rarely ever tells you exactly what's going on in her mind.

Kirsten sat there laughing while I tried to recapture the floor and thereby the conversation, "Melanie, just one second, okay? So she and her family moved in next door and since then life has been a living hell for me."

"More so than when Kelsey died?" Melanie asked innocently.

"Well, I am still dealing with that, so yes it has made it that much worse."

"We were all so sad to hear that, I mean I know we told you last year and all but it's still sad, you guys were so close," Kirsten said.

"I know but tonight is about making new friends and kind of getting away from all that."

"Moving on is good I guess," Kirsten added, "I guess that's why Mr. Addams has put his house up for sale."

169

B. GRIGOLETTI

"What?"

"Kelsey's dad," Kirsten said.

"Yes I know who her father is, what do you mean he put the house up for sale?" I asked with a quivering voice.

"When my mom and I pulled in to your driveway she noticed the realtors sign out on their front yard." She must have felt bad because she then said, "Geez, Caitlin I am sorry, I thought you knew already."

I swallowed a couple of quick breaths to stop the nausea. This night was not going to turn into a melt down. Not tonight. This was about learning how to interact with new people and start over. No, not 'over' that sounds terrible. To start 'again', yes that's what I was trying to do and I would not allow this news to derail that plan. Mr. Addams was hardly home. Once he went back to work it was inevitable that he would sell that house. If I were him, maybe I would do the same. I pushed the thoughts to the back of my head and let them go.

"So, tell us about this new kid, what's her name?" Melanie said coming to the rescue.

"Her name is Savannah Summers and she thinks that the sun was made millions of years ago in preparation for her birth, any day before that was merely a test run. She is manipulative, cruel and just so damned . . ."

"Perfect?" Danielle added.

My eyes lit up, "Dani, is she that way with you too?"

"She sucks up to everyone who she thinks will give her some power or advantage over the other kids around her. She's a phony."

"I was thinking bitch," We all laughed.

"The first day I met her she was all like 'You should thank god that I chose to move to this pathetic little neighborhood.' I so wanted to smack that smug look off her face," I grinned.

Kirsten turned to Danielle, "How did you meet her?"

"Field hockey camp at the high school. The coaches were doing skills work with us and she told them that I was holding my stick wrong. I was pointing my finger down on my lower hand. It helps me control the ball better. I've been doing it that way for years. The coaches warned me it was a good way to get hurt and then the next day who do you think smashes my hand in a scrum for the ball, Savannah. It hurt like hell. My mom thought I was going to lose the nail but I didn't. When it happened though, I was so mad."

"Well my family has become the 'Little Summers' and it's driving me freakin nuts. The reason they all left the kitchen before was because they are going to change into their comfortable clothes and head over to Savannah's house for their nightly yoga ritual."

"A ritual you mean like in a cult?" Melanie asked with a look of dread on her face.

"No, not like in a cult. I meant ritual because it's become part of their everyday routine. Not all rituals are cultish. Look at Christmas, there are many rituals that people perform at Christmas, right?"

"Well," she continued, "I've never heard of anyone doing yoga on Christmas. And aren't they more like traditions?"

We all fell silent and I jumped up to start putting the ice cream away in the freezer because we all heard my parent's door open up as they came waltzing back into the kitchen dressed "to yoga."

My mother called up to Mimi and Nicole who appeared less than a minute later. Mimi was carrying small towels for everyone and Nicole muscled me out of the way, as she grabbed four water bottles from the fridge. I mean let's face it the exertion of tai chi can be enough to break you out into a real sweat.

I could not stand here while the gruesome foursome got ready to leave so I invited the gang to head downstairs and maybe we could pick some movies to watch. As the girls headed down into the basement my mom called out, "Caitlin doesn't Dog need to be walked?"

"Nicole could you please get him, I've got company, thanks sweetie."

"But then I'll be late. Mom . . ." I quickly shut the door and went down to hook up with my friends.

"Now that's funny," Kirsten said.

"What's that?" I hated walking in on the middle of a conversation.

"Melanie was just reminding Danielle that your bitchy neighbor asked her to be friends on Facebook."

"NO WAY!" I blurted out.

"Yeah, but I'm not doing it. She's just trying to pad her friend numbers by asking every single person she knows," Danielle said.

I ran across the room from the bottom of the stairs and leapt onto the couch next to Sam. "You have to accept it, please! I'm begging you."

"Why?"

"Don't you get it? We can keep an eye on what she is saying and doing. We can see who she's playing with and who her friends are. Come on Danielle you've got to click yes." I was beside myself with joy. If I could convince Danielle to join the 'Savannah Summers Fan Club' I would have an inside track into the cretin's head.

"Come on Danielle it might be funny," Kirsten said applying just a bit more pressure.

"Why don't you do it Caitlin?" Danielle asked.

"Two reasons. One, I've got a mother who believes that technology like Facebook is nothing but a popularity contest for those with no self esteem, present company excluded and two, Savannah would NEVER invite me or accept an invite from me. Come on Dani, plllllleeeeaaaasssee!" I smiled, pointed at the computer in the back corner of the basement and nodded.

She sighed and got up, this was going to be excellent. I was going to see the inner workings of a devious mind posted nice and neatly on a community page. This was the weapon I needed.

I heard Nicole shout something but it was muffled. "Did anybody understand what the hell she was saying?"

Melanie said, "I think she said I leashed Dog up and walked him."

"Oh, good." I pulled the chair out for Danielle and helped ease her into it. The others came over and gathered around us. She quickly got on the internet and then logged into Facebook. With a deep and heavy exhale she went to her friends request page and hit accept next to the name Savannah Summers.

With two more clicks we were suddenly transported to her home page.

"What's that in her photo album?" Kirsten asked.

"She's tagged some photos," Danielle replied.

"Let's see them," Melanie chimed in.

"I'm sure that any photos she has posted are of herself or her gorgeous family. Who cares about her stupid pictures, I want to . . ."

"Caitlin, oh my god is that really you?" Melanie burst out laughing.

"Holy shit," Kirsten said.

I was speechless. There were no words for it. There I was standing in my pajama's squinting from the sun my hair sticking straight up in the air like I was a victim of a recent lightning strike. My face of course looked like someone was holding a sweaty gym sock under my nose and Dog was in the lower corner of the frame, trying to irrigate the yard near my feet. Under the picture was a single word, "Dweeb."

Danielle didn't say anything. She just sat there perfectly still trying not to draw any attention to herself.

"Wow, I didn't know Craig was such a bad typist," Melanie added.

"Shhhhh." Kirsten said.

"What, what do you mean?" I wanted to look away from the picture but it was like a train wreck, it was just too terrible to pull away from.

"Well Craig wrote under her tag line, LOLOLOLOLOLOLOLOLOL. He must be a terrible typist or a chronic stutter. Does Craig stutter a lot Caitlin?"

"Craig? Stutter? No, not yet, though after I kick him in the jock strap he might begin to. What other pictures are there?"

"Well let's see. Here are some pictures of her rock garden. Oh and look there's your family doing what ever it is that they are doing," Kirsten said.

"That must be the yoga class. Wow what a pretty back yard. I mean they even have a pond and a waterfall in there with fish and everything," Melanie added.

"What, where do you see a pond, I don't . . . oh over there in that picture. Okay, so it's a pond, I mean big deal." Yep, two strikes against my nerves, Mr. Addams moving and now Craig posting how hard he laughed when he saw a picture of me in my early morning 'Bride of Frankenstein' ensemble.

"Oh and look at the lovely Chinese thingie," Kirsten blurted out.

"Chinese thingie? What like a little lantern or a statue of Buddha?" I asked as I looked at the next snap shot. "Umm, that's called a pagoda and look there appears to be a prayer alter inside, and yep . . . that's a Buddha." Wow, they had transformed what was once a gnarly, overgrown, weed infested acreage into an absolute paradise. The whole thing looked like it belonged in Disney's EPCOT. Flagstone marked out pathways that allowed the curious to wander about and enjoy the entire quality of the garden without losing sight of the center focal point which was a small wooden arch bridge that crossed over the stream that ran from one side of the yard to a waterfall and pond. I don't know how they did it but I can only say it must have cost a small fortune just do to all that landscaping. *God, I hate them.*

Danielle kept clicking on various photos and then suddenly there on the screen was an image that when I saw it felt like someone had just stuck a knife in my chest. I don't exactly know why it was so offensive but the picture seemed to conjure the most evil and malevolent images in my head of Savannah getting stuck in a wheat harvester.

"Who's Peggy Sue?" Melanie inquired.

"Danielle, could you turn it off please," I implored.

"Caitlin, I thought you wanted to see who she is hanging around with and . . ."

"I know. It's completely my fault okay. Just please turn it off before I run over there and kick everyone in the shins."

"That can really hurt."

I took another sobering breath, "Thanks Mel, you're right it does hurt but I've got to come to grips with the facts about Savannah and her plot to destroy me."

"Oh, well yes that too, although I meant the whole kicking everyone in the shins. That really hurts," everyone nodded.

"Destroy you? Come on Caitlin it's not that bad. I mean not everyone in the world is going to be friends with you."

"I understand that Kirsten, but we are not talking about simply not getting along. We are talking about evil, the embodiment of a sinister and malignant soul. This girl is so mean that, well I can't tell you because you wouldn't believe me anyway."

"You can tell us Caitlin," Melanie said.

"Yeah, we would believe you," Kirsten added.

Danielle said nothing, she just got up from the computer and went back over to sit on the sofa. I wanted to explain to my new friends everything that had happened so far in the last nine months of my life. I wanted to let them in, to show them that I was not merely a normal teenage girl with the usual problems to deal with. No, I was dealing with things on a level that they could not even begin to understand or imagine. Yet, I was afraid. I knew that most likely they would scoff at me, laugh or think that I was crazy. Of course I know what you are thinking, take them up stairs and at midnight show them the doll, make them believe. I had thought about that course of action as well but it was not the right thing to do. Throwing someone into a lake is not the best way to teach them how to swim, no matter what your fat Uncle Clarence tells you. So, at that moment I made up my mind to only share with them the things that had occurred during the last month. The Soul Patrol would stay secret but the viciousness of Savannah Summers, I could explain without having to go into all the stuff about losing a twin sister and my family's choice to let her live next door.

"Okay, but if I tell you what's been going on you have to promise me not to tell anyone else. It's not just about being a snob or playing a simple practical joke or insulting each other. This is about dark forces at work and the struggle to protect my family."

"What are you talking about?" Kirsten asked.

"All right, I'll tell you everything."

I spent the next half an hour or so explaining every single detail of the encounters that had occurred between myself and the devil child from

Georgia. I then spoke about the first meeting where she was so haughty that it made me feel uneasy. I told them about the day she took the photograph of my hair standing up and doing the wave on the top of my head. I told them about her weaseling in with my sister. I explained about the jokes behind my back that Craig occasionally shared with me and then I went on to relate in graphic detail her attack on me in the middle of the night. Their eyes had gone wide in disbelief. They couldn't bring themselves to comprehending such a terrible person. Then with some hesitancy, I shared with them the story that Stephen had told me about her powers of voodoo and how she planned to turn her hellish gifts loose against me.

"So has she?" Danielle finally asked after my tale was over.

"Has she what?" I replied.

"Has she attempted to use any voodoo on you?" Every girl in the room was staring at me. They wanted to know, this was the moment where my story could turn from crazy to confirmed. But in all honesty, since the warning from Stephen, nothing really very serious had happened.

"Well Danielle, voodoo isn't something that you immediately sense. I mean she could have cursed me or begun the necessary spells to raise an army of zombies and ghouls to attack my house."

"I guess that means no, then?"

"Danielle I am not making this up. Her brother did come into my yard and warn me about his sister's intentions."

"I never said you were making it up," her eyes were stone, her voice soft and level. "What I am saying is that it's one thing to have someone tell you they are into voodoo it's another thing to actually have them do something to you. It sounds like they were just making a joke out of the whole thing."

Melanie jumped in, "Danielle, you yourself said you didn't like her."

"I don't. But that doesn't mean she's a witch doctor. It just means that she is a jerk," she retorted.

"Well I'm convinced that she is a Bocur, not a witch doctor, those are two totally different things by the way. And I have already begun making the necessary preparations to defend this house."

Kirsten asked, "Like what Caitlin?"

"Well for one I have ordered a dozen rubber chickens from Amazon."

"Wow, what for?" Melanie asked.

"Well, chickens are used in many of the rituals of voodoo. But since I like animals too much and my parents would freak out if I even thought to hurt a live chicken, I decided on the next best thing. When they arrive I will cut off their feet and tie them to weak points around the house to ward off bad spirits and harmful spells."

"Hold on, you think rubber chicken feet count?" Danielle the doubter inquired.

"Well I don't know but I plan to find out."

"I hate to say this but I'm sure there is a reason you are supposed to use live chickens. Probably the blood and stuff is all part of it."

"I know Dani but I've got that covered. I am going to fill the chicken with ketchup. Then, when I whack his plastic feet off, there's the fake blood. See, it will be fine."

She shook her head, "Caitlin this is silly."

"No my dear Danielle, this is war," I grinned and sat down beside her.

We talked for a while longer; mostly about boys, music and other people less fortunate than us in the cool department. Overall we were having a pretty good time when I felt the pull of nature upon me. Normally dear reader, I have more class than to make any mention of the porcelain throne and its ignoble goings on, but in this case it lead me to the third and most shocking discovery of the night.

As I excused myself and headed upstairs I opened the door into the kitchen and saw Dog lying down in the kitchen. Now this in and of itself was not a bizarre or upsetting discovery but as I smiled at him I noticed that the back door to our yard was wide open.

That's weird. Why would anyone leave the door open?

I went over and slid it closed. I turned and made my way back across the kitchen and down the hallway to the bathroom. Once there, I handled my business.

Two minutes later as I came out though, I noticed something else that was not only odd but down right perplexing. Dog was still wearing his leash. It lay in a crumpled pile near him but it was still securely latched to his collar.

What had Nicole done, walked him and then not unleashed the poor little guy? How irresponsible of her not to close the door behind her as well. Dog could have gotten out and run off. I was angry. Today was obviously not the day to bring it up but tomorrow after my friends left I was certainly going to let little 'Miss Rules Lawyer' know that she had made a major mistake.

I removed his leash and hung it back up. I spoke to him for a minute and scratched his head. He laid there pretty mellow, which for Dog was not entirely out of the realm of normal. Happy that things had been put right, I went back downstairs and started the first of three movies that my friends and I watched that night.

As the movie marathon started we heard my family arrive back home. Nearing the end we heard my father's voice echo down the stairs asking us if there was anything we needed, to which we shouted back as one great voice, "DOR-IT-OS".

About ten minutes into the second movie, Nicole shouted down her goodnights and as that feature was winding down my mother invited us up for our sundae spectacular.

We ran up the stairs like, well like; did you ever see the Lion King? Remember the part where Mufasa dies? That's what it was like. If that lion had been resting on my basement steps his ass would have been flattened like a crepe. To any boys reading this, please take a highlighter to the following passage and remember it for all of your adult lives; never stand in the way of a woman as she rushes towards her sundae extravaganza.

There, on the table were all the pints, neatly opened and already slightly thawing so as to be easier to scoop. Four bowls were laid out on the countertop opposite of the ice cream with a variety of toppings and crunchy things to shake on top.

Everyone began to dig in. Cold, creamy goodness was layered high as flavors began to melt and mix adding new and interesting combinations for our palettes to enjoy. Laughs were shared along with dozens of spoonfuls with each one of us professing a new and better sensation from our concoctions than those of our friends.

I was scraping the bottom of my bowl to get the last of the chocolate syrup and magic shell when it crossed my mind that Dog had not had any ice cream. *Odd.* Normally, he sits there and whines like a cast member from Annie until someone offers him a little taste of the dessert from their bowl. As far as canines are concerned, wiener dogs have only one passion higher than ice cream and as you, my educated friends already know, it's chili.

"Hey mom, did you already give Dog his ice cream treat tonight?" I asked as she was already busy removing the dirty bowls and silverware over from the table into the sink.

"No, why?"

"Why, because he hasn't been begging for any and unless the entire population of the earth's Dachshunds are in a communal mind meld, I can't believe he has not yet tackled somebody for their yummy, frosty treats." I turned and knelt down with my spoon still covered in the afterglow of fudge offering it to him. He didn't move, he just laid there looking up at me.

"Mom, Dog is not moving."

"Caitlin, maybe he's tired. He is not a little puppy any more. He is probably just worn out from visiting and playing with all your guests," she turned the water on and began washing the bowls.

I placed the spoon under his tiny little whiskered snout and held it there for him. Nothing. *What the heck?!?* I sat down next to him and began lightly stroking his flank. My friends were all still busy chatting about how heaven could only truly be experienced in one of two ways, the dreamy eyes of a drop dead gorgeous guy or a bowl of various Stone Cold Creamery flavors.

"What's the matter buddy?" I asked softly.

He looked up at me and I could immediately tell something was wrong. His eyes said it all, 'Help me.' "Mom, I'm not kidding. He doesn't look good and his nose is warm," As I continued to pet him I could feel how hard it felt for him to breathe.

"Mom, seriously it looks like he's in a lot of pain. Come here."

My mother shut the water off and dried her hands on a dish towel. She came over and bent down to get a better look at him. His eyes darted over to her as if pleading her to pick him up. "Caitlin, don't worry honey he will be okay."

Her voice had a definitive tone, a quality of command. It made me feel safe and secure and I'm not exactly sure why. Yet, even though everything I could sense and see told me that he was not all right, those words from my mother brought me a sense of calm. She nodded and smiled at me which had the added effect of making me feel almost silly for being so initially alarmed.

"Okay girls, why don't you all go upstairs and get your sleeping bags but please be quiet, Nicole is already in bed asleep."

I stood up and nodded to my friends who began moving out of the kitchen and down the hall.

"Caitlin, don't worry, Dog can sleep in our room tonight and Dad and I will keep an eye on him."

"Okay mom, thanks." I headed up and helped everyone gather their sleeping bags and even grabbed mine as well. We then headed back down into the basement and got ourselves organized to start the third movie.

Around midnight I went upstairs to make sure Dog was okay and he wasn't in the kitchen which made me feel a whole lot better. Mom had moved him into her room. I was going to knock and go in but the lights were off. I grabbed some more soda and headed back downstairs. I was certain that once my little man got a good night sleep he would be all better in the morning.

We laughed and joked and ended up saying the silliest things the later into the evening that it got. I remember busting out laughing all because Melanie rolled over at some point and nearly slapped Kirsten in the face with the back of her hand. That alone was comical, but when she screamed out "excuse me," I nearly peed my pants. We all started howling and screaming 'excuse me.' I hadn't laughed like that since before the accident.

It felt good. I mean it felt really good, like this is what life is really all about. It felt like all the other stuff, the crap and the pressure is merely to help remind you how precious the real and magical moments are. What is better than laughing yourself to sleep? I can't begin to imagine.

I'm not exactly sure what time we all finally did fall asleep but it was late. I slept so soundly and so completely that we all didn't even begin stirring until almost nine. I had just experienced an amazing night with some new and wonderful friends. It had been a great time and I didn't feel the least bit guilty, which was a complete shock to me. I had expected to wake up the next morning after having dreams about Kels or some other thing that I had left behind from my childhood yet there were none of those things haunting me.

We all got up to the smell of pancakes, bacon and hot chocolate. It was amazing. We ventured upstairs and sat down around the kitchen table in a much more civilized manner than the night before.

I was somewhat shocked to see my mother was the one cooking breakfast. This particular meal, especially on weekends was the responsibility of my father.

"Mom, where is dad?" I asked as I watched Nicole come into the kitchen as well rubbing her eyes and yawning deeply.

"Sleeping honey, he didn't sleep very well last night so I am letting him catch up on his rest."

I looked around as she set out the plate of pancakes. "Where's Dog?"

"Sleeping next to your father in the bedroom, I walked him already so he's okay."

"Thanks mom," I was relieved to hear it.

Everyone ate their fill except Kirsten who was afraid to have some bacon because it was the last Saturday in the month which meant that her mother would be giving Kirsten her at home cholesterol screening when they got back.

The parents began to arrive not long after we had finished breakfast. We all promised to keep in touch which would be incredibly easy since school was only a few days away. Everything had gone fine, even Mrs. Giovanni was impressed to see that her child had not broken out in hives or showed any outward signs of dehydration, rickets or sleep deprivation.

As my mother shut the front door I plopped myself down on the couch and let out a heavy and satisfied sigh. I had done it. I had come out of my shell, made some new friends and not had anything overly weird or catastrophic happen to mess it up.

Nicole wandered in and sat on the small loveseat next to the couch. Mimi followed her and sat beside my sister as mom came into the room with her arms crossed in front of her chest and a look of disappointment on her face.

She did not sit down, instead she kind of half stood, half rested herself against the arm of the chair that was directly across from me. It became apparent that there was something going on.

I sat upright and asked, "What is it, what's going on?"

My mother lowered her head for a brief second and as I looked around the room nobody wanted to be the first to speak. Why at these moments does time seem to slow down? I mean a second is a second, a minute is sixty of them and yet at moments of uncertainty, that small, thin, almost frail second hand seems to take forever to click off a single step in its march around the face of the clock.

"Where's dad?!?" I said instantly aware that he was missing from the room.

"In bed like I told you before, he was up all night at the vet's," my mom quickly replied.

"What?"

"It's Dog. Caitlin, he's very sick."

CHAPTER ELEVEN

CURSED

"What do you mean he's sick?" I shrieked.

"The doctor thinks he got into something."

"Is he going to be okay?"

"They hope so honey. But he was in bad shape last night by the time daddy got him to the hospital."

"This is your fault," I pointed and shouted at Nicole. You were in such a hurry to get over to your damn friend's house that you left the backdoor open."

"Caitlin, stop it," My mother said.

"Why, because your baby screwed up? Because the perfect Ms. Nicole did something wrong?"

Nicole looked up at me, "I shut the door."

"That's a lie! You were supposed to walk him for me and you must have not wanted to do it so you left the door open and you even left his leash on. So help me god if anything happens to my dog Nicole," I shouted.

"He's my dog too Caitlin, I've been up half the night worried about him," she fired back. "Don't you think I feel bad too?"

"Ah hah! Why do you feel bad? If you closed the door then you would have nothing at all to be upset about."

She stood up and took three steps towards me, "I . . . SHUT . . . THE . . . DOOR."

I jumped up and parked my face about an inch from hers, "Then who opened it?"

"I don't know you freak!" She fell silent.

"Nicole, enough," my mother interjected.

"What did you call me?" I asked through tightly pursed lips.

She turned and walked around to the stairs and went up to her room. I was not going to be deterred simply because she walked away from me, "Go ahead little Savannah, go upstairs and say you're sorry for lying and getting my dog sick."

"I said STOP IT." Mom's voice told me to cease any and all conversation. "You think that by yelling and screaming at your sister that you can make all this go away? Caitlin, she said she shut the door and I believe her. Why on earth would your sister leave the door open anyway? She knows Dog might run away."

"Because your daughter thinks that it is more important to impress that BITCH next door than it is to handle her responsibilities. Nothing but Savannah matters anymore. Watch how she acts, how she treats me and how much she worships that pig of a girl. It makes me sick. You want to believe that she didn't do it, go ahead, I know what I saw last night when I came up to use the bathroom.

"Christine, maybe Nicole is afraid to tell the truth?" Mimi offered.

"Nicole doesn't lie," mom softly said.

I blinked. She was right. There are constants in this universe. Gravity is a cruel foe, two plus two is four, the Great Wall of China is in fact in China and my sister doesn't lie. I took several long breaths and began to compose myself.

That of course could only mean one thing. As crazy as it sounded, she must have been made to forget, she must have been made to leave the door open and jeopardize Dog's safety. Savannah must have planted the suggestion in her head and made my little sister a pawn in her terrible plot to destroy me.

Sweet God in heaven, the attacks have already begun and here I was defenseless and without my mail order chicken feet!

I knew what had to be done. I knew that I had little choice. My family was vulnerable and could be manipulated without them even recalling the event. How could it take two weeks to ship a dozen rubber chickens? It's not like I ordered a pair of diamond earrings from Russia.

I couldn't just run from the room and begin a counter spell. In honesty I was not even sure I knew a counter spell or how to cast one. Worse than that, I had never cast a counter spell or any spell for that matter. But this was war. And in war you don't ask your enemy how they learned their craft you simply do what you can to defeat them even if it means making the ultimate sacrifice.

"I'm sorry. When will we know if he's going to be okay?" I calmly asked.

"The doctor said that if he got through the first twenty four hours he should be okay. I called about an hour ago and he was resting but still weak the nurse said."

"I want to go see him, he needs me." I said this next statement flat and firmly so my mother knew there would be no room for argument, I wanted, no, I needed to see my dog.

"Okay honey," she said, "I'll wake daddy and he can take you over once he showers okay? But Caitlin please, don't blame your sister, we were just getting back to some sense of normality."

"I know. You're right mom, Nicole wouldn't lie. She is innocent and I'm going to go upstairs and tell her I believe her. Please tell dad I'll be down in a few minutes to go to the hospital with him, I just want to shower as well."

Forty five minutes later we were heading over to the animal hospital. I had dog's favorite chew toy with me and his cushion bed he never uses. I brought it figuring it would at least smell like home and might be something he would appreciate.

My father and I rode in silence. He had been up most of the night and I was in no mood to talk. Talking had done little lately but cause grief and complicate matters. I had to put my mind to the task of getting Savannah to turn her attention away from my family before she caused more serious harm.

A single tear formed in my eye and I quickly wiped it away. I stared out of the passenger window and could feel my father watching me out the corner of his eye. He was trying to find the right words or at least the right moment to say them. Neither though, presented themselves before we arrived at the clinic.

I jumped out of the Jeep and met my father coming around the other side. Together we walked up to the front door. I pressed the small brass buzzer on the right side of the door which I had been told once before alerted everyone inside to hold on tightly to their pets since the door was going to open.

As we stepped inside, my nostrils were immediately aware of a strong antiseptic smell. At first I couldn't place it but I knew I had smelt it before. We shut the door and walked to the counter where a receptionist was stationed. She was busy doing paper work of some sort or another and it took her several moments before she glanced up and acknowledged our presence.

"May I help you?" She inquired.

"Yes, my name is Ian O'Connor and this is my daughter, Caitlin. We are here to check on our dog."

"Okay, and the patient's name?"

"Dog," Dad replied.

"Yes, I got that part thank you. What is your dog's name, we file all of our medical information under their names."

Dad nodded and I tried to smile but that only seemed to make the girl think we were less than coherent, "His name is Dog."

She blinked several times and then shook her head as if irritated which in fact made me irritated. Its' funny how that works, isn't it? You end up getting someone slightly perturbed and then as their body language, posture and expression relate that they are annoyed you get annoyed for them being annoyed until everyone in the whole room is thinking, *Can't we all just get along?*

"Ah yes, here we go. Dog O'Connor. Male, Dachshund, ten years young, brought in last night for lethargy and possible stomach disorder. Refused ice cream and sprinkles. Hummm. Okay, could you both please take a seat and Dr. Marshall will be right with you."

"Can we see him please?" I asked.

"Let me get the doctor for you. He can better answer that question than I can," she said as she stood up and pushed in her chair.

"He can answer whether or not I can see my dog? I don't mean to be rude ma'am but this is my dog and I would like it very much if you would let me in to see him, right now."

"Is he okay?" Dad added.

"Doctor Marshall is in the next room. I will get him in here for you," and she walked into the adjoining room. I felt a weight deep down in the pit of my stomach. The vet entered the room, "Hello Mr. O'Connor and you must be Caitlin?"

I nodded.

"Dog told me all about you last night," Dr. Marshall said.

"He did?"

"He said he loves you very much. He also wanted me to tell you that he is going to be okay."

I tried not to shake, I didn't want this doctor dropping a bomb on me but I couldn't tell whether or not he was trying to be cute or soften the blow. "So, can I see him?"

"Well he is asleep right now. He had a rough night but he should be okay to go home by tomorrow morning. Think you can hold off until then to see him?"

I smiled and nodded again, "As long as I know that he can come home tomorrow I can wait."

"Well I ended up sedating him last night so he would rest easier. He was having a lot of trouble breathing when your father brought him in. But after I examined him and did a small procedure he was breathing normal again."

"Doctor what was wrong with Dog?"

"Well Mr. O'Connor if I had to guess, I would say he got into some weed killer or other toxin."

Those words were darker than I had guessed. He hadn't been cursed he had been poisoned. Savannah had actually tried to poison my dog! She hadn't just sat in her room and chanted over a photo of him while sticking a doll with pins, oh no; she had actually fed him poison in an effort to end his life.

I guess I must have had a very dark or odd expression on my face because Dr. Marshall reiterated that Dog was going to be okay and asked if I was in fact all right.

"Thank you doctor. I'm fine."

I learned that day that inside us lives a twisted little gnome. He is not the cute garden variety. He is a gnarled, hooked nosed, watery eyed freak-a-zoid who makes his home in the darkest parts of our subconscious. Mine is named Quillerbee and he made himself known as soon as I had fully processed that she had tried to kill my pooch. He began to whisper all of these amazingly cool ideas on how Savannah should suffer for her attempted murder of my wiener dog. Quillerbee suggested for instance that I shave her head, bury her up to her neck in wet sand and dump a red ant farm on her skull and watch as they dance the Lambada across her face. He also helped me visualize tampering with her toothpaste tube and replacing the traditional mixture with something that comes out of the back of a bull. Of course, he explained we would need to add some mint to mask the smell but the thought of her smile afterwards made my heart soar.

My father paid the bill and we agreed to return the next day to retrieve Dog. I handed the incredibly un-helpful receptionist his chew and bed and laughed when Quillerbee made an interesting suggestion about tying bacon to her legs and dropping her into a den of angry Chihuahuas. We thanked Dr. Marshall and left his office.

On the ride home I sat and tried not to clench my fist as my father focused on the road and I focused on the words of my new imaginary friend, Quillerbee the malignant dwarf.

CHAPTER TWELVE

THE PROMISE

"Okay, so what you're telling me is that there is a midget living inside of you?" Craig sat there looking at me as if I had sprouted two heads. I settled myself back into a comfy chaise lounge at the side of his pool and thought of perhaps a new and different way to explain what was going on. I figured the only real way to get him to fully comprehend my situation was to go through it piece by piece.

After a lengthy explanation, he was brought up to date.

"So then I asked the girls to check out Savannah's wall on Facebook and I saw your post regarding my picture."

He lowered his eyes for a second but I must admit that he never tried to deny the fact that he typed the LOL's or that he was already confirmed as a friend of Savannah's. He was far too honest for that. Craig and I may never be emotional, spiritual or conversational equals but when it came to integrity I could not hold a candle to him. Not that I am a weasel mind you, it's just people like Craig only exist in books and those are usually fairy tales.

"Then Nicole was hit with some kind of dark magic that made her forget to close the back door and Savannah came over and fed him poison, that's how Dog ended up in the hospital."

"Is he going to be okay?" He asked in a very concerned voice.

"Yes, but before I get off track, that's when I discovered Quillerbee."

"The gnome that lives in your gut?"

I sighed, "Yes."

"While you were at the Vet's?"

"Yep."

He leaned back in one of the chairs that matched the chaise lounge I was reclining in. "And you gave him a name?"

"Uh-huh."

"And you don't think that maybe this thing is just an extension of your own mind looking for someone else to blame for the evil thoughts that you are having about Savannah?"

"Did you hear the part about Stephen telling me that I was a warrior of the light, a child of good?" I asked.

"Yeah, I heard that part of the story as well."

"Then you must surely agree that a warrior-ess of good would never be able to have such thoughts on her own. Therefore, it must be the gnome."

"Caitlin, I realize that freaky stuff happens to you and I'm okay with that. It's actually one of the things that makes me like you so much. I never believed in ghosts or magic or any of that stuff but thanks to you I've come to open my mind and allow myself to actually see that there is more to the world than simply what the eye can see. With that being said do you have to ramp up the creepy by talking about this "Quillerbee" as if YOU believe that he is real? Because if that's the case I want to go inside and get my mother's pepper spray and douse you with it until you run off. No offense, but this is making me think you've crossed over from being a brilliant girl to joining the ranks of those people who wear helmets to bed just because it's the right thing to do."

"Alright, yes I know the gnome doesn't actually exist. And yes, I believe you are right that he is a metaphor for my hatred for Savannah which is reaching epic proportions. This chick is burying herself into my skin like a tick and I need to do something to get her to leave me alone."

"You could always ignore her." He said flatly.

"What?"

"Come on, Caitlin, think about it. Savannah is having fun at your expense. The reason is because she knows which of your buttons to press. You are dealing with a person who gets her kicks watching you squirm. So, take away her pleasure, take away her only reason for ragging on you. Stop squirming."

"You think it's that simple? You think I can just make myself stop caring about what she is doing, what she is planning? She is stalking me, don't you see that?"

He shook his head, "What I see is my girlfriend spending all of her free time and energy wondering what is going to happen next while the girl who she thinks is plotting against her seems to not even be breaking a sweat or caring one bit what you are up to. Does that make any sense to you? How can you be locked in this so called struggle of light and darkness and she isn't even showing any signs of concern?"

"She tried to kill my dog," I growled.

"Caitlin. I don't know what to say about that, but man I can't see anyone wanting to hurt Dog. I'm not saying that you're wrong, but the proof is pretty thin don't you think?"

"Craig, I need you to believe me. When I came to you about Kelsey you never doubted me. What made me want to be your girlfriend was that you never asked me to prove anything, you just believed. Why is it different this time?"

The light shimmered off the pool behind him and I could see that my words had made him feel guilty or at least made him self conscious. "Why can't you see that I'm not making this crap up.? Savannah has it in for me. And if she didn't cast an actual spell on Nicole to leave the back door open she has made her stop caring about what matters and make the mistake."

"I don't know . . ."

"Fine, tonight then," I said.

"Tonight what?" He said with his patented confused look.

"Tonight, I bring the entire Soul Patrol together to see for themselves that this is not just a matter of me thinking she is after me. Right after your yoga class, make an excuse to head home."

"I always go straight home after the yoga class."

I was not about to be sidetracked by his post yoga habits at this point, "then I will call her over to the house on some lame excuse about Nicole's birthday and you guys can listen in from the bushes behind my house. No better yet, you guys go up into the Addams' tree house and listen in from there."

"Okay Caitlin, but what if Mr. Addams doesn't want anyone on those swings?"

"He hasn't been home in weeks and with the place up for sale, who's going to care?"

We spoke for a bit longer and even made some pleasant small talk that didn't include me wanting to choke him or him mentioning the whole 'you're going nuts thing' again. I guess I stayed about an hour in total and then headed back to my house where it was time to get all my chores done for the day so as not to risk getting grounded at the last minute which would definitely ruin my plans.

Nicole and I avoided each other for much of the day. I wanted to have a long conversation about how this was not her fault and that for the first time in our lives it wasn't my fault either but the timing was all wrong.

I knew that once she was in the tree house listening to the cruel tongue of Savannah Summers that she would come rushing down the slide and defend me. I envisioned the peace and harmony of our house restored and I must say it was a pretty cool thing.

Dinner came and went without an incident. I even smiled as she reached for the last bread stick; such was my faith in the upcoming sting operation. Soon everything would be as right as rain. I listened without getting nauseous as Mimi described another successful day of laying out the patterns and furniture magnets on a metal board which had every room in her new house drawn on it to scale. It was a tool that Mrs. Summers had shown her and she was in heaven ever since. I even enjoyed and participated in Nicole's talk about her first upcoming field hockey game and how much her skills had improved over the last month.

We cleared off the table and scraped the small scraps of unfinished food into the garbage can. Then we stacked the dishes neatly into the sink and wiped down all the surfaces of the kitchen that had come into contact with a spill or crumb. Finally, after a long day of keeping myself out of trouble, it was time for "the cultists" to make their way over to the garden of evil.

I rushed into the living room and grabbed the phone. "Hello Auntie Katrina? Yes it's me . . . Okay, you're happy I called and that he's not scratching his butt . . . Well, that's good. What, oh yes Dog is going to be okay. How did you know? . . . Oh, Craig called you . . . yes he is sweet . . . Listen can you come over here in about forty-five minutes please? . . . Well, I am planning a little surprise for Nicole and it would mean a lot to me if you were here . . . I don't understand, what do lawn darts have to do with bratwurst? Really, I never knew that? So, you can make it? . . . Great, thanks Auntie and don't be late, okay?"

After hanging up the phone I ran upstairs and down the hallway to my bedroom. I grabbed Kelsey off the shelf and placed her on the bed. I got out of my every day clothes and put on a nice outfit that I had picked out for school. New jeans, a nice simple black top that had a bit of a swoop neck line and a pair of white sketchers. I threw on a little bit of make up and even put a couple of curls in my hair with the curling iron. All in all, I looked damn good. The goal here was to give Savannah absolutely nothing to use as ammunition besides her festering hatred of me. If I looked good, she couldn't pick on it. If I stayed pleasant, she would not be able to sleaze her way out of it by making an excuse that I started anything. I needed to be completely natural while the Patrol listened in, otherwise this exercise would become a complete failure.

I grabbed Kels and went back downstairs for a time check and to round up snacks. I had just under twenty minutes until the yoga class let out so I quickly grabbed a couple of juice boxes and a bag of chips from the pantry. I went out through the back door, crossed the yard and climbed up into the tree house. I propped the doll in the corner and laid out the drinks for my team of spies. "Well Kels, I know you would never approve of this trick. You would tell me that it is under handed and nasty to lure someone into a set up like this one. But I hope you understand. I can't get the others to believe the level of hatred this girl feels for me. If I don't make a drastic move, I may lose Nicole forever and I can't let that happen. I'm sure you will give me an earful tonight but just understand I do this out of sisterly love and to prove I am not some kind of freak who imagines everyone dislikes her."

Freak? I was shocked when the word left my mouth. I had never referred to myself as a freak before. It was Nicole's word. She had really stung me with that one. More than I had known, more than she could have imagined.

How could my own sib think I was a freak? Okay, that actually was a stupid thing to ask. I mean I speak to a dead person, I hang out with a dysfunctional gypsy dwarf, I'm dating a guy I've never even kissed and to top matters off I make friends about as easily as Attila the Hun. *At this point in my life, freak was probably a compliment.*

I carefully climbed back down the ramp and went back to the house to wait for Aunt Katrina in the living room. I looked at the grandfather clock in the corner and noted the time. I had only eight minutes before my family came home. I tried to sit still but it was getting difficult. So I decided to twiddle my thumbs.

Now I know you are saying to yourselves as you read this, "come on, who actually does that," but let me tell you it helps pass the time. I sat there and twiddled and twiddled and twiddled some more. I watched in fascination as my thumbs spun around and around each other in a ballet of harmony and grace. I smiled as I tried the old, keep one thumb still and twiddle the other around it. This was a cool diversion for a few moments but a professional would tell you that both digits must be in motion for it to count as a real twiddle.

Time check? Great, seven minutes to go . . . "DAMMIT, twiddling sucks!"

"Hullo, Quate-lin dhaling?"

"In here Aunt Katrina," I replied as she peeked her head down the hall to look and see if I was in fact sitting in the living room.

"I knocked but dere vas no answer," she said.

"Did you try the bell?"

"Dhaling the last time that bell vent off a ghost valked through da front door, forgive me if I don't vish to repeat dat little incident. Now, vhere is Nicole and dis party?"

"Actually, this is all a surprise so we need to move quickly so as not to spoil it. Let's go out through the front door and make our way to where the surprise is going to take place, okay?"

I stood and she followed me out the front door and around the side of the house. Then I explained the plan that she should go upstairs into the tree fort and wait for Nicole. I had expected a bit of a hassle with this part seeing how most adults don't like playing along with what they view as childish games. Yet Aunt Katrina was very cooperative, that is until she saw the doll.

"Quate-lin the doll is up here dhaling! Did you know this?"

"Oh yes, sorry Auntie but I thought Kelsey should be here as well. You know, part of the family type thing."

"Vell dhaling I vish you vould have varned me. This doll and I have a history of violence."

I smiled and assured her that the doll had no malicious intentions. Yet as I turned to go I was certain I heard her laying down some serious ground rules.

"Von, I vill not allow you to throw me around dis tree house. Two, I am currently taking Brazilian Ju-Jitsu from a friend of Royce Gracie's third cousin and I vill place you in a submission hold if you make any move towards myself or von of the children. Three, dat creepy voice of your's, dat is not allowed today . . ."

I looked to my right and knew that my family was due to come home at any second so I rushed back across the yard and went in through the front door again to hopefully avoid any detection. I threw myself back onto the couch and picked up the phone. It wasn't difficult picking out Savannah's number, it was the one called everyday after their morning run at seven forty-five.

The phone rang three times and then her voice came through, loud and very clear. "Hello, Nicole what's up?

"It's Caitlin. Before you hang up I would like to discuss Nicole's upcoming birthday with you so we can get all the details in order, can you come to my back yard in about fifteen minutes? I mean, if you're not too busy to discuss your best little pal's party plans? If you are, I completely understand, its probably a bother for you after seeing her ALL DAY, so if you can't come over I will just tell my parents that you were fed up and needed a breather from her, no worries there."

There was a long and dramatic pause, "Fine, I'll be there." and the line went dead just as the back door opened.

"Hello, how was everyone's yoga lesson?" I beamed.

"Good, thanks," Mimi replied, "you really should try to come over with us one of these nights Caitlin, it's a lot of fun."

"Caitlin, why are you all dressed up?" My mother chimed in.

"Well, I think Craig is going to ask me to the movies so I wanted to look really nice."

"What movie?" Dad asked.

My mom was wiping some sweat from her forehead with a towel and gave him a little shove, "who cares what movie the fact is that he might ask her."

"It matters to me," he said dejectedly.

"Mom," I interrupted, "can Nicole come with me for emotional support please? I am going to go sit on the swing and if she could be there for me my stomach wont be so, fluttery."

"If you think it will help, sure." My mother answered as Nicole stood there and said nothing but I could tell that she was not very happy about my reason for going out to the swing set. I wrote it off as simply her immaturity over the whole Craig love triangle thing but I was soon to discover that it had absolutely nothing to do with that what-so-ever."

I grabbed her arm and hustled my way to the back patio door, just in time to see Craig making his way up into the tree house. I distracted Nicole for a moment longer and then slid the door open and stepped outside.

"Okay Caitlin, enough with the fibbing. You want me to watch while you try to prove that Savannah doesn't like you, who cares?" She said as she planted her feet on the patio and refused to take another step.

"I care and so should you. I mean, we are sisters for god's sake. We are members of The Soul Patrol and this is official business," I shot back.

"Why, because someone out there finds you annoying and mean?"

"Wait a minute, who told you?"

"Craig, and he said it was Patrol business otherwise he wouldn't have shown up either. This is nuts. Not everyone has to like you or believe you."

"Listen, there is more going on than even you know about but if you just sit in that tree house and listen all will be revealed, I promise."

She gave a heavy sigh and then followed me to the swings and thankfully up the ramp and into the fort where she was greeted with a big hug and a "Nicole Dhaling . . ." Words were shared and I could hear the bag of chips being opened as Katrina stuck her head out of the fort door, "so this is an elaborate plan to veed out da criminal? Clever, very clever dhaling but dangerous, let us hope da serpent shows her true colors and does not act like a Peruvian beaver."

I didn't respond but I think by now Katrina understands that means I am completely baffled by what she just said. She pulled her head back inside the fort and I could hear speaking in hushed tones to the other members of the Patrol like old friends who had not seen each other in months. I got a warm sort of glowing feeling at that moment. I realized that even if this trap, which was cunningly set failed, my dearest friends were together and speaking which meant a lot to me. Kelsey's death had brought them all together but it was true friendship that kept it all going.

The words, "What do you want?" came soaring from my backyard to where I was not positioned on the swing just under and off to the side of the fort.

"Hello Savannah, have you had a nice summer?" I asked, trying to show that I was not beyond a polite amount of small talk.

"My summer has been just excellent, thank you, and yours?" She asked, slowly making her way closer to my position. She was dressed in comfortable shorts and a tight fitting blue Old Navy shirt that did nothing to cover up her mid section. Her black hair was tied back off her face and she looked like she had just finished a work out, which made some sense because she just had. She was sipping on a bottle of Evian water and glaring at me which made me so hopeful that in fact, my plan was a mere insult away from working.

"I wanted to discuss my sister's upcoming birthday party with you and make sure that you save the date," I said showering her with kindness.

"Well that's very thoughtful of you Caitlin but isn't Nicole's birthday in October? I mean aren't you a bit early on planning a party?"

"Listen a girl only becomes ten once in a lifetime. In my family it is a milestone and we like to do something very special to celebrate it. But before I give you all the details can we clear the air about a few things?"

"Sure, like what?" she asked crossing her arms across her chest.

"Like the fact that you don't really like me do you?"

"Why whatever do you mean Caitlin? Listen, if this is about the time you tried to scare me half out of my wits the night of the block party, I thought we had put that behind us?"

"Savannah, come on?"

"Caitlin, let's be honest it's you that doesn't like me. From the moment we met I could tell that you were regarding me as some sort of threat. You never even gave me a chance to actually get to know you. You're an egotist and yet somehow you are very insecure. My mom has even spoken to your mother about it and I must say both sides are a bit confused by your behavior."

"Your mother spoke to my mother about us?" I asked in disbelief.

"Of course, when she saw that you were actually willing to avoid coming to our house for yoga with the rest of your family she pulled your mother and father off to the side and spoke to them in great length about your recent behavior. We are all VERY, concerned," she said.

"Concerned?"

"Caitlin, it's obvious that your envy of me is so overwhelming that you have begun to act strangely. Sending your boyfriend over to learn more about me? Asking your friends to spy on me from my Facebook page? Yelling and screaming at Nicole about your dog because you felt guilty for not walking him yourself? Caitlin you are teetering on the edge and I am afraid if you don't get help soon, you are going to go crazy and maybe do something drastic. Please, take a few minutes to think about what I am saying and try to see the wisdom in it. We all just want whatever it is bothering you to come to the light so we can deal with it."

I stood up from the swing, "STOP SAYING 'WE'. There is no 'we' with you. You are you and 'we' do not exist. How can you even stand there and spew this bullshit when you know perfectly well that YOU are what's bothering me? You think that you can twist this one around and make me look like the fool again, do you? Well I know your secret. How's that strike you? I know how you got Dog sick, I know how you're controlling my sister and I know why you had to leave the south and come here to Massachusetts. I know it all."

With a grin that could have chilled the devil's blood she asked, "Do you now? Then why don't you enlighten me?"

"Okay, your brother came to visit me about ten days ago and told me all about your past and how you have become a master in the voodoo arts. He explained how he's afraid of you and how basically your whole family has had to uproot their lives because of the crimes you committed against other girls in your last school. You were able to manipulate them and make them steal for you."

I looked in her eyes for a sign of fear but none ever came, perhaps it would have but I was unable to finish my full litany because I was rudely interrupted in the next few moments. "I suspect it was through a similar spell that you were able to make Nicole forget to close the back door, which allowed Dog to get outside and into who knows what kind of mischief . . ."

A scream came from behind me, "STOP IT CAITLIN! Stop it right now."

I had no choice but to turn around. My sister was coming down the slide and it was apparent by her look and tone that she was not happy.

"I've heard enough. This is insane. You've gone too far Caitlin, too far. I will not allow you to blame Savannah for this. Dog got out, okay? Not because of a spell but because someone didn't close the door. Savannah doesn't hate you, you hate her."

She then walked over to my enemy and said, "I'm sorry about all of this Savvy."

"It's okay Nicole, I knew it wouldn't work," Savannah said.

I moved towards Nicole, "You told her about this? How could you tell her? Dammit Nicole, don't you understand that changes all of her answers, all of her behaviors. This whole thing is worthless because she had time to plan her answers. Why would you warn her?"

My sister looked at me like I had two heads, and rightly so. She would have had no time to warn Savannah, none at all. No one could have warned her, so how the hell did she know?"

"Caitlin, stop yelling at Nicole, it was me. I warned her."

Please, someone tell me that wasn't Craig's voice.

He was already behind me standing very still. "I told Savannah that you were going to try and get to the bottom of all of this nonsense. I thought that if I warned her she could calm your fears and maybe we could all start to get along. We're all neighbors now. We should be friends, ya know?"

"This was Patrol business," I whispered.

"No Caitlin, this is you looking for someone to be your enemy. You're lying to your parents, sneaking around on secret trips with my aunt, making up stories about Stephen visiting you in the middle of the night to tell you that you are a warrior of the light and to make matters worse, you're speaking to imaginary people now too. I mean come on. Can't you see it? She's not evil. She's not into Voodoo; she is simply a girl that you don't like because she is pretty and you find that threatening."

I stammered, "How could you betray me like this?"

"I didn't betray you. I was simply trying to get Savannah to back off and give you some room. I know how hard this has been for you and

Nicole over the last eight months and I just didn't want anything else to make it worse than it already is," he said convincingly.

"You know nothing. Do you really care if we get along or is it that you just didn't want to have this feud make you choose sides? Well guess what, you won't have to worry about that anymore . . . it's very clear which side you've already chosen."

His eyes got a bit misty as he sensed what I already knew in my heart, that there was no going back on his choice. This one would have to be played out until the end. "Go away, Craig . . . Go away, before I find something heavy to beat you with." Those were the last words I would say to him for almost six months.

He slumped forward and slowly began to walk in the direction of his yard which of course, as fate would have it carried him right past Savannah who gently placed her hand on his shoulder in an effort to comfort him.

He paused and then said, "You're not as innocent as Nicole thinks, so save it. We we're all perfectly happy until you moved in to the neighborhood. Now all we do is fight and lie and sneak around behind each other's backs. Caitlin may be wrong about a lot of things but you have somehow cast a spell over us and because of you're bullshit, I just lost my best friend and I will never forgive you for that Savannah."

Craig walked off. It felt oddly like one of those movies where you watch one of the heroes walk away from his teammates and you hope beyond hope that he glances back so he can see just how much they are all going to miss him. But that's what makes a hero a hero, the ability to do what's best for others even if that means facing a grim and lonely future.

"Caitlin, say something to him." Nicole shouted.

"Like what?"

"Don't let Craig leave like this, he's our friend," she pleaded.

"Was. Get that through your head little sister, was. Craig knew what he was doing."

"God, you're so pig headed. CRAIG," she yelled, "wait up." She spun and tore off in the same direction trying to catch him before he reached his house.

It didn't take long for Savannah's face to change. A smile, wider than the Cheshire cat's crept out across her face, "This is just too easy."

I wanted to jump on her and pound that smug expression right off, but instead I chose to find out after all these weeks, the real reason why this bitch hated my guts so much, "Care to tell me why?"

"No, not really," she answered calmly.

"Come on Savannah. Let me in on the secret. What the hell could I have done to you to make you this mad at me? What did I say or maybe not say, that has you trying to utterly ruin my friggin' life?"

I waited for a minute or two before trying again to pry this crucial information out of her. "There's no one else here, I swear, it's just you and me. Seriously, what's the cause of all this? Tell me, please?"

"Okay. I hate you because . . ." and she paused.

"All right, because why?" I stayed very still waiting for the revelation that I hoped would at least give me a small amount of insight into the mind of this cold, hearted cretin.

"That's it, because."

"Huh?" I wasn't sure I heard her right.

"Jeez dim-wit, try to follow this okay? I hate you because, I just hate you. I looked at you and thought, yep this is the one. Make this chick suffer, it'll be a load of fun watching her squirm."

"WHY ME?" I shouted in frustration.

"Why not you? I was in a mood the day we met, you were there. I mean, does that really matter? What matters is how far I'm willing to take this. I'll tell you what. Beg me to stop and I'll think about stopping but beg me really good or else I won't believe you mean it."

I was too angry to think of anything else to say so I went with the old stand-by, "Go to hell."

"Okay, but in a few more weeks you will be begging me to stop and by then I may not want to. Last chance, feel like dropping to your knees and telling me how much you want me to stop, how much you need me to be nice?"

"I want to tell you something almost as important if I may?"

"What's that?" she asked.

"Eat shit . . . and die."

Savannah turned and went home. I was unsure exactly where this whole sick encounter had left me. I couldn't imagine the whole thing going much worse than it just had. I tried to envision what to do next, how I would continue to carry this hatred, this grudge into the upcoming school year especially now that it appeared that The Soul Patrol was in serious jeopardy of breaking up. I casually made my way to the swing set and sat down in one of the swing seats and began to rock very slowly back and forth. My mind began to wander which is probably why I didn't hear the panicked calls for help sooner than I did.

"Assistance vould be appreciated dhaling."

I looked back over my shoulder to see Aunt Katrina trying to step out of the fort backwards. A task that I soon discovered is easier said than done when you are as short and stocky as she is. Her feet were having a difficult time securing purchase and even though the small meeting house was only about four feet off the ground a fall of that distance could actually hurt someone who was pushing deep into her late fifties.

I clamored out of the swing and immediately got in close so I could help her find the second rung on the ladder. Once her right leg was not aimlessly swinging out into open space she seemed to calm down a bit and then gingerly climbed down the other five rungs until she was safely back on planet earth.

"Vell, that could have gone better."

"Sorry, I kind'a forgot you were still up there," I apologized.

"Not da ladder dhaling, I meant the meeting vith dis girl," she corrected.

"Oh," I stood there quietly and prepared myself for an insightful lecture or a clever anecdote, yet one never came. I wish one had and was sort of getting a bit discouraged that it wasn't. Up until this moment, Craig's aunt had never failed with her ability to sum up a potential problem and offer some enlightenment towards its solution. I cocked my head slightly to the side and couldn't help but watch as she did the same.

"At a loss?" I finally asked.

"Yes and no."

"Okay, so let's start with the easier one," I offered as I repositioned myself back onto the swing, "what part are you NOT at a loss with?"

"Vell, she is definitely not a beaver." If I wasn't already exhausted I would have ran out towards the street praying that some passing mime on a moped would have come along and whisked me off to France where we would spend countless hours making stupid faces at each other, but instead she continued, "Vhat I am saying is dat dis girl is not trying to make a home here and vhen it is done she vill simply go about her life."

Okay, sadly that made sense. "So what part are you at a loss about?"

"Vhat to do about her. Quate-lin dis girl, is as you said before, evil. Only true evil vould hurt something vithout being provoked. Only true evil looks to make problems vhen there are none. She must be stopped, and yet, vithout me contacting my cousin Sergei and renting a large banana costume, I'm not sure ve have many options."

I took the bait. However this time I was not going to allow her to trump me with some silly explanation, so I offered what to me would be perfect Katrina logic for why she would have to rent a banana costume. "Let me guess, your cousin Sergei works for a traveling circus and is in charge of training killer gorillas so if we put Savannah into the costume one of his animals would try to eat her for us, right?"

"Vhat? Quate-lin sometimes I vonder vhere you get your crazy ideas, really. No dhaling, Sergei has a potassium deficiency and has been forced to live on a diet which requires he eats eight bananas every day for the last twenty years. He now hates them so much that he goes berserk every time he sees one now. I can tell you that breakfast around that man is pure hell."

I smiled and walked over and gave her a really big hug. She had done it again. This crazy woman with a terrible sense of fashion and an even worse accent had just made me feel better. As odd as she is, somehow she is able to bring a sense of peace to me. I knew that Savannah was going to do everything in her power to ruin my life. I knew that Nicole was going to be a complete pain in the butt until I could prove to her just how twisted her bestest friend was. I knew Craig and I would never be the same again and yet I also knew that this chubby, salt and pepper haired matronly gypsy would be my friend forever. I can't explain it. We just have a connection. It runs deeper than merely both of us being able to see ghosts or thinking the world works in strange ways. It's a bond that forms when one generation sees itself in the other's eyes. She saw herself as a young girl, sassy and proud. And I saw in her what I might become, what I would become, if I ever plotted to dress Savannah into a banana suit and allow cousin Sergei a chance to get his revenge against the one hundred and forty four thousand pieces of yellow fruit he had so far endured in his life.

I needed a different plan for my revenge and fortunately, in a few weeks, fate would provide it for me in form of our drama club play, "Arsenic and Old Lace."

CHAPTER THIRTEEN

SCHOOL

School had progressed very much like I anticipated. The girls (by girls I mean, Danielle, Melanie and Kirsten) and I became closer, Kelsey lectured me nightly about my poor behavior towards Craig. Aunt Katrina called me several times a week with new hexes and potion recipes she hoped to try out on my neighborly nemesis and Nicole became even closer with Savannah who coincidently, ended up becoming an assistant coach for her hockey team.

Yep, the Braintree Fireballs were honored to have a junior varsity girl helping out with drills and skills. At first I refused to go to the practices. I gritted my teeth, held my breath and threatened to take up smoking Cuban cigars if my parents forced me to attend. In hindsight I will tell you this; I am glad I finally broke down and went to their opening game. Nicole was so happy that she gave me a giant hug. What really impressed me though was the fact that she had gotten a lot better. The practicing, the sweat, the running, all of it was paying off. Instead of her being this smallish kid that other girls wanted to charge and challenge, Nicole was one of the players they began trying to avoid. My parents, Mimi, Dog and even myself were so very proud of her, when in only the second game of the season she scored her very first goal. You would have thought that our beloved Bruins had won the Stanley Cup, we all shouted and screamed so loud.

However, as I am sure you have come to expect, all was not well in paradise. Hostilities between the aforementioned Ms. Summers and I had escalated to full blown insults now whenever we were fortunate enough to pass each other in the hall. At first it was more along the lines of light banter, you know the kind of thing; "Hey butt face, where you off to crack baby, out of my way ho-nugget" and of course the ever popular, "slut." However, as the second week began, the discourse began to turn a bit more, shall we say, hateful.

In fact, things got so heated in the third week of school that we were both brought down to the principal's office to explain our behavior. We were ushered in by the geometry teacher, Mrs. Carter who was a wispy sort of woman in her late forties. I didn't think she had it in her when she grabbed both of us by the arm and screamed about an inch from our faces that she had witnessed quite enough and it was time for us to grow up.

We were instructed to wait for Mr. Campelli in his office and to not "move a muscle" from the high back leather chairs she plopped us in. The whole room looked like something out of a Victorian novel. The office was paneled a dark sort of color, the accruements on the desk were brass and there was even a big model barge like the one in Ben Hur, directly behind the desk chair and slightly elevated so everyone could view it no matter their position in the room.

"Caitlin."

Turning my head slightly, I glared at her as if she were Colonel Sanders and I, a vegan activist from P.E.T.A. "What?"

"You know, if we don't act real cool about this whole thing, we are going to get suspended, right?" she added.

"Yes, that thought had occurred to me, toilet breath." I replied, thinking at first that this was another attempt to stick me with a jab while my guard was down and my brain occupied with thoughts of the beating I would get when I got home.

"Cut the shit and listen, all right? If I go home suspended, yeah my mom and dad will be a ticked off but I will simply say that it's a real tough adjustment for me move'n schools and all. But, wonder what are you gonna tell your folks about why we are carryin' on this way? I can't imagine that they are gonna take too kindly to your being thrown out, can you?"

I could not allow her logic to show me for the chicken shit I was. Of course I didn't want my mother storming in here with thoughts of smacking my behind with a large, floppy, radio antenna, but I could not allow Savannah to see that. So I bluffed, "Listen to me cockroach. This is EXACTLY the kind of thing I've been secretly hoping for. I want the principal to come in here and blast us both. I then want him to call our parents and make them sit together in this very room so I can relay to them just exactly how, cruel, cold and calculating you really are. Oh, you're right, I am going to get an earful for this but you; you are going down." I don't remember which hand gesture I used but it did finish with my finger aimed in a downward position so I figured I pulled it off.

"Alright, well once the principal and counselor come in, I'm sure they will want to hear your side of things, especially since they already know my side," she settled back into the deep maroon, leather button chair and sighed.

"What makes you think that the counselor will be in here anyway?" I asked.

"Because dummy, I will request that she is."

"And what the hell do you mean, she already knows your side?" I stammered.

"Well, since about the third day of school at least twice a week I've been going down to speak with her about how, terribly I've been treated since moving here. Up until today, I've never wanted to name names for fear that it might lead to further repercussions. But after all this, I won't be able to hold my tongue any longer."

"You are the smelliest, slimiest, nastiest piece of putrescence that ever came seeping out of a snail's ass," I whispered.

"Glad to see we're on the same page sugah. Now, this is all just a terrible misunderstanding, ain't it? We are going to both promise from here on out to be on our VERY best behavior, right?" She instructed, even though her voice sounded as if she were posing a question.

"Okay, you win, for now," was all I got out before the door behind us opened and in stepped Mr. Campelli, all five foot four of him.

He moved the same way a lame duck might in the water, all out of kilter. He had two distinguishing characteristics, thinning hair on the top of his head and square shaped glasses on the tip of his nose. He claimed that he only ever needed them for reading but in his line of work being a school administrator that probably meant he required them all day long. He was not a handsome man but he did dress handsomely. His suit was double breasted and charcoal gray, while his shoes were made of polished black leather. They were so shiny that you could see your reflection in them.

"So, it seems that we have forgotten how to behave like young ladies in this school?" He said as he walked passed us, rounded his desk, pulled out his chair and sat down facing us with this hands folded neatly in front of him on the blotter.

I chose not to speak since it was obvious that his question was rhetorical, but Savannah sensed my hesitation and jumped right in. "Mr. Campelli, I know a man like you has more important things to worry about than two young women squabbling like . . . like . . . is that a Roman Barge?"

"Yes it is, Ms. Summers but please stay on task. Finish what you were saying."

"It's just that I am fascinated by that period in history. I mean think of the opulence, the fashion, the power and the very spirit of Rome itself. Why, it's enough to make ones head spin," she said with passion in her voice.

"Well, yes it was an amazing time for my people and for my family," he replied, swiveling around in his chair to spend a few more happy moments staring at its majesty.

"Your family? Sir you can't mean that you were able to trace your ancestry all the way back to the days of the Ceasers can you?"

He answered like all boys do when you speak about their favorite subject, with a passion in his voice and his chest puffed out, "Well, I do know that one of my ancestors was in fact in the Roman legion assigned to a battle against the Phoenicians aboard a ship very much like this one, off the coast of Madagascar."

Savannah was throwing some amazing B.S. She honestly looked like someone who cared about this kind of thing. I hate her guts but the girl can really play someone when she needed to.

"I can almost hear the pounding of the drums as the long oars . . ."

"Sweeps, they were called sweeps," Mr. Campelli interrupted.

Savannah, undaunted by the correction, continued, "as the sweeps cut through the water in unison and the brave legionnaires prepared themselves on deck for the battle soon to come. Oh, Caitlin can't you see it too?"

Flatly I said, "Oh yes, I can definitely see it."

At first I thought she had overplayed it but I was sooo wrong. Instead, as she began to mimic the drums cadence it looked as if Mr. Campelli was about to burst into tears from his heart longing so much for those by-gone days. "Boom, boom . . . Boom, boom . . . Boom, boom . . . Sir, I can see you standing there on the bow. Water splashing around you as the reinforced iron hull cuts a swath through the cold waves. Your armor glistening in the first few rays of autumn sunlight and suddenly your voice rings out over the din, 'Prepare for battle.'

"Times were simpler then, you know?" He said as he spun back around facing us once more. "There was no PTA. No sub-committees on the interpretation of rules within the school system. No, there was Ceaser's word and Ceaser's word was final."

"Something we all should respect. The Republic was nothing without it's Ceaser," Savannah added.

"Exactly!" He had begun to develop a wild look in his eye. "They made him a god, so why not act like one. To do less would have been to insult the very honor they themselves bestowed upon him."

"How right you are Sir, isn't Mr. Ceas . . . I mean Mr. Campelli right Caitlin?" She asked.

"What, oh yes. He is most definitely right. Too much red tape these days, waaay too much bureaucracy."

"You see Sir, for a while we behaved poorly and we do not argue that point. It now falls upon some silly person who is not even in this room to doll out our punishment without even the chance for us to explain ourselves. Instead of them trusting that you will do the right thing, they have bound your hands and all you can do is tow the company line. It is sad, is it not Caitlin; that we can't throw ourselves to the ground begging for mercy from Mr. Campelli like in the old days and know that his wisdom would see us to a fair and honest outcome of these tragic events?"

"Yep, it's very sad."

I wouldn't have believed it if I had not seen it with my own eyes. Mr. Campelli, our principal stood and raised his chin up by at least six degrees. He also, for reasons unknown to me at the time, began breathing deeply though his nose. Long powerful breaths like a horse might take after an intense and exhausting gallop.

Savannah was done, her spell had been cast. Now, it was merely a matter of letting her target stew awhile while we waited to see how deeply she had moved this man.

It took all of about a minute for him to speak, "You two are free to return to your classes, this time. But I do not want to hear another report of either one of you acting in such a way again or by the GODS I will have you both shipped off to an outpost far away from the imperial city. Do I make myself clear?"

Savannah stood up and pulled on my arm so I would do the same. "We thank you for your mercy and your patience Sir." She then leaned over towards me and whispered a simple instruction in my ear and together we said, "All Hail Ceaser!"

We then did an about face and marched out of his office. As I shut the door, I saw him turning back towards the barge and running the tip of his finger over its deck.

We walked together past the secretary who appeared confused by the fact that she had NOT been instructed to call our parents and stepped out into the school hallway.

"I know now why I hate you so much," I said.

"Why, because, I'm prettier than you?" Savannah answered.

"No because you're an amazing improviser. I mean, wow. I am good but that was unbelievable."

Savannah studied me for a moment and then said, "You really mean that?"

"Hey, I know a master when I see one," I had been humbled. I actually had been in awe. I now understood just how devastatingly good this girl was at twisting people around her finger. If I had any chance at besting her and winning Nicole back I needed more time.

"All right then Caitlin, truce."

"You mean that?" I asked, my voice almost sounding incredulous.

"Yep. I think you finally understand just how great I am, so for now at least, until you get under my skin again, truce."

'Oh Savannah, don't you worry, I don't have any plans of getting under your skin again." This statement was a fact. I didn't have a plan, not yet, but I would soon, very, very soon.

CHAPTER FOURTEEN

OH, FOR PUCK'S SAKE

Nicole's birthday party in the last week of September was a nice one. Since Savannah and I were now 'close friends' we had a delightful time hanging together, NOT! Well, at least Savannah had a great time. She spent the afternoon throwing little comments about how awesome she is and how lame at times I am, and about how her hair was just gorgeous while mine had the same consistency as straw (which is just not true by the way). What really freaked me out I guess, is how little anyone seemed to notice. How can adults sit there and not recognize the needling that is going on around them? I ended up speaking to Kelsey about it later that night and even she said that Savannah's behavior was down right rude. I don't get it. My mom normally hates that petty tit for tat crap and if Nicole and I were to act that way she'd go bonkers. Why didn't she bother to stop it this time? I must say though, that whatever hostility I was already harboring that day only amplified by about ten fold when it came time for Nicole to open her birthday gifts.

Everyone was very generous and she got some lovely things. Allow me to share with you a quick run down of the highlights of the evening's gift giving: over one hundred dollars in cash, a gift card to Barnes and Noble, a new field hockey stick and bag (from the Summers) an autographed picture from the Bruins goalie which I arraigned for her, a vanilla Bundt cake from Aunt Katrina which had a stuffed gopher plushie in the middle holding a hyacinth blossom (the symbolism was lost even though she seemed very excited to present it) and of course six tickets to see the Bruins at the Gah-den. This last gift from my parents sent even my head spinning. I could taste the hot dogs, hear the screams of eighteen thousand crazed B's fans and when I closed my eyes I could see the boys in Black and Gold holding their hands aloft after scoring the winning goal with only seven seconds left in regulation. The tickets were for the second week of October against the Capitols and there amazing sniper Alexander the Great. *Let the countdown begin.* Fifteen days until . . . . *Wait a minute, why six tickets?*

I walked over to my dad and quietly, so as not to embarrass anyone who was not coming along with us, asked him who the six tickets were for.

"Well the four of us, Mimi and of course Nicole gets to pick a friend to come along since these are her tickets," he replied.

Before I could speak up about all the reason we should not let her make such an important choice without guidance, Nicole came running up and blurted, "She can go, she can go. Daddy, Savannah's mom and dad said absolutely she can go!"

It was time for me to come to grips with my situation. I had what I could see, were three paths laid out before me:

1) Make a scene. Refuse to go to the game. Beg my sister and parents to realize just how evil Savannah is and invite Craig to patch things up. This path would ruin my plans though, since any hostile action taken after they understood just how rotten she is would be considered revenge and not well tolerated. Not to mention that I have tried this tactic several other times over the last few weeks with absolutely NO success.

2) Go to the game, suck it up and try to have a good time while still plotting out a cunning plan. This method allowed me maximum emotional impact and shock value when I sprang it which in my humble opinion the creature had already earned several times over in spades.

3) Or, shave my head, drape a red sheet over my body and move to Tibet where I would proceed to learn the ways of the Dali Lama. In hind sight, this was probably at the time, my best option even though I chose number two

Plan Number two, the great number two; if I live to be a thousand years old I will never, ever forgive the number two. Not even two scoops of raisins in a package of Raisin Bran will make me forget the travesty that was plan number two. Two hates me, and I, now that I understand just how cruel it is, I will hate two back for all eternity.

So, game day arrived. There had been an electricity about the house over the last couple of days. Everyone was getting the bug to go to the game, even Mimi. We laid out black clothing, unpacked our jersey's from summer storage (they are normally called sweaters in hockey, but jersey is also acceptable) with our favorite players name on the back. I found my gold and black Toque, which is a knit ski cap with ear flaps and tassels. Why wear one you ask? Because it shows everyone else around you just how ravenous of a B's fan you are, so much so in fact, that you are willing to throw fashion to the wind and stand before your peers looking like a complete Ja-bobo. We even went so far as to bring out Dog's Bruins collar and place it around his neck. He wore it so proudly, for about six minutes. Then he began acting like a spazz and to ensure that he didn't strangle himself my dad told me to take it off of him.

The game was a one o'clock start time which is pretty common for a Saturday game. So, a little after eleven we were all getting into mom's mini van and headed around the block to pick up Savannah. I was thankfully sitting next to Mimi since Nicole had insisted I leave the seat all the way in the back for her and 'Savvy.'

As we rolled into her driveway, I had to catch my breath and shake my head. I hadn't been here since they moved in. Actually, I had avoided coming anywhere near this house for the last two and a half months, sort of the same way a vampire might avoid the Vatican, during the middle of the day, in August, while wearing a two piece bikini, covered in Bain de Soleil dark tanning oil, preparing to light a cigarette with a propane blow torch.

The house was amazing. The Summers had hired contractors to paint the outside of their home and it came out spectacular. It was now a creamy sort of yellow color, like buttermilk, with deep burgundy shutters. The front iron gate and fencing had been (I would later learn) sandblasted and repainted in black making it look brand new. The front yard was cleaned up and the grass was growing in. The reason for that, I noticed, was that the massively scary tree had been pruned back allowing sunlight to reach the ground. All the creepy roof angles that once haunted our daydreams, were still there but suddenly seemed to make sense. Instead of the house giving off an air of foreboding, it now joyfully sang, 'Hi, come on in for a Macchiato? Oh, and try this delicious biscotti we found while skiing in Northern Italy.' It was, I hatefully admit, beautiful.

Dad put the van in park and honked the horn which got him a lecture from Nicole about being rude. She slid up passed me and threw open the side door so that she could go get Savannah properly when the front door opened.

Everyone and I do mean everyone in the van sucked a deep and dreadful breath through their clenched front teeth. Savannah came out of the house wearing, dare I say it, an Atlanta Thrashers Jersey.

"Holy shit," I whispered.

"Sissie, don't start," Nicole rebuked.

"Don't start, for god's sake Nicole she's in a farkin Thrashers sweater. First off, anyone not a Bruins fan is the enemy <u>BUT</u> what's worse she's not eveing wearing the RIGHT enemy's sweater. We are playing the Caps today, who cares about the THRASHERS!"

"Wow, this will be uncomfortable," Dad sighed and smiled at Savannah through the windshield as she approached closer.

Mom leaned back and said, "Okay, just let's make her feel welcome she is our guest, no off color comments. Understand Caitlin."

"Your mom is right princess, she is a guest, even though our guest appears to be a chowder head who knows nothing about hockey etiquette," Mimi added. "You never wear an opponent's jersey to the Garden, especially if they aren't even playing that team. I am shocked."

It was worse than a train wreck that you can't take your eyes off. I watched, although it kills me to even recount the event, I watched as my sister, greeted, smiled and hugged a Thrashers fan while in her Savard jersey. *Is there no end to the power this girl wields over my sib?*

"Hello, everyone."

A single, unified voice sans one, mine, greeted her, "Morning, Savannah."

"Well good morning to you too, Caitlin." she said with a slight sneer in her voice. "Mr. and Mrs. O'Connor thank you so much for the ticket. I've never been to a hockey game before."

She and Nicole slid into the rear of the van and buckled their seatbelts while I closed the door. I was glad Nicole began to make some small talk before I had a chance to gather my wits and pose the question that everyone was already asking in their mind, "Oh, you've never been to a game Savvy but you're wearing a jersey. Most people don't ask for one until they've seen a game or two."

"What, this? Oh my mom ordered it for me on-line after she found out I were going to see this game."

"Your mom ordered you a Thrashers jersey because you were going to a Boston Bruins hockey game?" I asked trying ever so hard not to start this day off on the wrong foot.

"Yeah, I mean why not, we're from Georgia silly," I heard the word silly but what I think she was trying to say was more like, 'dipshit.'

"Yes, but you are in Massachuettes now. If you've never been to a hockey game than perhaps you might end up rooting for the first team you ever saw, especially since it's in your new hometown," I offered.

"Oh, we live in Braintree don't we? I mean, do they have a professional hockey team as well?

I could see that this was going absolutely nowhere, so I dropped it. Okay, Mimi poked me in the ribs which reminded me to just drop it, otherwise I probably would have continued and gotten everyone mad at me.

"Sooooo," my Mom chirped, "our plan for the day is to see the game then Mimi offered to take Nicole downtown to her favorite place, Pizza Regina."

"Sounds like fun, that is very nice of you Mimi," Savannah said.

I had not been around Savannah and my grandmother much as you can imagine, so I couldn't help but wonder, *when she had been given permission to call MY grandmother, Mimi?*

We drove into the city which took about twenty minutes and then spent another fifteen in traffic worming our way along towards the parking area near the TD Garden.

As we climbed out of the van, I slipped on my lucky Toque which illicited quite a condescending stare from Ms. Summers. "Something wrong?"

"Isn't it a little warm for that . . . hat?" She asked, rolling her eyes.

"Ummm, no and do you know why? Cause it's the right season to wear this hat," I snarled leaning in about six inches from her face. "Ya know what season it is, don't ya?"

"No."

"It's da season of da bear, BABY!!! LET'S GO BRUINS !!!" I felt my heart soar as people from all the cars around us joined in and began to chant along with me."

"LET'S GO BRUINS!!!" echoed over and over again throughout the parking deck as my parents smiled proudly at me.

We began to make our way towards the stairs and across the street to the Garden when I heard the first of many jeers thrown at Savannah that day. Can I just say that I am proud to be part of one of the most obnoxious group of fans in the entire world. "Hey, nice jersey moron! Oh look, an Atlanta Slackers fan! Far from home ain't ya Jerk-*#%! Wrong arena A-hole!"

I give my sister all the props in the world. While the rest of us tried to disassociate ourselves with Savannah by walking a bit faster and closer together, Nicole would not abandon her friend. She walked along side and a few times even fired a shot back at the fans who were heckling her friend.

We went through security and survived the odd looks and jeers that our guest received all the way up to our seats. We were dead center on the top teir but in the first row so even though we were up high we were going to be able to see all the upcoming action with ease.

"Great seats Dad," I beamed.

"Well, there are some better ones but we are all together and in the same row that was the tricky part when I was ordering them."

"You did well Ian," Mom added.

"When we used to go to the Atlanta Hawks games we never sat this high up, I always wondered what the view was like from here," she paused a moment and then said, "it's really not so bad."

We all got comfy, chose our seats and then Mimi said, "Okay, let's go princesses and of course you too, Savannah. Why don't the four of us go for a walk and see if there's anything we need."

OH yeah! It was time to take a trip to the bear den!"

Mom said that her and dad would hit the hot dog vendor and bring everyone back fries and dogs. She wrote down how many with mustard, onions, no onions, no mustard and of course relish or no relish. We split up and four went down the stairs to the left while two, (the spiteful number two) went to the right.

Upon entering what has been called by other Bruins fans as 'The Mecca' of Bruins paraphernalia" I could not help but dry the single tear that was forming in my left eye. The whole store was a sea of black. Banners, hats, jackets, photos, jerseys, pins, foam claws, sweat shirts, even, I blushingly recall, a Bruins thong. Now I am a die hard fan but I can't imagine what kind of woman walks around all day in a Bruins thong. For the sake of my own sanity, and yours dear reader, I shall let this one go.

I chose, since it was not my birthday, a modest Milan Lucic tee, name on the front, his number on the back. Nicole went for a pullover hoodie which was really cool but then the incredible happened.

"Savannah dear, what do you think about this?" Mimi asked, holding up a long sleeve shirt that had the logo on the front and Bruins down the right sleeve. It was very nice, actually I liked it more than the tee I had already picked out.

"Oh, that's nice Mimi do they have it in your size?" Savannah asked.

"I was thinking sweetie that I get it for you so you don't have to spend the next three hours getting shouted at. It's making Nicole nervous seeing how the people are reacting to you and quite frankly I don't want this day to be a bad one for her because some fans are a little less tolerant than others."

"Oh, I see your point. Thank you, yes that is very nice. I'll have my parents pay you for it when we get back, I'm sure my mother will understand the neccessity for the shirt."

Mimi smiled, "No need dear. Better to be hidden amongst the crowd this time. It's a gift. Your mom and dad have been very nice to us, I would never dream of having them pay me back."

BLECH.

So, we allowed Savannah to run into the ladies' room and swap her top and slide her Thrashers jersey into the bag, where no one would see it. We then made our way back to our seats and found mom and dad already sorting through the various hot dogs looking for each person's specific order.

For the sake of my tale I need to let you know the seating order. I was sitting on the aisle which was to my right, next to me was Mimi, then Nicole and of course Savannah, mom and then dad. While this information may seem superfluous at this juncture, I assure you it will become of monumental importance as you read on.

We ate in silence, well mostly in silence, for I could still hear Nicole trying to explain the rules of the game to her guest. If you have not watched hockey for any length of time it is played very much like soccer only with sticks, skates, fists and heart. The difference is easy to explain, in soccer a cramp is just cause for medical attention, in hockey the action continues until teeth are missing. 'Nuff said.

I looked up at the jumbo-tron television that hung over center ice and saw that there was only twenty one more minutes until game time, that meant the teams would be taking the ice, right on cue. Out came the Bruins and moments later, the Capitols for their warm up skate.

The excitement in the building was one of eager anticipation. The Bruins had opened their season on the road for the first three games and were coming back home with a 2-1 record.

At this point Mimi and I made some small talk and watched the guys take shots at the backup goalie first and then the starter. Not long later, the red carpet was rolled out onto the ice and the color guard marched out taking their position for the singing of our national anthem.

Everyone stood, took off their hats and cheered as Rene Rancourt belted home another wonderful rendition of the "The National Anthem." It was a tradition at the Gah-den to have Rene sing it before every game. Equally important though, was his fist pump and scream, "Let's go Bruins" that got the fans worked up into a frenzy.

And so the game began. It was a real back and forth affair for the first two periods. Boston though, began to push a bit and it created some holes that the Caps exploited allowing them to score the go ahead goal five minutes into the third period making the score 3-2.

About six minutes later nothing had changed. The Bruins were still down a goal and looking for a way to even it up when my favorite player got called for a completely BOGUS cross-checking penalty. I screamed what a load of horse crap that was; in fact, about seventeen thousand people screamed what a load of horse crap that was. It didn't matter though, the refs had called it and now we were going to be a man down for two minutes. (Two minute penalty. Two, spiteful number two!)

The Capitols coach, sensing one more goal would probably be enough to keep Boston out of the win column for the day, loaded his power play with four forwards and only one defensemen. The especially bad news was, one of those forwards, was Alexander the Great. An NHL sniper that could take a puck, shoot it from his own goal line and cut the eyelash off of a squirrel who was desperately trying not to be hit at the other end of the ice.

Hearts crawled into our throats as the faceoff was taken deep in our own end. Shot . . . save . . . another shot . . . another save . . . shot . . . . OH, off the post . . . held in at the blue line . . . shot . . . off the goalie's mask. The action was pure insanity. Players hitting, throwing their bodies down to block shots, the goalie getting peppered from almost every conceivable angle when the puck trickled back to the point and Alex wound up to take what had to be the hardest slapshot in his entire life. At the same moment, Sidenberg, a B's defenseman, burst from right to left and reached out in front of Ovechkin with his stick trying to block the upcoming shot. The effect was that the puck exploded off Sidenberg's angled blade, went somersaulting high into the air and over the glass. In all my life I had never seen a puck flip so many times through the air especially up so high. *Wait a minute. OMG it's coming this way!*

I heard my dad yell, "Mom, lookout!" I instinctively lunged to my left reaching my hand out to block the black rubber disc from striking my grandmother in the head.

DAMMIT, that hurt, was all I could think of as the puck smashed into my hand and fell down onto the floor off to Mimi's left. Nicole scrambled and suddenly emerged with my puck!

"I got it, I got it!" She shrieked as people all around her patted her on the back and gave their praises.

I rubbed my hand and of course said, "Can I have my puck now, Nicole?"

"What do you mean?" She answered.

"What do you mean, what do I mean? I caught it and stopped it from hitting Mimi in the face. If it weren't for me she would have been hurt."

"Caitlin, if you caught it then why was it on the floor?"

"Caitlin, come on honey you know the rules. You did a great job but the person who first can hold it up wins the puck."

"No Dad, the person who prevents a homicide should be the hero of the hour here, not the person who snarfed it off of the floor."

"Snooze you lose," Savannah chirped.

I had to stay calm, I could not let this get the best of me. Reason, I prayed would win out. "Guys, I could have caught it, or grabbed it once it slammed into Mimi's skull but I chose the more mature option of trying to protect a loved one."

"Geez, thanks princess for all your trouble," At the time I did not notice the sarcasm in her voice but now that I think about it, she did seem a bit miffed that I was getting angry about losing the puck over saving her.

"Caitlin, its Nicole's birthday," mom said. "Why don't you let her have the puck sweetie, I mean, she did get it."

"Because without me, she wouldn't have gotten it at all."

"Yeah and without the guy hitting the thing so hard you wouldn't have had a chance to have tried to catch it anyway."

"I am not speaking to you about this Savannah okay? This is between me and Nicole."

"Well then stop trying to push her around. It's her thing now, it's her birthday, be a good big sister and let it go."

"Savannah, the thing is called a puck okay? And since you know less about hockey then my dog maybe you could shut the hell up and let me talk to my family without butting in."

"Caitlin!" Three adult voices shouted at the same time.

"What? I shouted back.

"Savannah is our guest." I had to stay calm, I had to keep my eye on the prize. My ultimate goal is to ruin this chic when she was completely unaware.

So through the screams that reverberated through my head, I said, "Sorry Savannah. I should not have snapped at you like that."

"Apology taken." The first time it happened you'll remember I was trying desperately to believe that no one goes into a new situation looking for a fight, this time I was certain of what I saw. Her eyes lit up and her mouth curled as she spoke, "And I apologize to Caitlin. This is an argument between sisters and I am not Nicole's big sister, you are. Nicole," she said turning my sister around gently to face her, "you keep that puck as long as you want, it's your birthday. One day you might find someone that you are close enough to or care about enough to share or even give it to. Trust your heart, it will know when the time is right."

"It will?" Nicole replied her eyes filled with awe and reverence, "Then I want you to have it Savannah."

Everyone in my family's jaw dropped wide open. My father was so stunned that he actually spilled some soda in his lap.

"Nicole honey, why don't you think about it a minute. It's not every day that you find something so special, I mean some people come to games for years and years and never get a chance at a game puck," mom said.

The master spoke as well, "Your mom is right Nicole. You shouldn't just give something like this to me, I don't deserve it."

GOD, I CAN'T STAND THIS BEE-ATCH!

"Guys, is the puck mine, yes or no?"

We all nodded yes.

"Then I will do what I want with it. Here Savannah. Thank you for coming to my birthday and more than that, thank you for being my friend."

If my grandmother had not thrown her arm around me at that exact moment I would have jumped over the railing and done a swan dive onto the frozen surface seventy feet below, chin to ice.

"Nicole, are you sure?" Savannah just wanted my parents to witness the exchange so she could say that she gave her several chances to get out of giving it away.

"Absolutely sure." Nicole smiled and handed over the puck to the only Thrashers fan in the whole state of Massachuetts.

The rest of the day went by as a blur. The B's lost, the pizza was excellent but I couldn't taste it due to the crap burger I was still being fed by my sister's earlier actions and on the way home we got a flat. My father took almost forty minutes to fix it and all the while, Savannah went on and on about how LUCKY she was to have been able to go to a Bruins' game and at her very first one, get a souvenir so special. Even Mimi, I could tell, was beginning to lose her cool when she asked my father to turn up the music. I'm sure it was in an effort to drown out the endless prattle coming from the back seat.

We finally pulled into Savannah's driveway just after six o'clock. Her parents came out and thank us and flashed their gorgeous southern smiles when they learned that Nicole had given their daughter a gift as rare as the one she now carried nonchalantly in her left hand. Mrs. Summers even complimented Nicole which only made my seething rage hotter.

"Nicole, this was the sweetest thing you could have done. Nothing lets a friend know how special they are to you like a gift from the heart. Your parents should be proud they raised such a fine young lady."

We backed out of their driveway and everyone began waving goodbye. WWhile the people beside me were waving farewell to Savannah, I sadly, was waving to my puck.

CHAPTER FIFTEEN

A DOLL, A PIG AND A PICTURE OF DAVID HASSLEHOFF

"So, not only did Savannah show up in the wrong team's jersey like I was telling you but to make matters worse, Nicole gave away my puck!" I wanted to scream but I knew everyone had been through a long day. It would have done me absolutely no good to wake Mimi and Nicole up at this point.

The doll turned its head slightly as it listened, "I think what really bothers you is not so much that she gave it away, but who she gave it to," Kelsey said.

"Of course that's the real issue. I've been to what, thirty hockey games already in my life and not once has a puck ever come my way. I had it Kels, it was right there."

"Caitlin, honestly forget the puck. There is nothing you can do about it now, consider it gone. What concerns me more is that Nicole would want to part with something like that simply over a teenager who's shown her some attention. Doesn't that bother you at all?" Kelsey asked.

The pillows behind my back were all scrunched up and I found myself wriggling to get them in a more comfortable position as I answered her question with a question, "What do you mean?"

"Listen Caite, Nicole has always been like the little mother around the house. She's the practical sort of logical girl that rarely gets into any trouble. But, I think we found her weakness. Savannah is giving her undivided attention and for whatever reason Nicole is lapping it up like a kitten at a saucer of milk. I never would have guessed it but it's fairly obvious that Nicole is emotionally needy."

I chuckled out loud, "Come on Kelsey, that's never been Nicole. Why all of a sudden would she need to have someone to latch onto? What could have caused her to shift from a quiet confident kid into a girl who is desperate to be accepted?"

"There are only two answers, Caitlin. One, she has always been this way and we never noticed or two, a terrible tragedy."

I leaned forward and took the doll in my hands and lifted it closer to me, "You mean like someone dying?"

The little doll just nodded and then continued, "I think earlier during the summer when she snapped at you and told you that she had lost a sister as well, it was more than just some random outburst. She is reaching out and since she feels you won't be there for her it appears she found someone who will. I agree with you Caitlin, Savannah is not behaving well, in fact the more I hear, the more I believe that she is taking advantage of her. The worry I have is that if you go through with this need for revenge you might just lose Nicole forever. She sees any attack against Savannah as an attack against her. You need to get her to believe you still love her and always will."

"Kelsey, come on, of course I love Nicole she's my sister," I said.

"That's my point. Caitlin, listen to me. The love that comes from a member of your family is special but for most people it is assumed. It is fairly uncommon when our own blood turns against us in such a way as to make us feel unwanted or unloved. Now sure there are circumstances when people make mistakes or act poorly and hurt each other. What I am talking about though is dismissing or rejecting someone. So, if love from your own family or blood is assumed merely because the perception is that they "have" to love you, imagine how strong the pull would be towards someone who loves you not because they must but because they choose to?"

This revelation made me think. She was right. Kelsey was absolutely right. The love between siblings and parents, while beautiful and strong; is assumed. That's why Kelsey and I were so much more, we didn't even know we were blood we just loved each other. Nicole has found that connection or at least thought she had. It made sense now, all of it.

I finally realized I had been wasting my time. There was no way on earth Nicole would ever think less of Savannah for the things that she did to me. The only way to get Nicole back was to work on getting the creature to turn her ugly head against Nicole and then my sister would have her eyes opened.

"Caitlin, why are you smiling?"

Kelsey's question told me what I already knew, my face was bubbling with glee. I couldn't have contained my happiness even if I wanted to. I was so brilliant. This idea, this plan, this scheme, this divine plot, would win me back Nicole and awaken my entire family from the dark slumber that has been enslaving them over the last several months. Savannah Summers would no longer hold sway here in my house. Say goodbye to yoga, interior design sessions, field hockey coaching, morning jogs and the occasional sunset picnic with its variety of sensible entrée choices and melon basket. Soon the O'Connor's were going to go back to being the boring, slightly soft around the middle couch potatoes that we all once were.

"Caitlin?" The doll asked.

"Yes, oh I um, listen Kels no need to worry yourself over this, okay? I just was thinking of something, ya know, funny."

"Funny?"

"Ya, it's silly." I was struggling to make her believe me which was usually the case when I was up to no good and Kelsey was involved, "it's a joke and it really isn't very nice. It umm, involves a pig, a blind guy on a ladder and a crudely framed portrait of David Hasslehoff."

"What? I swear sis, sometimes you are so strange," she said and I saw the doll's head slowly lean forward and I knew that for tonight at least, Kelsey and I were done speaking.

The plan however, was still echoing around my head. I would go into school tomorrow and start to become friends with one of the strangest kids in my class who just happened to share my younger sib's first name. I would then over the next few days earn her trust and then, when I was sure she would do me a really "big favor" I would have her do something to Savannah that might just tick the southern beauty off so bad that she will probably freak out and call the girl names. All the while I will be standing there, taping her tirade about how stupid this new "Nicole" is and then bring the tirade home to my family and let them hear the entire thing. I actually shuddered I was so excited.

I rolled over and buried my face into my pillow and screamed as loud as I dared, "YOU ARE SO DONE BITCH!" Sleep avoided me for about another hour but when it came I dreamed that whole night of a life free of Savannah Summers.

CHAPTER SIXTEEN

THE EVILS OF FUDGE BROWNIES

I went to school Monday with a new vigor in my step, and why not? I was going to unhorse the dreaded Black Knight. I was going to destroy a despot and in the process, free my family from tyranny. I was the heroine of a great and noble quest. No longer the victim, no longer the down trodden. Today was the beginning of the end and I couldn't help but feel so good. Now all I needed was the proper weapon and that weapon came in the shape of Nicole Pederson.

Nicole Pederson was not an ugly or heavy girl. She wasn't a laughing stock or someone who picked their nose. She just was. Nicole was one of those kids that never stood out, never spoke and never wanted to. She was content, (so it appeared) to be the kid no one cared about. She dressed in basic clothes. She didn't have the expensive stuff, truth be told, but she didn't wear clothes that spoke of third generation hand me downs either. Nicole never had bad skin, bad breath or a bad hair day. She walked through the halls with her head usually down and her books clutched tightly to her chest. She was the ultimate loner. I assume you are beginning to disapprove of my plan already. Using someone simply to get back at someone else perhaps seems a bit on the shallow, "I can't believe you would so such a thing, side."

Please understand, I was stuck for a solution. Of course, I would have rather not had to go and pretend to become friends with a kid that for the most part people cared little or nothing for. Yet, in times of great emotional stress, people will do whatever it takes to survive and right now that meant removing a parasite from my life.

I didn't run into Ms. Pederson until the start of third period that day and by run into I mean just that. I was walking down the hall speaking to one of my male class mates from Sociology, which had just let out, when I saw her silently making her way down the hall.

As fate would have it, she was all the way over to my extreme left hand side of the tiled passage so I would have to do some quick thinking if I was going to "accidentally" make her acquaintance. So, being me, I began laughing out loud as if I had just made a rather clever joke at Brian's expense and then as Nicole P. ambled a bit closer, I lunged forward as if I had been intentionally pushed and screamed out, "HEY," as I ran head long into her spilling her books and mine all over the floor.

I turned towards my imaginary assailant and chided him for doing such a terrible thing, "Brian Flynn, are you crazy? Look what you did to Nicole's things!"

"I . . . but . . . I didn't . . . ."

"Oh, right, sure, like I just happened to have the need to leap across the hall and slam into Nicole for no friggin reason, right? God, you're such a jerk."

Brian moved on completely embarrassed while I bent down to help Ms. Pederson collect her belongings. "God, boys can be such creeps. Sorry about this Nicole, here you go," I added, handing her one of her several notebooks that had been strewn about the floor.

She took the offered item and was about to dash away when I said, "I'm Caitlin, Caitlin O'Connor, remember me? We've been in the same grade now for about . . ."

"Our whole lives," she answered in a voice that was direct but softly spoken.

"Yeah," I laughed, "I guess that's true. We have been in the same grade our whole lives."

"I am shy, not stupid," and like a flash of light, she was gone.

I stood up after recovering my own books and saw Craig standing there looking at me.

"What?"

"You okay?" he asked.

I was still so angry that I could only bark my answer at him, "Duh."

"Still not ready to talk?"

"To you? Nope." and with that he turned and walked away as well.

So, I guess you could say that my first attempt to gain favor with Ms. Nicole Pederson was somewhat of a bust. Oh well, all great plans require a few dry runs to iron out the kinks. I waited a full two more days before trying again to speak with Nicole during the school day. Since she didn't belong to any club or after school activity I was forced to try and use the few times during the day that our schedules intersected in order to make contact.

After nearly eight days of 'Hello's' and 'How ya doin's?' she finally lifted her head and greeted me first as we were both making our way to the library. I smiled and then fell into step with her making light small talk about this and that, she even asked that I call her Nicky which was a relief since I felt awkward calling her by my little sister's name. It's funny, she actually seemed to be a genuinely nice person, just amazingly shy. Over the next several days I was to uncover some of the reasons for that shyness and it made me realize that I was not the only person in this world with some seriously messed up problems.

It seemed that Nicky's parents were pretty screwed up. They both had issues with substance abuse and spent much of her early life taking turns behind bars for one petty offense after another. Not willing to stand idly by and watch this situation continue to worsen her Aunt Frannie appealed to the court system to allow her to take over custody of the young girl rather than place her into foster care. Because of some crazy laws the state delayed Nicky being placed with her aunt and she did in fact spend nine months as a ward of the state living in a house with two dads. I have to say, I have no real opinion with the two dad system since I've never been in that situation but I do find it odd that a child would be placed with complete strangers rather than a family member who already has a child of her own and is willing and capable of caring for them. The only conclusion I can draw from this is that the adult world must know better than I do (which on several occasions as you have already seen dear readers is a load of horse manure). So once the state of Massachusetts got it all sorted out, she moved in with her aunt and has since been doing much better. However, her father got cleaned up, found a new girlfriend and got on with his life in such a completely new direction that he somehow forgot the directions to his daughter' new residence. Nicky hasn't seen him in almost three years and has only gotten a few phone calls on birthdays and special occasions. She hasn't told me this but I am pretty certain she is very afraid that even these small little gestures of kindness are going to soon come to a stop.

Her mother, on the other hand has not gotten any better and is using the fact that her ex husband is jerk, as a crutch to continue to lead a really screwed up life. Nicky doesn't say much about her, only that she goes to bed every night hoping and praying that the police don't call the house and tell the family that her mother took too many pills and was found dead.

My plan was, to say the least, falling apart. How on earth could I even think to drag someone like this girl into a confrontation with Savannah? Even if I was as evil and devious as my nemesis, I could not bring myself to use this girl who had slowly, over the last several days, begun to open up and trust someone again for my own gain. And so it was, I was back to the drawing board. I had been defeated before I even had begun. In truth though, I was a friend richer and obviously a bit wiser as well, and as fate would have it, I was rewarded for my kindness.

I confided in Nicky while talking with her on the phone. I began to explain some of my misfortunes while leaving out the really spooky stuff like my sister's ghost and the fact that my life mentor was a deranged middle aged gypsy. I did though share with her my dislike for Ms. Summers and the horrible things she had done to me since moving into my neighborhood back in July. All the time while I was spinning my tale I heard a succession of ohs and ahs come across the phone. I even have to admit that the reserved and shy Nicky even tossed the word 'bitch' when she heard about my nearly being dragged into the bushes by Savannah.

"I can't believe this chic is that nuts?"

I chuckled and answered, "You have no idea, but that's not the worst of it?"

"How so?" she asked.

"Have you heard that the school is putting on a production of Arsenic and Old Lace?"

"I think so."

"Well that's like one of my ALL TIME favorite movies and I want to play the lead role of Mortimer Brewster."

"Mortimer is a boy's name, isn't it?" she asked somewhat perplexed.

"Yeah, I know, but I already spoke to Mrs. Pagolini and she said the best actor/actress would win the role regardless of their gender. She even said that the script could easily be reworked to include a Morticia Brewster as opposed to a Mortimer."

"Why change it, I mean I think that's great and all but isn't that a bit silly. I mean it would be like if you wrote a book and then Hollywood wanted to make a movie about your novel and they decided for whatever reason to change you into a boy, wouldn't that suck?"

"Yes my dear Nicole, I mean Nicky, it would suck, especially since the boy they chose would have to play me with all my hormonal glory," I sighed and pressed on, "you're really missing the point," I said.

"Okay, so what's the point?"

"The point is Ms. Savannah also has set her sparkling little eyes upon this role and has been telling everyone who will listen that she is going to be the star of this production."

"Has she now?" Nicky asked.

"Yeah, so I have to figure some way to make sure I am better than she is."

"How are you going to do that? I mean, and please don't take any offense to this but she is waaay more popular than you are."

"I know that. Yet, I would be the better choice. I know every single line by heart, I have studied the various nuances each of the actors brought to their characters and I even spent three whole days of my Christmas vacation when I was seven "charging up San Juan Hill", like Teddy does throughout the film.

"Cool, although I don't know what San Juan Hill is. Caitlin, let's be honest, a great play is only great if it is enjoyed by many people. Someone could put on the absolute best rendition of 'High School Musical' but if no one shows; who knows? Savannah may not be as good as you are but her being in it will put a lot of butts in those seats."

"I never thought about it that way before. Her star power alone will boost ticket sales by an ungodly amount. I can see it now, all the boys that normally would avoid this production like the plague will suddenly be sitting there in the front row, salivating. God, what a nightmare. Well, maybe Mrs. Pagolini won't think of it?"

"Caitlin, if I thought of it, more than likely so will she."

I was fuming. I believe the expression was 'fit to be tied,' although I can't imagine the origins for this little quip that don't involve a straight jacket and a struggling person screaming some foul obscenities about their deep rooted hatred for dark haired divas from the south.

"Caitlin, you still there?"

"Yeah Nicky, I'm still here."

"Okay, thought I was talking to myself for a second there."

"I spaced. What were you saying anyway?" I was still locked deep in my thoughts of jealousy and pettiness. I should be willing to do what's best for this production, even if it means standing there while Savannah gets all the glory. Unfortunately, Quillerbee was attempting to corrupt my thoughts and drag me down a much darker path. I would have followed him willingly, cackling all the way when I heard five magical words slither into my ear through the speaker of my phone and save me. Those five words quite possibly, changed my life, forever.

"What did you say again?"

"Sounds like you need Ex-Lax."

"Ummmm, okay?"

The next day I found myself standing by my locker with my nerves in a complete jitter. I had been waiting for at least five full minutes for Nicky to arrive and still there was no sign of her. I knew Savannah would be walking by any minute and with today being the day of the school tryouts, our plan was looking more like a 'no go' every second that ticked away.

I forced myself to try and remain calm by utilizing the ancient oriental breathing technique known as "hyperventilation." It's a miraculous little body over mind exercise in which you let your entire being completely fill with endorphins (a chemical compound that enters your blood stream when you are excited or scared) so your heart rate increases to a full blown samba beat and then you allow all your fears and worries to settle firmly in your mind, which of course ends up making you forget to breathe. Soon the tell tale signs begin to occur: sweat, nausea, blurry vision, dry mouth and of course shortness of breath; the result is pure hysteria.

"Hey Caitlin."

"Where the hell have you been? I've been standing here for like an hour."

"Relax, and you have not been here an hour, your bus let off one in front of mine," she said in a rebuking sort of way.

"Is that them?" I asked while gazing on a plate of magnificent perfection. For in Nicky's small, lithe hands was a plate overloaded with a giant pile of fudge brownies. Each one had to be at least an inch and a half thick and two inches square. They looked fully cooked on the top but soft and gooey in the center. At least that's what they appeared to look like, displayed as they were under the semi-clear plastic film that covered them.

I grinned from ear to ear as she lifted one end of the wrap and let me sniff them. They smelled heavenly. As a girl, it is difficult to fully explain the allure of chocolate yet archeologists have discovered various rooms devoted to its worship in every matriarchal society that they have ever uncovered. Chocolate, to put it simply, is God's way of telling females that 'it's gonna be all right' and after getting a nose full of their exquisite aroma, I was fully prepared to believe him.

We laughed a bit and waited, knowing full well that our target would be arriving any minute. Unfortunately, we had to shoo away at least a dozen boys from our brown pile citing that they were for one of our teacher's birthdays, thankfully the ravenous hounds believed us.

Suddenly, the air horn the administration had chose as our hall bell sounded, indicating that we only had four minutes until we were expected in our homerooms. My eyes began scanning the hallway for a sign of the she devil. I knew she had to come passed us to get to homeroom, there was simply no way she could avoid our nefarious trap, unless . . . unless the stupid cow had overslept and caught a ride in with her mother. *Not today, please. Of all the days to be punctual, God let her be on time for this one. I know you can't openly take part in this plot but at least show me you understand why I am doing it even if you can't condone it.*

My sign appeared around the corner at that exact instance. I would never know if it was synchronicity that placed her so close to me. I thought through my prayer that day, or the hand of some higher power pushing her along but I knew at that precise moment, the universe wanted to see Savannah eat those brownies.

So, well rehearsed from the night before, Nicky set the trap, "No, Caitlin you can't have one of my aunt's award winning brownies, they're for the party."

"Come on Nicky, don't be a jerk just one. Who's gonna notice if one is missing?"

"I said no! We put a lot of work into these brownies I promised my aunt that no one would have one and I don't want to break my promise."

Savannah sauntered up and stopped in front of us, right on que. "What are you two going on about?"

Nicky immediately went into her shy mode as we discussed. Even though she wanted to help me, speaking to someone as popular as Savannah would have been completely out of character so I replied, "Nicole Pederson's aunt made these brownies and I wanted one but the little dweeb says she made a promise to her aunt not to give any out because they're for a teacher's birthday party or some dumb shit like that."

Nicky lowered her head and really turned it on. I mean she sunk all the way back into her shell, on purpose mind you but it was amazing to watch.

"God Caitlin," Savannah said, "with your lifestyle of sitting around doing a whole lot of nothing all day, plus with your oily skin problems its probably best if you don't have one." *Ah Savannah, how predictable you are . . .*

"Give me a break, she's not gonna give you a brownie Savannah, her aunt made her promise."

"Caitlin, you approach everything like the world owes you something. I totally understand why, what's your name again?"

"Nicole, Nicole Pederson," she whispered.

"You see Caitlin, Nicole can't just hand out brownies to everyone, especially people like you who would stuff it into your mouth and not even begin to appreciate the artistry that went into making such a delicious looking confection. I understand your plight, my mother won several baking competitions in Georgia and people were always asking to try her recipes. You're doin' the right thing by not giving in."

"Oh, please. Savannah you're just trying to weasel a brownie out of her by telling her that B.S. about your mom," I said.

"This is why you will never be an equal to me, Caitlin. I don't have to make shit up for people to like me, they just do."

I threw my hands high up in the air and shouted, "Give me a freakin break," and set off down the hall leaving Nicky to close the snare.

The exact conversation that transpired I will skip, I will share though that Savannah did in fact get not one, not two but three laxative filled brownies. Nicky then, threw the rest of them out as she quickly made her way to homeroom.

I saw Savannah several times throughout the day and I must admit that each time she appeared to look greener and greener. By noon I had heard rumblings (forgive the pun) that she had sequestered herself in the girl's lavatory and was in fact, reciting novenas and other prayers to make the cramping go away.

At twelve thirty I couldn't stand it anymore and had to see for myself if the rumors that had been running all over school that day were true. I raised my hand, received a hall pass from my math teacher and made a beeline for the girl's toilet hoping to catch a glimpse of Savannah's suffering, I was not disappointed.

"Wow, what's that smell," I announced as I stepped across the threshold and entered the small porcelain filled torture chamber, "did something die in here?"

"Caitlin . . . Caitlin is that you?" a pitiful voice weakly inquired from inside what has now become known now as "Savannah's Stall."

"Savannad? Od my gawd, whet's going one in dere?" I said, clutching my nose tightly with my left hand while wildly waving my right in front of my face to stop the fumes from burning my eyes out. I knew that no matter what transpired next, I had to maintain consciousness.

"T . . . he brown . . . . ies," she said stuttering.

"Whet bow-nies?

"Th . . . e brown . . . ies that dumb ass girl brought with her this mohhhhh."

"Dis whet?" I had to force myself not to laugh because as you all well know if you laugh while holding your nose shut you could blow your brains out through your eyes and end up very, very dead.

"Thi.sss MORNING!" She screamed and I saw in the gap between the floor and the door to her cubicle of pain her ankles and shoes lash about as another abdominal cramp tried to strangle her lower intestine.

"Od, dis morning. Wow, dey got you sick?" I asked innocently.

"Listen to me; I don't have much time left. I need you to get the school nurse, a cold compress and some ice water and bring them to me quickly before I dehydrate. Can you do that for me, please?"

"Wherd should I get the water frum? The foundin is not very cold. You wand me to try da cafederia?"

"Caitlin please, JUST GO GET THE NUUUURSE!"

"Oday, you wait righd dere, I'll be back."

I walked out into the hall and ran as fast I could, not to the nurse's office but to a safe place where I could laugh my head off. Thanks to Nicky I had finally gotten a small piece of revenge on my tormentor. I did eventually go for the school nurse and as I expected Savannah was sent home to recuperate. Two hours later, as the tryouts convened, I was the only logical candidate for the lead role and won it with ease. What can I say, friendship can be a wondrous thing.

CHAPTER SEVENTEEN

ALL THE WORLD'S INDEED A STAGE, AND THE WORLD SUCKS

S o over the next three months, right through Christmas and the winter break, things continued on as normal. By normal of course I mean normal for my family and me. Savannah had convinced Mrs. Pagolini to allow her to audition for the lead role but only as understudy. An understudy for those of you unfamiliar with the theater is someone who takes the lead player's place should they be unable to fulfill their obligation. As a wise man once rightfully said, 'The show must go on.'

Nicky and I stayed good friends but things did not go so well when I introduced her to some of the other girls. For whatever reason, they could not seem to handle her reluctant shyness and need for a certain amount of anonymity. I guess her mannerisms made some of the other girls feel like she was up to something, which of course was not true. Besides the brownie incident, Nicky has never, as far as I know, plotted to do harm to anyone. Hmmm, that doesn't sound so convincing when you factor in that I've only know her for about 3 months. Well, I still like her.

Craig and I still were not speaking, though I did get him a Christmas present. I don't know why I did, perhaps because in my subconscious I felt not everything that had transpired had in fact been his fault. Also, my dad had won an autographed football in a charity raffle and since we don't follow football, I convinced him to let me give it to Craig. Okay, in truth, the gift was marked from Nicole and me but I delivered it to his house. So there, you see I can be very mature when the mood hits me.

Mimi had gone back to Ireland a few weeks ago and finalized the construction and more recently, the interior design of the house. She had been sending pictures to us every couple of days via the internet and all I can say is, wow! The house was awesome but the land that it was built upon was simply, magnificent. Lush fields of green, rolling hills and off in the distance, mountains that seemed to reach out and touch the sky. I was so looking forward to going there on vacation this coming summer that I began a calendar counting down to the end of school and the start of our Irish expedition.

In the mean time though, I still was dealing with the Savannah/Nicole issue. I was forced to endure Ms. Summers' presence twice during the holiday break. Once at a Christmas party that her parents threw for all the neighbors and the other time when we all went out to a New Year's Eve party in which all the families of the neighborhood rented a hall and spent the evening supposedly enjoying each other's company.

We returned to school on the third week of January as a result of several large snowstorms hitting us one after another. That meant the school play was less than a month away. Fortunately for me, being such an avid fan of the movie, I needed little practice to make this role work. My fellow actors however, were, to put it nicely, hopeless; all except Savannah, that is. The chick could really act. I'm in no way saying she is better than me, not by a long shot but compared to any of the other people in the cast she was hands down superior. I spoke to Katrina about it over the phone one day and she actually made sense out of the whole situation.

"Quate-lin, lissen to me dhaling. The reason Savannah . . ."

"Aunt Katrina . . ."

"Yes?"

"Sorry to interrupt and I mean no disrespect, but how can you say Savannah properly and not get my name right, it's a bit frustrating," I asked.

"Vhat do you mean, I've never said your name wrong dhaling."

"Right, my bad, please continue . . ."

I heard her take a deep breath and hardened myself for another story about some relative with a fresh fruit disorder but was actually quite intrigued when she gave me this crucial insight into the mind of Savannah Summers. "Quate-lin, the reason dis girl can play sports, act, do yoga like a Zen Buddhist and affect all da boys with mind numbing stupidity is because . . ."

"She is perfect," I interrupted again.

"No, she is confident. Quate-lin, the reason successful people are successful is because in dere hearts dey believe in demselves and dere abilities. That is infectious my dhaling. Suddenly everyone else starts to see they can handle anything and then, they come to them to handle it. Savannah makes her own destiny, she does not vait for destiny to come to her. If she wants something, she goes out and gets it and people want her to do so because they see she believes she can get the job done."

"Hold on a second. This is the same message you and Santeria Maria gave me weeks ago but from a different angle, isn't it?"

"Yes dhaling, dis time though I hope you listen and believe us," she laughed and hung up the phone. I hate when adults point out that you have forgotten or misunderstood one of their life lessons.

I sighed and tried to convince myself that she was just a lovable nut job but the words kept haunting me over the next few days.

February was cold. How cold you wonder? Very. That's about all any of us who suffered through it could say. Even the weatherman was at a loss for words one morning when the anchor man asked him how cold it was going to be that day, he simply replied, "extremely."

And as fate would have it, I got a cold. Not just any cold mind you but the grand-daddy of them all. My nose was leaking snot so fast I went through a box of tissues on the very first day of the illness alone. The complete rag of this situation is as my cold worsened I had only three days to go until I was expected to be on stage for opening night. I took medicine both over the counter and homeopathic. I tried hot tea and honey for the sore throat and even listened to Katrina's advice about garlic and its amazing curative powers. I wish I had asked her to clarify though that it was the essence from whole garlic cloves that you are supposed to spread on your chest as opposed to chopped garlic from a jar. All I ended up doing was making my room smell like an Italian eatery and over the next several days having my mother and father laugh whenever I entered the room.

Two days from our big production and you guessed it, I broke out in a fever and was 'shackled' to my room. I was in hysterics as you can imagine. I had worked so very hard at this. I had spent years honing my skills hoping beyond hope that one day my school would actually do a play that didn't involve singing elves and a talking grasshopper. I had finally, with all my odd and offbeat luck, achieved a chance at stardom and now because someone up there finally decided to balance the books and found out about my sabotaging of Savannah I came down with a wicked cold and most assuredly lost my role as lead in the play.

The call from Mrs. Pagolini came at about three in the afternoon. She just wanted to check in on me and to see if I would be able to make it down to rehearsal. With a hundred and two fever there was NO way my mother was going to allow it.

I cried, I gurgled (since screaming was not easy with a sore throat) and I even offered to give her my left pinky finger as an offering to whatever demon god she served. Yes, I actually accused my mother of being in league with a nefarious underworld power. Well come on, wouldn't you in this situation. I mean she kept yelling at me that if I went out and tried to perform I would most likely end up with pneumonia. What a load of horse droppings. How bad can pneumonia be? I knew a real mom would have made some allowances for my condition and let me perform so therefore it must be an evil prince she was conspiring with to stop me.

Who the hell am I kidding? My mother would never have let me go out with a fever. *"DAMN MOTHERHOOD AND ALL ITS CODES OF ETHICS!"*

So I sat in my room and sulked and brooded which is a really effective combination. It helps you focus on all the crap that seems to be adding up in your life and then gives you the time to rationalize through it all to the most positive and efficient solution; which in this case was to lie on my bed, wipe my nose every three seconds and repeat the phrase, "my life sucks eggs" over and over again.

"Caitlin," I heard my mother's voice shouting from downstairs.

"Go away! Caitlin has taken an entire bottle of Nyquil and is on a merchant marine ship bound for Ecuador." I'm not sure why I picked Ecuador, it was just the first place that came to mind.

"Caitlin, it's the telephone for you, or should I just have the call forwarded to your south bound ship?"

"Very funny! I don't want to talk to anyone right now, tell them to go away."

"Sweetie, the cast is worried about you and they asked this person to call and check to see if you're okay," She yelled from the bottom of the stairs.

"Fine." I got up and went into the spare room which had a phone in it that had been installed for when Mimi came over. I was totally bundled up in my bedspread as I plopped my rear end down on the queen sized bed and picked up the phone."

"Hello," I said with a voice that sounded as pitiful as I felt.

"Caitlin, oh you sound dreadful."

Oh God, not now!

"Caitlin. Hello?"

"I'm here Savannah, what do you want?" There was enough venom in my voice to flatten a fully grown bull elephant.

"Want? Caitlin there is nothing you have anymore that I could possibly want. Why, now that I've got the lead in the play, I've pretty much got everything you could ever have desired," she replied.

"Well, that's just great for you. I hope you have a great time in MY role. You know the one I was picked for and you weren't. Remember that as you go on stage. That the entire school is coming to see the best production they can and unfortunately they're going to get you instead."

She chuckled slightly, "Oh, they will know they saw the best possible performance because Mrs. Pagolini herself said I brought a much more believable angle to the lead role. She even was kind enough to say I looked more natural up there on stage than you do, the cast of course was in full agreement."

I had taken enough and was not going to sit here and put up with anymore of her vicious shit, "Well, I am going to hang up now bitch, you take care and try not to get hit by a bus, okay?"

"Brownies."

I felt my stomach tighten, "What did you say?"

"I said, brownies. You know, those things you eat with milk and if you're not careful will end up making you stuck all day in the toilet wishing you have never been born." Her voice was dreadfully serious and I could tell that there was no avoiding the truth of it all. Somehow, she had discovered my secret. Even so I was not about to openly admit to my participation in the crime, well not yet anyway.

"What are you implying?" *Nice touch Caite. That sounded almost believable; maybe the nonchalant tone in your voice will throw her off the trail.*

"There is no implying here. You and your little toad poisoned me. My mother ran into Nicky's aunt about three weeks after the incident and she inquired about her 'famous' brownie recipe and guess what, the dumb bitch can't even bake."

Well there's a time and place for denial, this was not one of them, "You think that was poisoned? You have poisoned everyone, and I mean EVERYONE against me. You don't even have a good reason to hate my guts, you just do! So yeah, I had Nicky whip up some brownies and by chance you ended up crapping your brains out for a day or so. Well, guess what jack ass; that was a small price to pay for all the grief you've caused me! And now, by a poor stroke of luck I've even lost the school play to you. God I must be cursed."

There was another one of those dramatic pauses, the kind that make you realize the revelations are far from over. "Luck? You think it was bad luck that you caught a cold? Wow, you are stupid. I'll let you in on a little secret dweeber. You know Tim Shulic, don't you? Well I paid him ten dollars to sit behind you in every class he could last Friday. Wanna know why? Because he came to school that day feeling downright miserable, he even thought he might be sporting a fever. I know 'cause he told me so in homeroom. Now unless I'm wrong, you share four periods with him, don't you? Oh dear, imagine four periods of his fetid breath, oozing all over your neck, your jacket, your . . ."

I lost track of what she was saying. She continued to spew her vile thoughts and practices at me for about another minute or so before laughing and hanging up. I was at a loss. There is no way a person with any goodly convictions can stand against such vile and despicable evil. A thought hit me at that moment and it is one that I shall remember the rest of life. *You can't mud wrestle with Satan and possibly hope to win.*

As fate would have it, my fever broke the night before the school play and even though I was feeling much better the next morning I was allowed to stay home and relax. My father realized the stress I would have been under if I actually went into school that day and decided that no one should be made to deal with that. I was very thankful for his astute judgment. I was also thankful when my mother decided not to attend the school production even though Mrs. Summers called and asked if she needed a ride. She apologized and said she needed to be here for me but after Nicole begged and pleaded, she did accept her offer to give my sister a lift to and from the play so she could watch her very best friend in the whole wide world on stage.

The play was a huge success, so I was told. Nicole didn't mention it. In fact, she barely spoke when she got home from the play, she merely said good night to everyone and went upstairs to bed.

Unfortunately, when I got back to school the following Monday morning everyone was still talking about how funny and cool the whole story was. I avoided Savannah as long as I could but we finally ran into each other and when we did she laid into me with all the hatred and viciousness that she could. The encounter sent me home, physically ill from her string of insults. Some of the kids had even started a rumor that I made up being sick because I was terrified of being the lead in the play. Other kids actually said that Mrs. Pagolini had paid my parents to keep me home because I was so awful during rehearsals she was afraid I would ruin the performance. The dollar figure was from two hundred to a whopping thirty-five thousand dollars for my lack of participation. It's so easy for these kind of rumors to start and almost impossible to end them. If you argue, then they say it's because you're trying to cover it up. Say nothing and it's because you know that the so called truth has been uncovered and you're too embarrassed to argue about it. Either way, you lose.

And so, I went home after just one day of this assault and decided to prepare for a verbal challenge so intense I actually stayed up late into the night practicing my jabs. I had decided to stop running. Tomorrow, as the lunch bell rang I would become the hunter and she the prey. I would stop this once and for all. No prisoners, no excuses, no more fear.

Well there you have it. Now you know exactly how I ended up in the cafeteria crying my eyes out. Now you know just how evil Savannah Summers is and how I tried so very hard to not let her best me. Now you know why several really nice, funny, cute and soft spoken girls were driven to the brink of their limits and decided that violence was the only logical conclusion for dealing with this girl. They all agreed that she would never stop on her own and so they figured THEY would have to stop her, once and for all. There comes a time when it is better to face the terror than be consumed by it and that time was now.

CHAPTER EIGHTEEN

SISTERS

I got home from school that day and ran up to my room not wanting my father to see me like this. I shut the door over and threw myself on the bed and cried for at least another hour. How could Craig do this to me? I know he and I had broken up but to run to Savannah's arms was just unbelievable. It might have been true but it didn't seem like Craig. He may be a guy, but he was always a good guy. It hurt like hell to think of him possibly kissing her, holding her hand, sharing popcorn at a movie or a table at lunch.

I looked up at Kelsey and so wanted to talk to her but it would be hours before she was able to reach out to me. I felt very alone, very small and very, very meaningless.

My door opened and in stepped Nicole. I didn't want to hear her words right now nor did I want to see her face. "GET OUT!"

"Are you okay?"

"Do I look okay? Your best friend has just officially ruined my life. So NO, I am not okay," I shouted back

"That bad, huh? What happened?" She asked as she came into the room and shut the door over so as not to let our father hear my outburst she knew was coming.

"She stole my play, she stole my boyfriend, she tried to kill my dog, she ridiculed my twin and she stole YOU from me. She has humiliated me over and over again and my own sister is her best friend. HER BEST FRIEND!" I screamed with tears pouring down my face.

"Did you poison the brownies?" she asked flatly.

"What? How could you even worry about such a small freakin' thing like that? Didn't you hear me? She has ruined MY life!"

"I heard you, Caitlin and we will talk about it if you would just answer my question first. Did you poison the brownies she ate and please don't lie?"

"You little jerk! The only thing you are worried about is if that bitch got the runs? Well, guess what, I did poison her. I let Nicky put Ex-Lax into the brownies and then tricked Savannah to eat them so I was assured a chance at winning the lead role. There, are you happy?"

"Actually, no. On the way home from the play Savannah finally told me that you had tricked her with bad brownies and I said I didn't believe her. I defended you and actually got mad that she would accuse you of doing something so underhanded and despicable. But then her mother chimed in and said that she believed Savannah after running into Nicky Pederson and her aunt at the grocery store. Mrs. Summers thinks you're a lunatic and Mr. Summers wanted to call the police about what you did, because it was so downright mean. But I kept telling them, over and over again that you would never do that and look at what I find out. You did try to sabotage her. I can't believe I called my friend a liar over this and now I have to apologize to her because of you." She couldn't even look at me, she was so upset.

"Don't you even care about what she did to me?" I shrieked.

"Caitlin, how can I care about what she did to you when you don't even care about what your actions have done to me? Did it ever occur to you that she is my friend and that your petty jealousy might reflect on me and cost me the only best friend I have ever known? Through your whole speech it was my play, my boyfriend, my life. Well guess what, now my life is ruined as well, thanks to you. You never learn. You say you're sorry for acting so spoiled and petty and then two days later you're at it again. When will you learn it's not always about you? I'm tired of saying it, Craig's tired of seeing it, Dad's tired of dealing with it and Mom is just, tired. Grow up Caitlin, before everyone around you starts tuning you out."

"Nicole, I thought one day you would come to understand just how manipulative she is but you know what, the girls are right, the only way to deal with Savannah is to kick her freakin' ass . . ." I tried to stop myself but the words were already out of mouth, spoken in a moment of haste.

"What? Caitlin, what did you say?"

"Nothing." I wasn't about to discuss this any further with my nine year old sister.

"Caitlin this is wrong, this is so very wrong." Nicole burst from my room and dashed next door into the spare bedroom and grabbed the phone. Part of me wanted to stop her. Part of me though, wanted Savannah to know exactly what was coming; to agonize over it, to feel the same level of dread that I tend to feel on a regular basis. I was not to get my wish though, less than a minute later Nicole was standing in my doorway, her eyes empty and her face devoid of color. Her hands were clenched and she was visibly shaking.

"She won't come to the phone. Her mother said not to call back. She wouldn't listen to me, she just politely told me to go away. Are you happy now? I don't know what you're planning Caitlin but I hope to god that I don't lose MY sister tomorrow like I just lost my best friend today." And with that, she was gone.

CHAPTER NINETEEN

THE TRAP IS SET

Wednesday morning found, Kirsten, Melanie, Danielle and even Nicky Pederson huddled around my locker trying to act as normal as possible. I was shocked when I saw Nicky there but Melanie had called her at home the night before and told her their idea about ambushing Savannah and she had agreed to help. Since Savannah had discovered the brownies were laced with Ex-Lax she had been terrorizing Nicky during the school day, spreading rumors, having boys tease her, pointing out her general discomfort of being around other people while in class and even bullying her in the girl's locker room. Nicky, like the other girls had taken all they were going to take.

"So here's the plan," Danielle said, "There is an away game coming up next Monday against Ashton Vale High School. Ms. Freakin' Perfect and her squad of prima donnas will be there, of course cheering on the boy's basketball team. Our job is to lure her out into the parking lot early and then jump her."

"How are we going to do that?" Nicky asked.

"With bait," Danielle replied.

"Like we could tell her someone is giving away free donuts outside and then build this really cool wooden donut stand and Nicky you could put on like this fake moustache and talk with a heavy accent saying, 'Fresh DOOO Nuts.'"

"Melanie! No," Danielle interjected.

"Sorry, I just love donuts," she giggled and smiled.

"I was talking about the other kind of bait. What does Ms. Summers love more than anything else?"

Voices began to rapidly, albeit softly, throwing out answers to this inquiry as if they were playing on a game show, "Clothes, hairstyles, skinny jeans, fondue, gum, expensive shoes, kittens, jocks?"

"Exactly, jocks," Danielle grinned and continued, "and especially older jocks."

Again, Melanie felt that she was on to a great idea and thought the rest of us should be sharing in her epiphany, "Oh what a great idea Danielle. We could tell Savannah that Mr. Reese the basketball coach is looking for her outside cause he has a crush on her. That will so totally work!"

All eyes went to Melanie and I can tell you without a shadow of a doubt that they were all filled with the same sense of horror that you might encounter if someone with a chainsaw ran into a car dealership screaming, 'It's judgement day!'

"Melanie," I whispered, "Mr. Reese is like fifty years old and married. That's just creepy."

"Oh damn, I forgot he was married. Okay, we need to pick someone else," she agreed.

Danielle had heard enough, "Melanie, for the remaining two minutes we have before the homeroom bell goes off, you are not allowed to speak. I was talking about a senior, someone with a hot new car."

Nicky jumped in, "Oh you mean, Steve Evans. His parents just bought him a brand new Dodge Charger. God, he's sooooo dreamy. I mean, did you guys know he can bench almost two hundred pounds and holds three school records. One, for the longest pass completion from the line of scrimmage, the second for the most completed passes in a season and third for the most touchdown passes in a career. He is even going to Boston College on a scholarship, so he can stay close to his family. He attends church every Sunday at Saint Judith's Episcopal where he was an altar boy until a year ago and now he is a reader helping with the masses. Oh and get this, his dog is a sheltie named Beeboo, and he has a 3.58 GPA."

I blinked. She knew more about Steve Evans than my mom did about Brad Pitt and that's pretty downright spooky.

"Do you know his bicep measurements as well?" Kirsten laughed.

"Seventeen and a half inches," she replied nonchalantly.

The warning bell sounded and we each had exactly ninety seconds to reach our homerooms. We agreed that a note would be used to draw her outside for a ride in his new car and once there she would be alone and easy pickings. More of the finer details would be discussed after school at four o'clock in the public library which was located more or less centrally between us all. And so I parted ways with my co-conspirators, already getting butterflies in my stomach as my mind filled with images of Savannah lying on the ground sporting a battered ego and a few bruises thanks to my crew. How could I have ever guessed that the actual encounter with Savannah would lead us all down a path that was far, far more terrible than a simple bloody nose?

CHAPTER TWENTY

A HOSTILE REUNION

I got home from school to an empty house. *That's right, it's Wednesday and that means dad is in the office today working on his assignments for the next weekend edition of the globe.*

So, I grabbed the purple leash from in the kitchen and hooked up Dog for his afternoon walk. He did his business rather efficiently which meant that the little mooch was looking for a cookie. We went back inside, shut over the door, I unleashed him and reached for his treat jar and threw him a bacon flavored Milk-Bone. As far as Dog was concerned, all was right in the world.

I poured myself a glass of orange juice and added a single cube of ice. I love the taste of OJ, as long as it's pulp free and thoroughly chilled. Oh, and it has to be Tropicana or else forget it. And, it has to be from the upper half of the carton. I mean, the upper half is where the water rests while the heavier, denser fruit juice sort of stays on the bottom. So yeah, upper half is good, lower half not so much. *I'll never understand why my parents say that I am high maintenance. Odd, isn't it?*

I looked up at the clock and saw that Nicole was due in the house in about thirty minutes so I went back outside for a minute and grabbed the mail from our mailbox at the end of the driveway. I brought it back in and plopped down at the kitchen table. I was flicking through the mail very much in a moment of zen when I got a weird nagging feeling at the back of my mind. I'm sure you've experienced that twitch or tingle that reminds you that you are missing a key detail to some forgotten puzzle. It was all rather irritating. I sat there sipping my juice and contemplating why I was so preoccupied with any other details beyond the fact that the girls and I were meeting at the library in about an hour to discuss the . . . *OH SHIT!*

How could I have been so stupid? Dad and mom are both at work and Mimi is in Ireland. Flip me! *Okay, okay Cailtin, think . . . think. I can't call Craig's mom because Craig is a fart sucking, donkey faced, spineless freak who thinks it's perfectly okay to do a topographical survey of my worst enemy's mouth. I can't ask Mrs. Pederson to drive me because she works, oh and I have Nicole to look after. There is NO way mom or dad would agree to allow me to leave Nicole home alone or ask one of the other moms to drive me and watch my sister. Who would mom and dad allow to come over while they aren't home and watch . . . Katrina. Oh lord, please, please let this be as painless as possible.*

I would still have to get permission from my parents to be allowed to go to the library with her. Unless, I worked it just right . . .

I grabbed the phone off its charger on the kitchen wall and quickly dialed Auntie Kat. This was going to take absolute precision and even a possible jedi-mind trick.

"There he goes again, da poor thing. Hullo Quate-lin Dhaling."

"Hi Auntie, how are you?" I beamed.

"I am vell dhaling. I just got done doing a few readings from this morning and I am feeling a bit thin, but udder den dat I am vell. So, vhat do I owe da pleasure of dis call?"

"Ummm, I was checking to make sure you were going to be on time," I said.

"On time? On time for?" She asked obviously perplexed by the question.

I replied, "For taking Nicole and I to the Library, to get those books on Hungarian Folk tales that we spoke about a few days ago."

"I don't, I mean, did ve speak of such things?"

"You mean you didn't get the dream transmission that I sent you last Thursday? I did it just like you told me and I even got a confirmation number and wrote it down when I woke up like you instructed me to do."

"Oh, I see. I just need a moment dhaling to recall the message."

I grabbed a pad of paper from our junk drawer and rustled the pages a bit and then added, "Here we go, the number you gave me in my dream was, AK21657. AK—Aunt Katrina, right?"

"Yes, yes dat vould make sense for a shared dream confirmation; ah, here I remember now of course, you and Nicole need to go to da library for books on Hungarian Folk tales, da, da I remember. I vill be dere shortly dhaling. You and Nicole be ready? Was I taking you for dinner afterwards as well?"

I couldn't drop the burden of paying in her lap on short notice, that just felt wrong so I said, "No, no remember, you are having dinner here with us when we get back. I hope that part of my dream message wasn't garbled?"

Her voice perked up, "Dhaling you are a young mystic. An incomplete dream share is not uncommon. Give yourself time, you are already doing quite vell. I am getting my coat and I vill be on my vay. Let me hang up Quate-lin, please. My poochie is tearing at his backside so franticly that it looks like a scene from a bad zombie movie." The phone went dead.

Now, all I had to do was convince my parents that they had somehow forgotten that Katrina was coming to dinner. Succeed and I would have pulled off the most amazing bait and switch of all time.

Knowing my parents, I figured my father was the best choice for this little operation based on two very important reasons:

1) He is used to working at home most of the time. That means on the one day when he is in the office he is usually very busy with meetings and stressed out. Any phone call I make will only be half-listened to.
2) He is not a mother.

"Hi dad," I said in my most cheerful voice.

"Hey Cate, what's up sweetie?"

"Dad, I know you are busy and all . . ."

"No, Caitlin don't worry. My meetings are done for the day, as a matter of fact I was just getting packed up and heading home."

Can anything ever go smoothly? I quickly regrouped, "Dad, don't forget to stop off at the store and pick up the stuff we need for dinner tonight, Aunt Katrina's coming over."

"Tonight? Okay sweetie, I'll get some stuff for a salad, mom took out a London Broil, right?"

I covered the phone's microphone so he could not hear my joyous exhale, "Yeah, I'll make sure to put it back in the fridge before she gets here to run me over to the library with Nicole. She has been so looking forward to going there."

"Okay, Caite. Make sure though that your homework is finished and the living room is picked up, understood?"

"Yep, I'm on it." We hung up and I did the dance of joy through the kitchen. I was so elated to have made this work. Now, I had a ride to the library, a gang of girls ready to help me enact revenge, my favorite family dinner being made tonight by my father and a highly evolved nine year old sister tagging along to potentially ruin the entire scheme.

I frantically began working on my homework while simultaneously trying to concoct a third fabulous story about why Katrina was coming to our house for Nicole. I had to make sure when she saw the other girls in the library she didn't begin to get suspicious. *Got it. I'll tell her that we are working on a fund raiser for unfortunate weiner dogs. No, she would only ask to get involved. It has to be something like that, without it being like that.*

Minutes ticked away. Sweat formed. Headache began. Throat went dry and my palms began to itch. How on earth could I be more afraid to face my little sister than my own father? *Oh, that's right, it's Nicole.*

The front door opened and in she stepped. Her backpack slung over her shoulder the same as gunslinger from the old west would carry a saddlebag. She then kicked her sneakers off while placing her burden in the foyer. She looked tentatively down the hallway before making her way towards me.

"Hey Boo," I greeted.

"Hi sis," she responded as she made her way towards the pantry and grabbed three chocolate chip cookies. When it comes to the cookie, Nicole had decreed years ago that the number to be consumed during an after school snack was three. Of course, you were allowed special dispensation for crappy days or on days when it rains, or when there was a gibbon moon, or if Dog has to go walkies more than once after he ate, or if dad has a glass of lemonade, etc, etc. Listen, stop laughing, these are chocolate chip cookies we are talking about; rules are allowed to be broken.

"Don't get too comfortable Boo, Auntie Kat is coming over to take us to the library."

"Oh, really, what for? She asked.

I involuntarily stammered, "For? What for, you ask?"

"Yeah," she replied, as she balled her hands into tight little fists and rested them on her hip.

"Why, to spend some time with Aunt Katrina and of course allow her the opportunity to introduce us to her ancestor's in the newly renovated Hungarian Cultural Wing at our library.

"They have a wing?"

"Yes," I said, nodding probably more than was necessary while scratching my head, "that is my understanding." I was happy to see that she believed me. In fact, we began talking about how excited we were to be seeing Craig's crazy aunt again, who could have known Craig was also being included in this covert field trip thanks to a head's up from his Aunt. I think my expression said it all as they pulled up in the car and I saw Brutus sitting there. (My apologies for the gratuitous Shakespearian reference.)

"My god you guys, will you please stop sitting there like two irate babies. Okay, so neither of you had any idea that the other one was going along, can't you at least act civil for the hour or so we are all going to be together?" Nicole said as she spun around in the front seat to admonish both Craig and I.

When I had climbed in the back of the car twenty minutes ago, I had not expected to find my ex sitting there. I could tell by the expression on his face that he was as annoyed as I was for not being told about the others participation in this little field trip.

A thousand questions and probably twice that many comments passed through my mind as I stared out the gigantic passenger side window that dominated my entire field vision. Ironically, if you asked me to describe a single thing I saw while glaring through that piece of glass I, even now, could not. So incensed was I by Craig's mere presence that I was unable to focus on anything else. I was livid, ticked off, enraged, infuriated and in a way relieved. Yes, I said relieved. Why, you ask? Well I thought that would have been fairly obvious, Craig was still alive and that meant that all the terrible and cruel thoughts I had been having over the last several days had not caught up with him and somehow initiated a series of events that caused him any physical or emotional scars. It also meant I had not been robbed of the chance to kill him myself at some later date.

"Nicole is right dhalings. Da two of you are acting like children. Ve are like family da four of us. Quate-lin, are you happier now dat Craig is out of yer life and not acting like a stooped boyfriend anymore?"

"Absolutely," I answered, flexing the muscles in my forearms which in turn tightened them even more across my chest. If body language could in fact be interpreted mine at that moment said, 'I am sitting next to a leper who just tried to play footsie with me while I was wearing open toe sandals.'

I saw her try to peek at us in the rear view mirror as she asked, "And Craig, are you not at least satisfied knowing that Quate-lin is at least happy, even if that means without you in her life?"

"Yeah, I mean who wouldn't want to see their friend happy. I mean, I don't know why she is so mad at me but if this is how she wants it, I'm cool."

"Excellent, den everyone is exactly getting vhat dey vant. So, now I ask like Nicole did, vhy da long faces if you both are happy?"

As if in unison, our heads shifted so that we were both glaring directly at the back of her head and if it were at all possible, laser beams would have shot out and burned four small pin sized holes into her skull. Craig and I said nothing, we just sat there.

"Right den," she gave Nicole a brief smile and continued to make her way towards our destination and my meeting with destiny.

CHAPTER TWENTY-ONE

THE SOUL PATROL RETURNS

We arrived five minutes late but having been driven there in Aunt Katrina's car I considered any journey completed with all my limbs intact, a good one. I climbed out of the 'spacious' back seat and without saying another word walked into the single level brick building. I was holding my breath, hoping beyond hope, that the girls had showed and if they did, they had been patient enough to wait for me. I was not to be disappointed. They were all there and better yet, they all broke out in big huge smiles as I approached the table where they had all gathered.

"Awesome, you're here. We were beginning to think you had chickened out," Danielle said.

"Danielle, why the hell would I chicken out of seeing the beast of the apocalypse slapped around and made to pay for her crimes," I responded as I took my seat.

"Okay, so here's what we've come up with . . . wait a minute, why the hell is Craig here?"

"Sorry about that. I forgot my dad is in the office on Wednesdays so I had to bum a ride with Craig's Aunt. It was the only way I could get here. Oh, and my sister is here as well." Craig waved from the main entrance to the rest of the girls sitting at the table. Aunt Katrina and Nicole came in behind him and together the three made their way towards the table that was used for the catalog computers.

All the girls were a bit taken back by this situation but no one as much as Danielle. "So, let me get this straight. You brought Savannah's boy friend AND her best friend along to a secret meeting where we are plotting to kick her ass?"

"Caitlin, that was brilliant. I mean with Craig here he can vouch for us all and be our alibi." Melanie explained.

"No Mel he can't. When Savannah wakes up, if she wakes up, I don't want her telling Craig that a GROUP of girls jumped her. Don't you think he might remember seeing us all sitting here like this, I mean come on, where's your head!" Danielle's voice was getting louder even though she was trying to speak in a low and effectively intimidating growl.

"What you mean, if she wakes up?" Nicky asked.

Danielle leaned in, "Let me ask you morons a question, what are you hoping happens that night? Each of us gets a chance to smack her on the hand and say 'Stop harassing us you bitch?' Do you honestly expect her not to fight back? Knowing Savannah and our luck she is probably a grand master at some ancient form of kung fu."

"She does practice Tai-Chi."

"Exactly Caitlin; all the more reason to make sure that when we do this, we do it right. I for one, am taking no chances. I plan on bringing an aluminum bat with me."

Everyone's face simultaneously went bleach white. I was not prepared for that kind of a revelation at the meeting.

"Why are you all looking at me like my head just came off? This isn't a gathering of the 'I hate Savannah Summers Club.' We came here to stop this shit from happening to any of us again. Nicky, aren't you tired of being picked on?"

"Yeah, but . . ."

Danielle refused to be derailed, "Melanie, how many times does this creep have to call you stupid and belittle every single thing you do or say in class?"

Melanie reminded her, "I would like it to stop, sure, but Danielle you are talking about bringing a baseball bat to confront a single girl. There are five of us."

"And not one of us is trained on how to protect ourselves. Guys, get a grip. Let's go about this from a different angle, okay? What if she turns us all in for assault? Are you ready to go to juvee? Are you ready to have it on your permanent record? Well, that is why I am bringing the bat. No one is going to pin this on me. Remember, she pressed our buttons, she started it. Now we put it to bed once and for all. We have to be committed or else she will win and will be laughing at us from in front of steel bars we are sitting behind. That's why the bat. I don't want her telling the police, anything, ever."

"Danielle, come on no one hates Savannah as much as I do but a bat seems a bit over the top." I said.

"Danielle, when did you become so angry at Savannah? I mean what the hell has she ever done to you?" Kirsten asked.

"What she did to me is not the point but yes Kirsten I do have a good reason to hate Savannah. More importantly, what we are going to do is send a message to every other bitchy, spoiled, pretty, little rich girl who thinks that because her parents have money she can act any way she damn well pleases and get away with it. Someone has to teach her and her brother a lesson."

"Her brother, what does Stephen have to do with this?" I asked, hurriedly.

"Nothing, everything, damn it, just forget I mentioned it. The only thing that matters right now is whether or not we are in or out." It was clear that Danielle was deeply hurt by some grievance that the Summers' had perpetrated against her at some point over the last six months. Although, I couldn't imagine what it could have been to make her this upset.

If I had only known, I more than likely would have tried to get Danielle some help and not followed her down this dark and terrible path of revenge. My berating at the hands of Savannah had set off in her a monster that wanted nothing more than to destroy the very evil that had created it. We were all perched precariously on the edge of a cliff and one more move might surely send us all tumbling down into a hellish future that included the loss of innocence, self respect, family, friends and freedom.

I can't even begin to explain to you the level of fear that began to worm its way in to my chest. Were we all really going to take this as far as putting her in the hospital? Were the other girls ready to carry out a vendetta to this level and if they were, were they doing it just for me?

"You said there was a whole wing," my sister's voice chirped, startling me and the other four girls huddled around the oak reading table. "But there isn't. Aunt Katrina doesn't even remember asking us to come here Caitlin. She said she felt bad not being able to recall your dream message or whatever the heck she called it. What are you up to, inquiring minds want to know?"

"Nicole, please find some place to get lost won't you? The girls and I are busy at the moment and don't need you hanging all over us asking stupid questions."

My co-conspirators nodded and gave her dirty looks. It was quite obvious to my intellectually sophisticated younger sib that bad things, dark secret things, were being discussed and she was not intended to hear them.

She tilted her head slightly to the side and refused to move a muscle. This was a particularly deadly pose that she inherited from my mother. It alerted me to the fact that she was 'on to me.' Nicole had put together the fact that my comments from the previous day about her best friend needing a butt kicking from 'the girls' was a fore-shadow of this very meeting. I had brought along Sherlock Holmes to a crime scene and I was still carrying the lead pipe that had been used in the gruesome murder. What a stroke of genius.

"Girls, we better call this a day. She is not going to go away."

"Then you take her out of here but I did not ride my bike all the way out here to have your sister screw up our chance at getting this done."

I couldn't believe what Danielle was saying. She was actually dismissing me from the revenge plot. She was going to go through with this whether I agreed to it or not. As a matter of fact, I began to get this suspicion that my consent meant nothing at all. Danielle was going to get Savannah even if she had to do it alone.

I took Nicole by the hand and led her away from the table. I could tell that the others were almost as nervous, almost as scared as I was. To see such a need for violence in someone's eyes like I saw in Danielle's was not only troubling, it was downright horrifying. She was possessed and her ability to rationalize the brutal beating of another person seemed almost too easy, too simple.

We found Craig and Aunt Katrina over by the non-fiction section looking up books on Russian history. When she saw me leading Nicole and the expression on my face, it was like that ancient Chinese dude said, 'a picture is worth a thousand words' and the words Katrina read were no good.

"Quate-lin, is everything all right dhaling?"

"No, can we go please? I have to get home as soon as we can and get dinner started."

"But of course, dhaling. Craig and I von't be much longer. If you vant you can vait for us here or out in da car, we just have to check out a few books that ve found."

Nicole and I chose to wait out by the Pacer. I was actually surprised she said nothing as we stood there. I am constantly amazed at my sisters ability to transcend years of time and somehow insert herself as my mother or at least the voice of my mother whenever I am doing something with which she strongly disagrees.

Aunt Katrina and Craig came outside only a few minutes later and we all piled into the car. Katrina inserted the key, and giving it a good hard turn, beckoned the beast to life. She took a moment to collect herself before placing her hand on the gear stick preparing to fight the transmission into reverse. "So, are ve all ready den dhalings?"

"Caitlin and her friends are planning to beat up Savannah," Nicole flatly announced.

"What? Vhat?" Craig and Katrina asked in unison.

"Caitlin and her cronies are planning to beat Savannah up."

"Quate-lin," she said, "is dis true?"

I had a choice to make. I knew that my melodrama had put most of those girls at that table. All perhaps except Danielle. She was there for her own reasons and was likely using me and my influence over the other girls as a rally cry for a deed she had been plotting for some time now. If I say no that it was not true, Katrina would believe me and I would buy the girls enough time to most likely pull off the attack. If I said yes, I would be breaking their trust but more importantly I would be spitting in the face of their friendship. They had come to my aid in a moment of crisis. Even if they were being somewhat misled down a darker path, Savannah did need to be dealt with. She had done so much damage; caused so much pain for myself and my friends. How could I possibly let her continue to get away with it? In many television shows they show a tiny devil on one shoulder and an angel on the other. They show these Christian symbols whispering in your ear offering advice both good and bad, leaving you the pawn in between to make the appropriate choice. Those shows are all B.S. There was no devil telling me what to do or an angel preaching forgiveness. Nope. But I can tell you what I did see. I saw Craig kissing Savannah. I saw Nicole handing her the infamous puck. I saw as clear as day, her laughing in my face after tricking me into believing that I was about to be sexually assaulted. I saw all of these things and more. I saw rock gardens, voodoo dolls and her grinning maniacally as she went on stage as Morticia Brewster.

"Nicole God, quit being so dramatic, that's not like you. They said they would like to kick her butt. They would never do it though. Girls don't do crap like that, at least not here in Braintree." I could tell that Craig and Katrina were not entirely convinced so I added laughing, "I mean could you imagine me in a fight? I have never hit anyone in my entire life."

"That's a lie." Nicole said.

"No it's not. They are NOT going to attack Savannah, Nicole you heard wrong!" I yelled back.

"I meant that you have never hit someone, you hit me at the wake remember."

"Yes, I remember," I said trying to pull in my reaction, "I meant someone outside the family."

"Why doesn't family count? I would think if you hit a perfect stranger it's bad but smacking someone you love is far, far worse, isn't it Auntie?"

"Okay. You're right. But we are not planning on attacking Savannah Summers, honestly. I give you my word."

Katrina nodded and Craig spun back around facing the windshield once again. A few moments and a couple of Hungarian swear words later and we were on our way home. Now before you condemn me for this action, put yourself in my shoes, would you have acted any differently? Sure, you all can say you might have, reading this from the safety of your own bed or chair. But, how many times did you make a bad choice or follow your friends because of peer pressure? It's not easy being a teen, especially an emotionally stressed teen with a messed up family and a ghost in her bedroom.

We pulled in the driveway and emptied out of the car. Craig waved goodbye, spoke a moment to his aunt and then made his way home. Nicole and I entered the house in silence to find dad already busy cooking. Aunt Katrina came in and shut the front door behind her. I said hello to Dog. Nicole brooded and my mother finally came home in time to eat dinner and tell us how bad her day was.

The meal was good, more than good, actually. One benefit of having a father who occasionally rates food places for his column is that he brings home all kinds of scrumptious recipe ideas for us to try.

After dinner Nicole fed Dog and within ten minutes, as was usual, he had to go outside for his after dinner drop off. I put my coat on, flipped on the patio lights and as I began to slide open the door was surprised to see Aunt Katrina also reaching for her coat. More surprising even than that, she followed me out into the cold night air and slid the door shut behind her.

"Ouf, dis is cold. Not as cold as Siberia of course, but cold nonetheless. Quate-lin, I think you know that ve need to talk, yes?"

"Yeah Caite, what's really going on?" Craig came around the side of the house, bundled up like we were.

"What the hell are you doing here?" I asked curtly.

"Aunt Kat sent me a text message a few minutes ago that Nicole was feeding Dog. Knowing his need for an evening walk right after he eats, I made my way here to discuss this whole Savannah thing."

"You want to talk about Savannah. Really, Craig? Really?" Dog tried to run over to Craig and say hello but I pulled him back and refused to allow him to get any closer to the traitor.

"Ya know, you've been a real psycho these last few months. I tried to talk to you. To repair the damage that happened to us but you've wanted no part of me," he was intent on pressing the issue and so I let him. "And now we find out that you are planning to attack Savannah, come on Caite, this isn't you?"

I shot back, "Isn't me, huh. Well I guess you don't know me as well as you think you do. Guess that makes us even, 'cause I never thought you would fall for Savannah!"

Katrina said nothing, just stood there listening, watching the argument I am sure she knew was months overdue. "Fall for Savannah? Well, its official, you've gone nuts. Auntie Kat, I'm sorry this has gone too far. I don't have to listen to this crap."

I raised my voice, which was no big deal considering I was a professional shrieker, "Don't you dare deny it! You made out with Savannah after a basketball game a week ago didn't you, cheater?"

His eyes rolled up, "Hey nut job, I can't cheat. We are not going out anymore remember?"

Tears began to form in my eyes. I was surprised how much this conversation was hurting, "So you're not denying it? You did make out with her?"

"Yes. We kissed."

"Craig, vhy?" Katrina asked.

"I don't know; curiosity I guess. She made a move and I let her kiss me. But we didn't make out. It was a kiss, that's all." He stood there defiantly, unwilling to take the blame for his scandalous behavior with my worst enemy.

"So why did you feel the need to tell that bitch about Kelsey? Why in god's name did you tell her about our dead sister, huh Craig? To show her just how screwed up the O'Connor's are? To laugh it up and give her more friggin' ammunition against me! Jesus, like this whore doesn't have enough to hurt me with already?" I unleashed my fear, my guilt and sadness. It felt good to get it out even though it tasted like crap as the words left my mouth.

"It wasn't like that Caitlin," he replied.

The back door slid shut and standing there was Nicole in her pink coat holding Kelsey in her hands. I quickly wiped the tears from my eyes and tried to sniff away some of the leakage back into my nose.

"Nicole, go back inside please," Craig pleaded.

"You said, our sister," Nicole's eyes locked on me for the first time in nearly eight months with an emotion other than disdain on her face.

"Nicole dhaling, perhaps it is best that ve go back inside. This conversation is going to get a bit uglier I fear, before it gets better. Come dhaling," and she moved to whisk Nicole back inside the house.

I felt that it was important for my sister to hear the truth finally from someone elses mouth, "Wait. Let her stay. I want her to hear this."

"Savannah was planning a few months ago to get you back for the whole brownie thing. She came to me and told me about this plan to frighten you with more of that voodoo stuff that she and her brother had you believing. When I asked her not to retaliate like that, she wanted to know why she shouldn't. I was trying to protect you from more of her crap that's all. So, I told her about the tragedy of Kelsey. I never meant to tell her about the ghost, I swear it. But after not telling anyone, it was hard to keep it all in. She seemed genuinely shocked and concerned for you. She even let it go, told me that she wouldn't try anymore crap. If I knew then that she was going to use the information to hurt you even more I never would have told her."

Surprisingly, it was Nicole that spoke first, "Craig, you broke a major rule of the Patrol. You should know better. It makes sense now why Savannah asked me if I had another sister beside Caitlin. She was testing me, testing to see if you were telling the truth. All so she could throw it in Caitlin's face at some point."

No one moved. We all just stayed where we were except Dog who was determined to try to find a piddle spot, which he did.

The oldest of us spoke first, "And so you enlisted the help of some of Savannah's other enemies and decided to take fate into your own hands?"

"Yes."

"Vell. The first thing is that I think ve can agree that ve need to start treating each other vith more love and respect. The more I learn about dis girl the more I see that most of vhat has caused us all to become estranged are merely moments of poor communication and a lack of trust. We are all members of da Patrol, Nicole is right. Ve need to be honest vith each other and stand united.

Nicole was the next to break the silence, "Caitlin, I won't let you do this. I won't let you go ahead and attack Savannah."

"I know Boo, she's your friend . . ."

"No, she is a human being but more than that, you are my sister. I don't want you getting into trouble and possibly going to jail."

I smiled at her, the first honest smile I had shown her since she discovered I had been seeing Craig behind her back.

"So den ve have a problem on our hands. Ve have to stop the other girls from going through vith dis plan or else it will come out dat Quate-lin was involved."

"You mean guilty by association?" Her nephew asked.

"No dhaling, I mean guilty because the other parents to protect dere children vill claim that Quate-lin vas the mastermind behind the whole sordid affair."

"Who said anything about stopping this? I'm not so sure I don't want to see her with a few teeth missing, especially now that you all are beginning to see just how manipulative this chic has been."

"Have you not been listening?" Craig blurted out, "You can't just attack someone because you're pissed off at them. No one wins if you're blamed for all of this mess."

"Sissie, do you honestly think Kelsey would agree with what you're thinking about doing? Would she be proud of us right now? Or is she watching us, sad that her memories of how we used to be are so much better than the behaviors we are showing her now. Haven't we learned anything by losing her? Haven't we talked about how precious life is and how each day is so special? And here we are Sis, about to let a girl get beat up all because she's a pest? This isn't us Sissie, this isn't you."

"I agree Quate-lin. Much of vhat you have done is based on love for your sisters and your family. You can not allow dis. I already know that you have concluded in your own heart dis is wrong."

I sighed, "So, even if I'm not there but I let this thing go off, I'm screwed. Because let me tell you, Danielle is not going to stop. She is determined to punish Savannah."

"Then we have to stop her Caitlin," Craig said.

"Oh really? Why, so Danielle can come after me? Guys if I double cross her she and the others will never forgive me. I don't need to swap one jerk for four new enemies. If they are this ready to grab Savannah, imagine what they will do to the one who tips her off and betrays them?"

"Quate-lin is right, Craig. If she vere to do dis thing who knows how bad it vould be for her. No, none of you can make dis happen vithout facing terrible repercussions. An adult must do it and in such a vay that Savannah believes da threat is real but not so dangerous as to tell her parents or da authorities. It must be me. I vill warn her. Quate-lin, tell me vhat they are planning and I vill get the information to Savannah."

"No Aunt Katrina, I have to do this myself somehow. I can't let you get involved, not to mention the fact that she barely knows you and probably wouldn't believe you . . ."

"Vhat? Vhat is it?"

"I know a way to warn Savannah and make her leave me alone all at the same time." I started to laugh hard. It was almost mystical watching my breath freeze into the night air and hover around me like some aura of spiritual energy. It then slowly snaked its way around my head giving my idea almost a life of its own, as if my thoughts had taken physical form.

"Caitlin, how the hell are you going to do that?" Craig asked, while Nicole and Katrina stood there looking completely confused.

"That's easy. Nicole is going to give her a present."

CHAPTER TWENTY-TWO

EYES WIDE OPEN

I knew the plan was risky. I knew it could affect the rest of my life in such a way that I would never be able to repair the damage. On the other hand, I had to do something. Time was running out for my both my friends and Savannah.

Nicole and I rehearsed the drill about fifty times between Thursday morning and Friday afternoon. She knew her lines and understood how important it was for Savannah to honestly believe my little sister was sorry for disagreeing with her assessment of my mental state. Nicole was ready to agree with the Summers' that I was a lunatic who needed some serious counseling. It was all part of my plan.

We were sitting in Nicole's room with the finely wrapped box between us. I smiled at her and she hesitantly smiled back.

"It's gonna be okay Boo," I reassured her.

"What if something happens to it? Caitlin, I would never forgive myself for letting you talk me into this. You know what, no. I can't do this, there has to be another way Caitlin, please."

"Nicole, you said so yourself the other day. Savannah doesn't want to talk to you right now. If she won't believe you, how the hell would she ever believe me? This is our best chance. You have to trust me Boo."

"And you honestly think you can reach her bedroom before something dreadful happens and we lose it?"

"Yep, Craig will be there to help me climb the tree and get to her window in time. He is going to tell her that he wants her back, and is going to stop by for a late night kiss. So, she will leave the damn thing unlocked. This is going to work, I promise."

She nodded and her shoulder length blonde hair leapt around her face. "Okay Sissie, if you say so." She leaned forward and hugged me tightly. It felt nice to be near her again. She was my sister after all and as Mimi pointed out to us on more than one occasion, "Friends come and go but sisters are for life."

I walked her down the stairs, put on our coats, and out of the back door with the package in her hands. I could tell as we made our way that she was still very nervous and tentative about this plan. To be quite honest, so was I. I knew in a way this was about as cruel a trick as I could play on someone but with everything at stake, including my friends' futures and Savannah's face, I had no other choice.

We crossed through the hedgerow where seven months ago Savannah had scared me into thinking that I was going to be assaulted, and we stopped just on the other side. I could go no further.

She nodded at me without saying a word, though she could see in my eyes that I was wishing her the best of luck. She collected herself and her thoughts and began walking. I watched her for the first thirty steps or so until she reached the end of the driveway and made the right hand turn.

Now all I could do was wait.

I won't drag out all the thoughts I had while sitting there. I will say however that it seemed like a long time to deliver a package to someone even though a time check on our return home showed we were gone less than seven minutes.

Back in her room, with the door firmly shut, I was finally able to ask a few questions. "Who answered the door?"

"Her dad."

"And what did you say?"

"I said hello Mr. Summers would you please give this to Savannah and please tell her I'm sorry for fighting with her."

I was, of course looking for far more detail than Nicole was willing to give me. "Well, what else did he say?"

"Thank you, I'll see she gets it," she added.

"And that's it? That was the entire encounter?" I asked dumbfounded.

"Oh, and he said something about the weather and how cold it's been."

The weather, a typical Summers' decoy tactic. It's hard to not get mad at that family. Even the parents drive me insane. "So, do you think he will give her the package?"

"Yeah, I think so. Mr. Summers always seemed to like me a lot. I guess it is just up to Savannah now to open it."

"Oh, she'll open it all right. Savannah is the kind of girl who HAS to open a present. Now all we have to do is wait until midnight," I said grinning.

Okay Kelsey, it's all up to you now . . .

I met Craig at the bottom of the old willow tree in front of the Summers' house exactly at eleven forty-five as we had planned. We were both bundled up tightly as there was an Arctic type wind blowing in from the northwest.

"Hey."

"Hey Craig, thanks again for coming, it means a lot to me that we can still be friends."

"Caitlin, even if we weren't friends and we are, I'm a member of the Patrol. It's my duty to be here even though it's starting to flurry."

I gave him a hug which was very awkward. Not because I was hugging my ex boyfriend in front of the girl's house he reluctantly kissed a few weeks ago. No, it was because he was wearing a down filled jacket that made it feel like I was snuggled up against the Stay-Puff Marshmallow man.

"Okay, Caitlin this climb is not going to be easy," he said, as we released each other from 'The Hug'. The branches are sort of frozen and with this wind, I don't know this seems kind of dangerous."

"What would you have me do Craig, break in through the front door and stealth my way up there like a ninja? I have to go. Do you have any idea what will happen to Kelsey if Savannah goes ape shit? We have to do this, it's the only way. I promised both Nicole and Kelsey I wouldn't let any harm come to her."

"I know Caite but hear me out, okay? The footing is gonna suck up there and I think her parents are still awake so I can't even shine the flashlight to help you navigate your ascent."

"My ascent?" I giggled.

"Your climb, okay? I'm sorry my parents watch a lot of Survivor Man.

"Well, thank you for your concern but we have no choice. Come on, give me a boost."

Craig bent his knees, interlocked his fingers and made a stirrup for me to use as my first foothold. I stuck my left shoe out and into his waiting palms and then, leaning my weight against the central trunk of the tree I said, "Up."

Craig straightened his back and legs out and I was a good eighteen inches higher than I was a mere second ago. That extra height allowed me to put my right foot up and onto the tree, hoisting myself with ease. I reached out and grabbed for the largest branch that jutted back towards the second floor of the house and immediately agreed with Craig's previous assessment, it was very slippery. I was never a good tree climber to begin with so I was going to have to take it very, very slow.

I began inching my way up and out over the front property. I laid on the large branch almost like a baby baboon lies across its mothers back as she travels across the Serengeti, the only real difference was I was not going to pick any bugs off the tree limb and eat them as a quick and healthy snack.

I braced my feet and snail crawled my way little by little. Several times I had to pause and work out in my head which was the best way to approach a difficult part of the branch, like where off shots of limbs were forming. You see, in my original draw up of this plan, there had been a moon and flashlight if needed, but with Craig afraid of alerting the Summers' and the canopy of weeping willow branches over my head shielding the soft glow of the moons light, I was left in a dark and creepy place. I have to tell you with the exception of the wake, this was by far the most frightening thing I had ever done in my life.

"Three minutes until midnight," I heard whispered from below me.

Thanks Craig, that's just great. "How much farther do I have to go?"

"Well, right now you've gone less than half way."

WHAT!

I closed my eyes and gathered my courage. I had made promises. I had given my word. I had to make sure my friends were not going to do something utterly stupid on my behalf. So, I exhaled and redoubled my efforts.

I grunted and groaned, swore, prayed and swore some more but finally got to the window and it appeared just in time, the show was about to begin.

Savannah was fast asleep in her bed. Her comforter and blanket pulled securely up to her chin and her hair was displayed almost angelically against her pillow. On her nightstand stood the note that we had my sister write only a few hours earlier:

"Dear Savannah:

I miss you. It's hard not being able to speak to you. Please don't be angry at me anymore. Caitlin is nuts. She thinks a terrier down the street is a werewolf named Cornelius who was responsible for the assassination of President Lincoln. My parents are thinking about sending her to a place where scary, crazy people live. Good riddance. Please accept this doll, my absolute most prized possession in the whole world as an apology. She means as much to me as you do. I will be away for the rest of the day but hope you will call me tomorrow. I'm sorry we argued.

Nicole."

And as fate would have it, holding the note in her tiny plaster hands, sitting there perfectly still was Kelsey. My plan had worked. Savannah had bit. She fell for Nicole's note and unwrapped the present just as I had predicted.

Now all I had to do, was watch and wait, fortunately I didn't have to wait long.

The window blocked out the first utterances from the doll. Yet even in this reduced light I could see that Kelsey's mouth was moving along with her neck as she tried in vain to locate the sleeping Savannah. It's an odd thing. Kelsey can speak through the doll but unfortunately cannot see. The glass eyes somehow make peering through the veil almost impossible. When I asked why, she could not explain it. She said though that her voice emitting from the doll was merely a parlor trick, she could whisper to me directly in a disembodied form, she just thought it was better this way and less creepy. I believe as you may, my readers, that the difference between a doll speaking or an unseen ghost, with regards to the creepy factor, is negligible.

I saw the doll's head loll and settle back as its arms began to make stiff and quirky gestures. Kelsey was making the doll look like it was being controlled by a puppeteer who was an amateur at his craft.

I leaned forward to make certain the window was in fact unlocked, to my horror it wasn't. *Oh God, no. That meant that Savannah was going to find Kelsey speaking to her and react in one of two ways. First, she would believe it was a trick and try to examine the doll for some sort of speaker or antennae. When she didn't find one she may try to take more drastic measures to prove her theory. The other outcome could be that Savannah believes the doll to be real and she freaks out alerting her brother and parents to my twin's presence. Either way, Kelsey's doll was suddenly in more danger than I was prepared for. This was quickly spiraling out of control.*

"Craig, the damn window is locked!" I growled as I leaned down a bit hoping he would hear me. Not that I expected there was much he could do from the ground at this point, I still felt better letting him know what was going on.

Through the window I could see the doll's mouth opened again and this time I saw Savannah stir. She groggily rolled over, readjusted her pillow and then allowed a deep sleep to take her again. Reality, at this point, was not even a close second to the things Savannah's mind or body were interested in experiencing, how quickly that was all going to change. In the next five minutes, she was going to get all the reality she could handle.

Kelsey tried to prop herself up on her legs and took a few wobbly, tentative steps towards the sleeping Savannah. She let go of the note and stood there with her hands on her hips in a pose that was reminiscent of my mother just before she began chewing me out for one reason or another. The odd, surreal difference was that Kelsey's glass eyes kept wandering left and right trying desperately to make out some shape or recognizable shadow that would allow her to know she was actually facing Savannah and not the wall.

The doll's mouth opened again. I knew I was nearly out of time. I had to come up with a plan quickly. I looked around and saw nothing that would help me gain access to the house. All the windows were shut tightly against the cold.

I was about to start pounding on the glass when I saw a small light emerge from under Savannah's blanket. It was an eerie blue color; almost like the color you might paint an infant's room. Powder blue I think they call it, which is odd, cause all the powder I've ever needed to apply to my body has been white. She stretched and then extended her arm out of the covers and the source of the strange light became apparent, it was her cell phone. She had gotten a call. *God, is this chick ever NOT popular?*

She sat up, her back to the doll that was standing there on her night stand and smiling nodded and even though it was midnight and as far as she was concerned she was totally alone with no one watching, she tossed her hair. I mean she honestly tossed her freakin hair like she was some sort of super model.

I was lucky that this whole head toss thing didn't over take all of my thoughts because I saw her nod, throw back the covers and stand up heading for the window.

From below me I heard, "Hide!"

I instinctively slid back about six feet on the branch and to my surprise she unlatched the window. She disappeared right after that, most likely to make sure that she looked awesome in her Victoria's Secret "Pink" collection sleepwear.

I grinned in the darkness. Craig, that clever little rascal, had called her and told her to unlock the window. *I have to remember to thank him if I get off this tree branch alive.*

I pulled myself back up to my former position just in time to hear her scream. It was the kind of scream that told volumes about the person who voiced it. It wasn't the kind of scream that said, "there's a knife toting psychopath in my room about to remove my kidneys", it also wasn't the kind of scream you might hear upon winning a million dollars in the lottery. No, this was the "I can't believe this is real, wake my ass up RIGHT NOW," kind of scream. I totally enjoyed it, but I knew if she did that again she would wake the whole house up. So, without thought to my own safety, I reached out with both my hands, threw open the window and pulled myself in.

The sight was something right out of a campy horror movie. Kelsey was already talking to Savannah and even though she was still facing the empty bed, had pretty much succeeded in getting her complete attention. Savannah had backed herself into the opposite corner, hands up in front of her face as if somehow that action would keep the images of this talking doll from resting in her eyes.

". . . need this to stop now! Do you understand?" Kelsey demanded.

"Caitlin! What the @%*# are you doing here?" She shrieked as I climbed through the window.

"Just take it easy Savannah, I'll explain."

"Explain? How the hell are you going to explain that?" She seemed unhinged. I must admit it looked good on her, well at least as far as I was concerned. I would have enjoyed her torture a few more seconds but she interrupted my thoughts. "Ya know what, explain it to the police freak, I'm getting my parents." Seeing me had helped to bring a sense of normality to the situation which bolstered her courage and made her far more confident than she should have been. I was going to lose control of this situation fast if I couldn't get her to listen to my story. Fortunately for me, Kelsey was already way ahead and ready to come to my assistance.

"Savannah Summers, if you so much as call out for your parents I will come back tomorrow night and every night thereafter to haunt you. You will never again know restful sleep or an evening without nightmares, this I swear," the doll said in a spooky, almost guttural voice.

Not one to miss such an obvious cue, I jumped right in, "Okay Kelsey, let me explain things to her before you unleash such a powerful curse."

The small doll spun, honing in on Savannah's rapid breathing and with a growl that sounded as if it came from a rabid Pit Bull, she took three quick steps, lunging at her frightened advisory.

"Savannah, allow me to introduce my sister, Kelsey. Kelsey, this is Savannah Summers, the girl . . ."

Kelsey quickly finished the sentence for me, "that has been tormenting you for the last eight months."

I nodded, "Exactly."

Savannah stared at me with wide eyed disbelief, "That, thing is your sister?"

"No. That thing is a doll that just happens to look like my sister. My sister is the ghost that inhabits the doll," I said correcting her.

I saw her back straighten. She had recaptured her self control and was slipping back into that state of arrogance I had come to loathe. "Oh I get it. You think I am going to fall for some lame puppet trick and back off from humiliating you? Think again reject. I am going to destroy you for this. Now get out of my damn house. Oh and tell Craig that his little stunt to open the window just got him a whole lot of problems as well."

"Why have Caitlin tell me? I'm right here, tell me yourself," Craig said as he pulled himself into the room, shut the window and stood beside me.

"Oh, there you are Craig? I didn't know you were slumming this evening with this," she said in an angry voice as she pointed at me with her chin. "And here I thought you were over the flat-chested little freakazoid. But this stunt tells me otherwise. Did the two of you honestly think that I would fall for such a lame and pathetic stunt as this? Did you?"

Without either of us moving a muscle, Kelsey lurched again but this time she had pinpointed Savannah's location and scurried towards her, howling. "This is no silly parlor trick, you fool. I am the ghost of Kelsey Adams O'Connor, come to curse you for all the misery you have inflicted on my family."

"Bullshit," was all she said.

Craig and I exchanged bewildered glances. We were completely dumbfounded. We had her, yet somehow seeing Craig enter the room put so much reality into this para-normal situation that Savannah was actually writing the whole thing off as, plausible. God, what the hell does it take to scare someone these days?

I was about to call it off when I saw the glass that covered several of the family portraits that hung in Savannah's room, begin to crust up with ice. I hadn't noticed at first but the temperature of the room had dropped at least thirty degrees and all of our breaths were now clearly visible as we exhaled. A smile began to form on my lips that coincidentally matched Craig's almost exactly. We both knew what this sudden cold spot meant; it meant that my sister, my twin sister, was tired of playing nice.

"Get out, both of you and shut the freakin' window, it's freezing in here," she snapped.

Craig responded in a half chuckle, "Oh, it's already shut, believe you me." And at that precise moment, I saw my sister's doll, her corporeal shell, collapse near Savannah's feet. I couldn't understand it. She simply fell down limp, totally inert. It was as if, she had somehow been quickly removed, ejected or exorcised from the doll's body.

"KELSEY!" I shrieked much louder than I should have, as I started to take a few panicked steps forward.

There was a loud nervous swallow behind me as a soft female voice said, "I'm right here sister."

I slowly turned my head to the left and there she was, standing there, glowing and ghostly. It was Kelsey. I mean, she was there, physically manifested beside me even though it was obvious she was not of this world by the way her hair moved perpetually as if being blown by some unfelt breeze and her eyes were milky white. I couldn't help but stare. It had been over a year since I had seen my fraternal twin. Many were the nights I would sit in my room and beg God for another chance to see my sister.

How strange it took a vicious and sadistic girl to make those wishes come true.

Kelsey was dressed exactly like the doll. She wore a medium length plaid skirt, a white blouse and stylish black vest and white knitted socks. She looked very much like a girl ready to go off to a proper boarding school. Of course, the fact she was floating six inches above the ground with her feet dangling limply made the whole vision more terrifying than anything I had ever seen before.

Savannah opened her mouth to scream and by the large amount of air she inhaled a mere fraction of a second before, it was going to be the scream to end all screams. She bent her head back, scrunched her eyes and balled her hands into tight unbreakable fists. This chick for lack of a better term, was about to go postal.

Kelsey raised her finger to her own mouth and whispered, "Shhhh," the same way a mother hushes a crying child. I don't know if it was a spell or a command that could not be ignored but when Savannah shook violently, wrenching her head from side to side, nothing came out. Not a single, solitary sound was emitted. I was in awe.

"You will not speak. You will not run. You will however listen, because if you do not, I will follow through with my previous threats and you and your family will never know peace again. Do we have an understanding?"

Savannah carefully nodded twice and then stood there transfixed and paralyzed with pure, uninhibited, fear.

"You are a terrible person. You are cruel and your heart is filled with malice. I cannot imagine how you have become so sinister, so twisted, but I want you to know, it ends tonight. You are no longer going to waste all of your gifts and talents on torturing others. I have seen what will happen to you Savannah if you continue on this course. I have walked in the grey lands and spent some time listening to the trees tell me of your fate. When your time comes, your end will be unpleasant; but not nearly as much so, as your life in the hereafter. You will be made to suffer and pay for your acts of malevolence. That is, if you fail to heed my warning. Savannah Summers, I will say this to you only once. You have but a single chance to make this life better for you and your family. Do it or else."

"Orrr, ellsssse, whhhwhhhattt?"

"Or else, you may find that Caitlin will not be able to stop several girls at your school from causing you tremendous bodily harm."

Kelsey shot her right hand up as she rushed forward placing her entire palm over Savannah's face, "See now what will occur if you fail to heed my warning."

I heard a tiny whimper escape Savannah's lips as Kelsey showed her a glimpse of the future. Within a few seconds Savannah was no longer whimpering but convulsing, her body reacting to each blow she witnessed in the vision as if it were really occurring. She doubled over in pain, tried to protect her skull, fell to her knees and frantically ran her fingers through her hair only to bring her hands in front of her face and tremble. I can only guess that in this alternate reality she was experiencing she must have been bleeding from the scalp.

Savannah tried to stand up but tumbled to the ground again, reaching for her left knee and opening her mouth as if she were howling in pain. Tears rolled down her cheeks as pain, fear and regret ran like quicksilver along her veins. She threw a hand out as if pleading for help only to have her arm smash down to the carpet and then hang there useless from another unseen blow.

Craig and I were transfixed. This was not what I had wanted. As much as I hated her, to see another human being in this kind of wretched agony was too much. My morbid curiosity had been sated and now my heart only broke to see her fall down to the carpet and curl into a small ball. As the pain kept coming, she looked more and more like a small child who was just trying to survive a beating by some abusive adult. This was not justice, it was becoming revenge.

"KELSEY, STOP IT!" I shouted.

"But my sister, this is not the last of what she would endure. Should she not know everything that will happen?"

"No. Enough, I can't take it anymore. It looks like you're killing her!"

"That's because, they were," Kelsey pulled her hand back and instantly Savannah stopped feeling the pain. She lay there panting deeply, crying. "You were right Caitlin, to fear for your friends. Once they began to hurt Savannah, they became fueled by the rush of power and the memories of her actions and would not have stopped until she laid still, her breathing shallow and the internal wounds on her body so numerous that she would have died in the hospital from hemorrhaging several hours later."

Kelsey floated back to me and hovered there waiting to see Savannah's reaction when she finally was able to collect herself. It was not what I expected.

She tried to get to her feet but the pain memory was strong and she would have fallen back down if it were not for Craig stepping forward to catch her.

"She's shaking," he said.

"Makes sense, she's just been through a lot," I replied, not moving.

"Caitlin, can you stop them from coming after me," she asked.

"Yes. Don't go to that game. Start making nice in school and I will tell them we spoke and you are ready to mend your ways."

She looked at me and all she said was, "Okay."

I turned to thank Kelsey but noticed that she was more translucent than before. She appeared to be fading and fast, "Kels, are you okay?"

"I need to . . . rest Caitlin. That was more energy than I have ever given before. I feel so wea . . . k," and with those words, my sister was gone.

Now it was my turn to cry. Craig took me in his arms and gave me a hug. I sobbed, praying that she had not given so much of herself that I would never be able to speak with her again. I had decided to forgive Savannah for all the bad things she had done to my friends but if this intervention had harmed Kelsey and cost us our nightly visits, I would hate Savannah for the rest of my life.

Savannah bent down and gently lifted the doll from the floor. She then handed it to me with a reverence I had never seen from her before. Craig nodded his thanks and then the two them led me downstairs and out of the house.

As Craig helped me outside, Savannah spoke, little did I know that these were some of the last words she would ever utter to me again, "I hope she's okay, Caitlin."

I let a calming breath pass into my lungs before I said, "Me too."

"And Caitlin, I'm sorry."

"I wish I could say it was alright Savannah but right now I'm just too upset. I hope you never bully anyone again. You have no idea the damage you nearly caused."

She lowered her head and whispered, "I meant for losing your sister, I can never apologize for the other things I've done," she stepped back, shut the door and was gone.

CHAPTER TWENTY-THREE

FIVE AGAINST ONE

"You told her? What the @&^$ were you thinking, O'Connor? Now we are all gonna get suspended," Danielle shrieked into the phone.

"Calm down. I merely warned her that if she didn't stop all her B.S. that something bad might happen, that's all," I replied into the phone.

This call I had been dreading. Having been warned about the ambush, she failed to attend the basketball game and thus made the girls not only suspicious but downright angry.

"You think that's going to stop her? She's evil Caitlin, you've said so yourself. There is no reasoning with her. She is going to start her shit back up again in a week or two. If not against us, against someone else." Danielle was the most upset, as you can imagine. She was beyond reproach, beyond rational thought, she simply wanted blood.

Nicole was sitting with me in our basement as I tried to keep this call as reasonable as possible. "Danielle, we got what we wanted, didn't we? She is not going to move against us, it's over. When we chose to confront her it was to stop the bullying and harassment, not to injure her, job done. Come on relax, we won."

"You're a stupid, naïve little girl, Caitlin O'Connor!" I pulled the phone from my ear out of necessity. She was screaming so loud I could barely think straight. "But worse of all, you're a traitor. All of us were willing to deal with this together, we made a pact and you went off on your own and warned that bitch. She will always be looking over her shoulder now. What if she tells her parents or the principal, now she's the victim and not us! Did you think about that? Did you? Or was it by warning her that now you are free and clear as well? You protected yourself and washed your hands clean leaving the four of us looking like this was all our idea."

I took another deep breath and sighed, "That's not how it happened, Danielle. I had the opportunity to fix the problem without us all getting in trouble or worse, so I took it."

Nicole smiled and nodded. I could tell she was doing everything in her power not to grab the phone from my hand and shout back at her. Nicole had been nothing but happy to see me come home a few nights ago with the doll intact and the report that Savannah had agreed to cease all of her tricks and torments. Unfortunately, she and I were still waiting for Kelsey to speak to us again. Three days was the longest period of time I had gone without hearing from my twin and every night brought me a bit closer to fearing she had somehow exhausted herself beyond repair to save me, to save my friends and family.

"You're a selfish bitch Caitlin," she barked.

"I know. It's been brought to my attention a few times before. It's a habit I am hoping to change," I smiled at Nicole and she leaned in and hugged me.

"Well, just so you know, the other girls and I have decided to write down our version of what happened in case it ever comes out and you can be damned sure we won't forget to put in there how you were the main reason for the idea of the attack and the orchestrator of the plan."

"Whatever. You do what you have to do Danielle. I'm just sorry you can't see that this was the best solution."

"Yeah, for you!" She screamed. "Watch your back O'Connor, nobody likes a rat," and with that she hung up the phone.

"So, now what Sissie?" Nicole asked.

"Well it looks like the other four girls are all pissed off at me as well."

"Do you think they will do anything bad?" She asked worriedly.

"Nah. They won't try anything during the school year. It's too soon and this summer we are leaving to go to Mimi's house in Ireland, so they won't see me. They'll calm down. Especially if they see we were right and that Savannah has in fact stopped tormenting people," I smiled and sat back on the couch beside her.

"Good. Sissie, do you think that they might try to talk to Savannah one day?"

I was shocked by this question, "What do you mean, Boo?"

"To find out what you said or did to make her change her mind. Or even worse to prove their own innocence by telling her it was all your fault and teaming up against you?"

I thought for a moment and absent mindedly pet Dog who was sitting along side me, "God, I hope not. That would mean I would have to face five girls at once. Not so sure I would be able to handle that," I laughed half heartedly.

"Sissie, don't be stupid. It wouldn't be five against one silly, we're The Soul Patrol. You, me, Katrina, Craig, Dog and Kelsey. That's six of us, together we can do anything."

I couldn't help but smile. My little sister was right as usual. We were six strong friends, united by circumstance but devoted through love. I felt safer at that moment with Nicole beside me than I had in quite a long time. I had to just remember that needing your friends to help with a problem is not weakness, nor is it cowardice. Well, as long as it's the right friends.

"Girls, dinner," I heard dad yell.

"Come on Boo, let's go eat," I said standing.

"Caitlin," she asked as she stood to come upstairs with me, "what if Kelsey doesn't come back?"

I paused and looked her straight in the eye and said, "Does Kelsey love us, Boo?"

"Of course."

"Then she's not really gone, is she? We just can't hear her at this moment. But I know she's out there watching over us. Want to know how?"

"How?"

I leaned down and whispered, "Close your eyes."

She did and I hugged her tightly, "Cause we're sisters."

The End